# Too Many Curses

## A. Lee Martinez

TOR®
fantasy

A TOM DOHERTY ASSOCIATES BOOK
NEW YORK

This is a work of fiction. All of the characters, organizations, and events portrayed in this novel are either products of the author's imagination or are used fictitiously.

TOO MANY CURSES

Copyright © 2008 by A. Lee Martinez

A Tor Book
Published by Tom Doherty Associates, LLC
175 Fifth Avenue
New York, NY 10010

www.tor-forge.com

Tor® is a registered trademark of Tom Doherty Associates, LLC.

ISBN 978-0-7653-5795-3

Tor books may be purchased for educational, business, or promotional use. For information on bulk purchases, please contact Macmillan Corporate and Premium Sales Department at 1-800-221-7945, extension 5442, or write specialmarkets@macmillan.com.

First Edition: September 2008
First Mass Market Edition: September 2013

Printed in the United States of America

0  9  8  7  6  5  4  3  2

To Mom. You may not be able to transform into a robotic dinosaur, but you're still pretty cool to me.

To the many fine writers of the DFWWW. Since this is book number five, I'm running out of funny things to say here. I guess I could just offer a sincere thank-you for all your encouragement and support over the years, but that's not really my style. So I guess you don't get to make it into this dedication after all.

To Paul Stevens. Thanks.

And to Booster Gold.

# ONE

Margle the Horrendous had a habit of collecting things. There were his books on various subjects of study arcane and lore obscure. His castle was filled with various monsters, or pieces of monsters, for purposes only wizards might fathom. Other chambers were filled with jewels, enchanted knick-knacks, gold and other precious things, and all the peculiar odds and ends that ultimately meant little to wizards yet which they insisted on hoarding. He also had a great assortment of enemies who he had gathered over the years. Margle rarely killed his foes. Death rarely amused him. Instead, he kept them close, a grand collection of old rivals and fallen heroes. And as with all his collections, it was Nessy's task to take care of them.

Margle was an exceptionally generous master, meaning that he was generally too busy to bother yelling at her, and when he did, he usually threw things not dangerously hard or sharp and missed more often than not. And Margle was frequently absent from the castle, leaving Nessy the run of the place— or at least the rooms that weren't forbidden to her, where she wasn't interested in going anyway because there were certainly many horrors waiting in Margle's castle. There were even one or two rooms the wizard himself never went into. And one place, The Door At The End Of The Hall, that even he avoided going anywhere near.

Nessy enjoyed maintaining Margle's vast library. And if she should take a peek at a secret volume or two while alphabetizing the shelves, Margle had yet to notice or care. She'd even picked up a handful of magic tricks. Nothing serious, but small spells of practical use. Feeding the horrors in the bestiary was the worst of her tasks, but even that she did without complaint. It was honest work and gave her a roof over her head and food in her belly, and though she knew that one day Margle would certainly kill her in a fit of rage or for some fiendish experiment or maybe just because it would amuse him to do so, she was glad to have it.

Except for the occasional overly chatty gargoyle.

"Did I ever tell you about the time I slew three ogres while armed with only a wet towel?" Gareth asked.

"Yes." Nessy polished his stone head with a rag as the gargoyle continued.

"Well, it was a terrible struggle. . . ." He blathered on for some time, and Nessy nodded as if listening. She pitied the poor soul trapped in a stone demon perched over an archway. Such was the fate of Margle's enemies. At least this particular enemy.

"Are you listening?" Gareth sighed.

"No." Nessy was ruthlessly honest, not so much because she valued the virtue as because she seldom considered lying before she spoke.

"I was a great hero, you know."

"I know." She spat in his eye and wiped away the dust.

"I hate when you do that."

"Would you rather have dirt in your eyes?"

"No."

"Well then . . ." She nimbly climbed onto his back and shined his horns. Gareth didn't move, couldn't move. He could only talk, and talk a lot. And stare down the corridor at The Door At The End Of The Hall.

"Ever wonder what's in there?" he asked as he always did when being polished.

"Best not to imagine."

"Maybe for you. That's all I can do."

"Well, maybe if you were quieter you'd get more visitors."

Gareth grumbled, "The others are just jealous of my legendary feats."

A disembodied voice spoke up. "Ah, yes, that's it. Certainly nothing to do with your personality. Or lack thereof."

"Hello, Echo," said Nessy. Margle had taken away everything but Echo's voice. While she lacked anything in form, she was at least free to roam the castle.

"He's back."

Nessy's tall, fuzzy ears cocked. She heard the distant thunder that always signaled her master's return. "Thank you, Echo."

The voice didn't reply. Or she was gone. It was impossible to know, but one was never really alone in Margle's castle. Nessy jumped to the floor.

"You aren't finished," protested Gareth.

"I'll be back. And you can tell me all about that time you died and had to wrestle the lords of the underworld to return from the grave."

"That is a good one. See, I'd just been slain while fighting an army of lizard men. I'd defeated them, but at the cost of my very life. . . ."

Nessy walked away. He continued. Gareth enjoyed hearing his stories more than anyone else. An audience was mostly a technicality.

"What a bore," said Echo, somewhere over Nessy's right shoulder.

"You could listen to him occasionally," Nessy said. "He gets lonely."

"Oh, I do. I'll ask him about one of his tales of adventure, and then I'll go find something to amuse myself, leaving him to prattle."

"That's not very nice."

"Well, I'm invisible. You only know I'm around when I'm talking, and he never lets anyone else speak. So he never knows. Sometimes, I come back later, and he's still going on. Then I pretend I've been listening the whole time. If I do it right, I can keep him amused for days without ever really having to listen to him."

This struck Nessy as a touch unethical even if she couldn't see the harm. But she had to admit that she didn't polish the gargoyle as much as she should because there were times she wasn't in the mood.

A small bat swept down and landed on her shoulder. "Are ye lasses speaking of the old gray blowhard? Can't stand the lad meself. His stories are all fuss and bluster."

"Hello, Thedeus," said Echo.

"Sir Thedeus!" squealed the four-inch bat.

Like all the castle's fallen heroes, he was stubborn about letting go of his greatness. They were all alike. Gareth was only a little worse.

The hallway torches flared. Margle liked a bright castle. It was expected that Nessy be in the tower to greet him on his arrival. If not, he'd threaten to shave her fur or throw her into the bottomless pit in the castle bowels. He wouldn't do it. Probably wouldn't, she corrected, knowing that he would kill her one day. She also knew that when he did, it would have little to do with anything she'd done. But there was no sense in making him mad. Her stubby kobold legs gave her a slow walk. She dropped to all fours and scampered at a brisk trot.

Sir Thedeus disliked the bumpy ride and took flight. "Given any thought to me suggestion, lass?"

"Not that again," said Echo. For a bodiless voice, she sounded curiously out of breath.

"Aye, it's high time we kill that evil bastard."

"And how exactly do we do that?" asked Echo.

"All I need is an opening, a moment of weakness. Then I pounce from the shadows and rip out his throat."

"You're a fruit bat."

"I've still teeth, lass."

"Nessy has to peel oranges before she gives them to you."

"Ach, have ye ever tried nipping an orange rind?" said Sir Thedeus. "I'm telling ye, it canna be done."

"Nessy does it."

"Fine. She can rip out the foul bastard's throat then. I don't care. As long as he dies and the spell is broken. Don't ye want to be a person again?"

Nessy pulled farther ahead. At full speed, she could outrun Echo and Sir Thedeus. She darted through the labyrinth of corridors. Margle was close, but she took the long way. She wasn't worried enough to go near the Wailing Woman today.

A clap of thunder told her that Margle's arrival was imminent. She bolted up the stairs, having lost Echo and Thedeus somewhere along the way.

An apparition rattled his chains at her. He howled pitifully.

"Not now, Richard."

She ran through him without pausing and reached the top of the tower not a moment too soon.

A great, black bird flew through the tower window. It clutched a stone the size of a kobold's head in one talon. It glared at Nessy with burning red eyes and shrank into Margle's shape. He was tall and thin, rather bony even for a wizard. His billowing robes only made him look more fragile. In Nessy's experience, a wizard's mystical powers were inversely proportional to his physical presence. Margle was a powerful wizard and a slight man. Sir Thedeus's teeth might just be able to bite the scrawny wizard's head off if the bat put his mind to it.

Margle's glare strengthened. "Where's my wine, dog?"

Nessy lowered her head, covered her muzzle with her hands, and tucked her tail between her legs. "I'm sorry, master."

He wrung his hands. His stringy forearms tightened. "And I thought I told you I wanted this floor polished."

"I did polish it, master."

He sneered. "Don't contradict me, beast."

"No, master. But the stones are slick, and I thought they might be too slippery."

"Ah, there you go again. Thinking is not your purpose."

"No, master." She licked her lips. "Yes, master. Sorry, master."

"I should boil you alive for eternity."

15

"Yes, master."

Margle gritted his sharp teeth. "You're fortunate, dog, that I'm in a good mood."

Nessy peered at the stone in his hand. The shape, color, and markings showed it to be a nurgax seed. She'd read of them in Margle's books but didn't mention that to the master. Nurgaxes were rare beasts, valued by wizards more for their rarity than their power. Nessy remembered the passage in the book. When the seed was broken, the nurgax would spring full grown and devour the first living creature it saw. It would then imprint on the second living creature it saw, forming a bond that could only be severed by death.

"Shall I put that away for you, master?"

His sneer deepened. "Beast, you're never to touch this. Do so and I'll flay you."

"Yes, master."

"Layer by layer by layer."

"Yes, master."

"Then I shall make a hat from your tanned hide and matching bookends from your bones."

"Yes, master."

Margle was in a threatening frame of mind and kept on for another minute. Nessy nodded and acted appropriately fearful. The threats didn't mean much. When Margle did finally kill her, it would probably be without warning.

". . . And I'll serve your eyes in my soup," he finished.

"Yes, master. Shall I fetch your wine?"

"Wait, beast. I haven't dismissed you yet."

Nessy's fur bristled.

Sir Thedeus flew into the tower and perched on her shoulder again. "Oh now if ever there was a throat needing ripping out," he whispered. "Should I go for it, or would ye like to, lass?"

Margle held up the nurgax seed. The skin on his face tightened. A lock of gray hair fell across his eyes. "Tell me, dog. Tell me how you live to serve me."

"Of course, master."

"Would you die for me?"

"Ach, what a great prat," said Sir Thedeus.

Nessy bowed. The day she'd been waiting for had finally arrived. She was mildly relieved. Good to get it over with and being devoured by a nurgax was a quick death.

Margle repeated the question. "Would you die for me?"

"Yes, master." But only because she had no choice. She looked up at Margle. He was ready to smash the seed on the ground.

"I canna take it any longer." Sir Thedeus hurled himself at Margle's throat. Despite the thinness of the wizard's neck, the small fruit bat merely nipped ineffectively. Unimpressed but startled, Margle backed away. His foot slipped on slick, polished stone, and he tumbled. The nurgax seed broke open and a giant purple monster sprang forth. It had one eye and one horn, tiny wings, and a body that was just a giant snout on two heavy legs.

Nessy scrambled behind a table out of sight.

The nurgax growled curiously.

"No. Stay away!" All the confident malice was gone from Margle's voice. "Stay where you—"

Then came a crunch. And a second crunch. And a slurp. Then a contented purr.

Nessy poked her head out. The nurgax stomped over to her. It licked her once, drenching her fur in its slimy drool.

She laughed. It laughed.

"What did I miss?" asked Echo, her sudden wheezing breath beside Nessy.

Sir Thedeus swooped around in circles. "Nothing much, lass. I just killed the bastard!"

There was nothing left of Margle. Not so much as a scrap of cloth. The nurgax wasn't much bigger than Nessy, and it didn't seem large enough to hold a whole man in its belly unless its body was all stomach. A possibility she didn't dismiss. Even then, there should've been bits of wizard, an arm or a leg, dangling from its lips.

Nessy wasn't sad to see the wizard gone but she was now an unemployed kobold. This wasn't the first time she'd lost a master. Wizardry was a dangerous occupation, almost as dangerous as wizardry assistance.

"If he's dead, why don't I have a body?" said Echo. "And why are you still a bat?"

Sir Thedeus landed and examined his wings. "I'm sure it will just be another moment or two before the spells are undone."

A jar filled with eyes, teeth, some brain, and a tongue began to bubble. Everyone was too distracted to notice.

Thirty seconds passed, and the bat stayed a bat, the voice remained without a body.

"Any minute now," said Sir Thedeus impatiently.

Nessy went to Margle's chair. She'd always wanted to sit on it, wondered what its cushioned seat would feel like. More comfortable than the smoothed stone she normally used. She grabbed hold of the armrest to pull her delicate three-foot frame into the chair but changed her mind. Margle was dead, but wizards weren't always permanently so. If he rose from the nurgax's throat, he would certainly be upset. Finding a lowly kobold sitting in his favorite chair would only enrage him further. She sat on her stone. Uncomfortable, but she'd grown accustomed. The nurgax stayed by her side. Its thick tail swung with wild abandon, occasionally thumping the ground.

It whined. Nessy rubbed its snout, and it immediately started purring.

"We're not changing," said Echo.

Sir Thedeus squinted at his furry little body. "Do ye think I dinna notice?"

"He is dead, isn't he?"

"Aye, being digested as we speak."

The nurgax hiccupped.

"Shouldn't we be changing back then?" Echo said.

"That's the way it usually works, lass. Slay the wizard, and all his magic is undone."

"How do you know?"

"I've killed wizards before."

The jar of eyes boiled to attract someone's attention and failed.

Nessy considered her next job. She could go back to her tribal caves, find a husband, begin a life of moss farming, and birth a litter or three. That wasn't a bad life, and she wasn't wholly against it. But it was boring. Working for wizards was a sure road to a grisly death, but it was a stimulating career with all the ducking and groveling and gargoyle polishing and other such requirements. She'd seen things that most could only imagine. She couldn't go back to the caves.

Finding a new position wouldn't be difficult. She had experience, a bonded nurgax, and a grand surplus of wizardly books and equipment that any arcane scholar would dearly love to get their hands on.

"Nessy, why aren't we changing?" asked Echo.

The kobold shrugged.

"Ye mean ye dunna know?" Sir Thedeus flew in anxious circles. "Weren't ye the unholy bastard's apprentice?"

"Assistant," she corrected. "I assisted. He didn't teach me magic."

"But you've looked through his books," said Echo. "And I've seen you do magic."

"Nothing more than trifles."

The jar trembled hard enough to rattle the shelf. The eyes tapped rhythmically against its glass sides.

"What's he want?" Sir Thedeus grunted.

"Isn't that Margle's brother?" Echo said.

"Aye, or what's left of him."

"He was a wizard, wasn't he?"

"Not a very good one, judging from what Margle did to him."

"Still, he has to know something."

The jar hopped twice.

"Quick, Nessy. Get the jar."

Nessy hesitated. Margle had told her never to touch that jar.

Echo's voice grew soft. "We'd do it ourselves, but we need your help. Please."

Nessy glanced at the nurgax. She gently put a small hand on its enormous lips and opened them. The beast complied obediently. She gazed deep into the black chasm of its throat.

"Master, are you in there?"

No reply. Still unsatisfied, Nessy performed a final test.

"Margle?"

She flinched instinctively. Margle would never allow her to use his name if he were still alive. She was quite certain he was dead. For now.

The nurgax licked her with its wet tongue and laughed. Its laugh was a lot like a kobold's, half bark and half chuckle. Was that because of the bond, she wondered, or just coincidence?

She set her fears aside, and using the cooperative nurgax as a ladder, retrieved the jar from its high shelf. It boiled furiously, shaking in her arms. She walked down the nurgax's tail, set the jar on the floor, and unscrewed the lid.

The yellow fluid calmed. The eyes, teeth and tongue rose to the surface in the arrangement of a vague face.

"Thank you. Ah, I've missed the fresh air." The eyes bobbed, and the teeth floated into a smile. "Yazpib the Magnificent, finest wizard of a thousand kingdoms, at your service."

Sir Thedeus was less concerned with introductions. "Why haven't we changed back?"

"Only works that way with inexperienced wizards. New wizards build their spell matrices around themselves, tying them to their own life because it is a relatively easy technique. Now Margle was an old hand at the magic arts. He'd learned to create self-sustaining arcane webs, thus allowing his spells to exist independent of his well-being." Yazpib sensed he was losing his audience. "So killing Margle doesn't necessarily end his curses."

Echo sighed. "We're stuck like this."

"That largely depends on how well Margle crafted his spell construction. Generally, the magic begins to fracture without the periodic reinforcement of will, the glue to shore up the leaks. So to speak. How long this might take varies with the metaphysical solidity of these spells and the applicable thaumaturgical pressures."

Though Nessy had looked in Margle's books, she hadn't ventured into advanced magical theory. But she got the gist of it. Margle was a great wizard, and while his spells would probably crumble eventually, it could be a very long wait.

Yazpib continued. "However, any spell can be countered. I was never as talented as my brother, but with his death, I might be able to break your curses. But I'm a touch indisposed."

"Yer worthless to us then, lad?" said Sir Thedeus.

"I know magic. I just can't do it anymore."

Sir Thedeus gnashed his fangs. "Useless wanker. If ye were any good as a wizard, Margle would be in that jar."

Yazpib's floating teeth clicked against each other. "Thirty years ago, I'd have turned you into a worm for that."

"Ach, screw his lid back on."

"Will you two stop bickering?" asked Echo.

"I was just trying to help," said Yazpib.

"If I have any eggs to pickle, I'll let ye know," snapped Sir Thedeus.

Yazpib literally boiled. "Oh, go eat a cockroach."

"I'm a fruit bat, ye git."

"Will you two shut up and let me think?" said Echo.

They kept shouting over each other. The nurgax glanced at each. It mimicked the snarls and sneers with its wide mouth. Nessy couldn't take the noise any longer. She dropped to all fours and strolled from the chamber. Kobolds were equally comfortable upright or prostrate. It was mostly a matter of personal preference. She'd grown up a quadruped, but assisting wizards required a lot of carrying. While she could use her mouth, there were a lot of things Margle asked her to carry that she'd rather not have tasted.

She mostly went bipedal now, only going back to her child-hood when she needed to run or contemplate.

The nurgax followed without prompting. Nessy started down the stairs in no particular rush. A ghastly transparent corpse of moldering flesh, tattered clothing, and clinking chains appeared before her. He wailed, and the temperature dropped.

"I said not now, Richard."

The apparition frowned. "Oh come on, now. I was rather proud of that one."

"It was very good, but I'm distracted at the moment."

Richard descended the steps with her. He could only go as far as the bottom. For reasons only Margle might under-stand, Richard was consigned to haunt the castle's many staircases. Why he bothered trying to be frightening, Nessy didn't know. Boredom, she supposed. She usually humored him, but was too distracted right now.

The nurgax snapped at Richard's dangling chains. It alternately growled and purred at him.

"So what happened up there? I heard quite a commo-tion."

"Margle is dead."

"Dead?" Richard stopped and wiggled his immaterial fingers. "Why am I still here?"

"Something to do with spell matrices," said Nessy. "Ask the jar."

He disappeared. Perhaps back to the top of the stairs or to another staircase entirely.

Oddly, Nessy felt saddened. She hadn't exactly liked Margle, but she would miss him and her castle, her home. And her friends. Bodiless, transmogrified, or staircase-bound as they might be.

Echo's panting voice bounced suddenly beside Nessy. "We figured it out."

The nurgax jerked around for the voice's source. It snorted cautiously, and Echo chuckled. "Stop it. That tickles."

Nessy stood. She snapped her fingers. "Sit."

Whatever bond they shared, it responded immediately.

"We need your help, Nessy. You have to help us break our curses."

"I told you, I don't know any true magic."

"But Yazpib does. He just needs an able body."

Nessy's ears tilted forward. They always did when she was considering things. Then they flattened. "It won't work. Kobolds don't have a talent for magic. And even if I did, Margle is dead. It will only be a matter of time before his rivals arrive to claim his castle."

"They don't know that yet."

"They will. Wizards smell death like vultures. They'll pick this place clean."

"We can't do this without you. Please?"

This was a bad idea. Nessy couldn't possibly match Margle's wizardry. She would most likely die experimenting with magic as most apprentice wizards did. Or Margle's rivals would descend on the castle and kill her. But she'd long ago accepted her unpleasant death when embarking on her career. And Margle was usually gone anyway, so it wouldn't be very different. And he might even come back. Until she was certain he wouldn't, it was her duty to care for his castle and his collections.

"Very well."

"You won't regret it. I'll go tell the others."

Nessy rarely regretted. As long as things proceeded on an interesting course, she didn't care where tomorrow might lead. In any case, she could always change her mind when the other wizards finally came for their plunder.

The nurgax licked its lips and belched. Nessy could still smell the wizard on its breath.

# TWO

**W**ord of Margle's death spread quickly through the castle. There were no secrets where every tapestry talked, where a witness lived in every flowerpot, where the spiders, rats, and serpents peeking from behind the shadows were known to gossip among themselves and walls bled with rumor. Actually, it was only one wall, but that was more than enough, since Nessy had to clean up after it.

*Is he really dead?* the glistening red letters asked.

Nessy wrung out a rag she kept nearby along with a bucket of fresh water for convenience. "Yes, Walter." She wiped away the gray brick.

*Why am I still a wall?* The question mark at the end of the question was twice as large as the rest of the letters.

"It's complicated."

*Complicated? He's dead! I should be a man again! Oh damn! Oh no! I'm going to be like this forever!*

"Calm down, Walter."

But it was too late. When a bleeding wall rambled, it was sure to be a mess. Letters ran together into a flowing crimson stream to puddle on the floor. Nessy grabbed some towels she kept folded nearby and put them down to stem the tide. Loath as she was to have an untidy castle, the Thing That Devours needed to be fed. And the key to maintaining the castle was prioritizing. She made a mental note to come back later with her three best mops.

The last time she was late with the monthly meal for the Thing That Devours, it'd shrieked for a solid week, loud enough to rattle the castle's lower depths. The Beast Which Annoys, in an effort to not be outdone, howled for another eight days after that. That affected all the various ghosts haunting the nearby rooms, causing them to grow ill and vomit gallons of ectoplasmic residue. Nessy spent hours scouring the slime and still found bits in the cracks on occasion. She never forgot to feed the Thing That Devours after that.

She made her way to the vaults, where Margle had stockpiled a seemingly endless supply of meat. Not every beast in the castle ate flesh. The unicorns lived on the purest morning dew and lightest dandelion wisps, and the mind worms sustained themselves on memories of food, thriving on Nessy's recollections of rabbit stew and peach cobbler. But most every other magical beast in Margle's menagerie enjoyed more unsavory appetites.

The nurgax, ever loyal, followed quietly behind her.

In the hall of portraits, she was assaulted by more questions of Margle's death. It had amused the wizard to consign his enemies of royal blood to prisons of ink and paint.

"He can't truly be dead," said Lady Elaine while filling her cup from her bottomless teapot. She'd spurned Margle's affections, and he'd trapped her in a lovely image of a tea party. True, the other guests painted in the party were just that, soulless, immobile paint, and it was a torture to be certain. But Margle must surely have loved her in his own twisted manner to allow her the luxury of a perpetual sunny day.

Lord Gilgamesh, on the other hand, was painted into a dank, dusky room with a small window to let in light. There was only one door in his portrait, and something terribly horrible had been drawn on the other side. The only thing holding the monster at bay was Gilgamesh keeping the door closed. "I wish I could've seen him get it," he said through gritted teeth. He shifted his shoulders, and the door opened a crack. A tentacle slipped through. Gilgamesh bit it fiercely, and the horror recoiled with a shriek.

Caliban the Ogre King, who lived in a charcoal sketch of a gloomy forest, and a poorly drawn sketch at that, poked out his head from behind a tree. "Did you see him die yourself, Nessy?"

"Not exactly, but I did hear it."

The nurgax hiccupped sheepishly.

"Everyone knows a wizard isn't dead until his head has been removed and his body stuffed with pine needles," remarked a scholarly dwarf duke consigned to an oil painting of a library with tall shelves and not a single stepladder. "Then you have to burn it under a half-moon while a cock crows."

A dragon emperor imprisoned in a very small cave with only a single copper coin to roll between his talons hissed, "Balderdash. You have to boil the corpse in river water and chant the wizard's name backwards six times."

"Are you a fool?" said the dwarf. "That's the surest way to bring him back to life!"

"Ridiculous mortals!" bellowed a demigod in a watercolor dungeon. "The only way to truly kill a wizard is to eat his right kidney while whistling a Titan funeral dirge! Or is it the left? Which is the evil kidney?"

She left the painted denizens to their bickering. She passed a looking glass, and her image said, "He has to be dead." It was Melvin of the Mirrors, who found form in reflections. "I saw the whole thing from the full-length mirror in the corner of the tower. Two bites and he was gone. Wizard or not, I don't see how any man could survive."

"I suppose."

She wasn't truly certain, and she wasn't especially interested in theorizing. Her only concern was with maintaining castle upkeep as she always did. Neither Margle nor his constant threats had ever been her true motivation. She enjoyed her work for the work itself, and she considered the castle her home as much as Margle's. More so, in fact. While the wizard had spent much of his time off collecting arcane artifacts, bringing kingdoms to ruin, and other assorted dark wizardly doings, she was the one who was always here, day in, day out, keeping disorder in check. A difficult job truly, but rewarding and enjoyable.

The oddest thing about the Thing That Devours was that it didn't devour all that much. Just a bucketful of brains once a month. It wasn't even a very big bucket. Not nearly as large as the brain bucket used to feed the corpse drakes. And only half the size of her entrails pail for Huxtable the hog.

She hurried to the vaults where Margle had stockpiled a grand supply of brains, skin, hearts, kidneys (both good and evil) and so forth in giant, presorted copper cylinders. This hadn't always been so. Years ago, the vault had been a terrible jumble. Nessy had a strong stomach, but she'd never enjoyed picking through the mountains of organs for very specific meals. Many of the creatures in Margle's collection had very special diets. She'd learned the hard way that feeding a mere spoonful of wolf brains to a nether zombie made them explode.

The vaults were huge, stretching for leagues. Fortunately, walking them was unnecessary. Margle had devised a miraculous mechanical device that moved the brass walls with rapid efficiency. His name was Crank, and he had once been a sea captain before being transmogrified into a machine, a tremendous gearbox with a face of tin and copper.

"Ahoy, Nessy!" he shouted up as soon as she appeared atop the vault's tall, steep stairs.

"Hello, Crank. And how are you today?"

"Can't complain." His green copper mustache wiggled. "I suppose I could, but I fail to see the point."

Nessy prided herself on civility, but she took extra care with Crank, whose punishment seemed a shade cruel even by Margle's standards. Yet he maintained a positive attitude and was always helpful.

His hook swiveled forward. "I believe it's brains you're wanting today."

Nodding, she put the appropriate bucket on his arm. The floor rumbled as his gears turned with a steady click, click, click. A well in the distance rotated out of line and made its way towards them at a steady pace.

Sir Thedeus flew into the vault and sat on Nessy's shoulder. "What are ye doing, lass?"

"Tending the castle." It seemed strange to her that she should have to explain it.

Echo made her presence known by speaking. "He's dead. You don't have to do that anymore."

"Who's dead?" asked Crank, perhaps the last resident to learn of these latest events.

"Margle." Sir Thedeus puffed out his small, furry chest. "I killed him meself. Tore out his throat in a great gush of blood. It was glorious."

"Yes, well, glorious victories aside," said Echo, "he's dead."

"Should I still be a machine?" Crank's mustache lowered a few notches as metal eyebrows waggled. "Don't a curse end when its wizard dies?"

"Apparently not," said Nessy.

Metal brow wiggling deep in thought, Crank lowered the bucket. "Maybe he isn't dead? A privateer once told me the only sure way to kill a wizard is to feed his corpse to seagulls and then slaughter the seagulls and feed them to sharks and harpoon the sharks and . . ."

"Not a one of us cares about yer daft sailor stories," said Sir Thedeus. "Margle's dead."

"He's dead, but the Thing Which Devours must still be fed." Nessy took the freshly filled bucket from Crank.

"It was human brains you were wanting, wasn't it?"

"Yes, thank you." She walked to the foot of the stairs, put the bucket down, and chanted briefly. Dust pixies in the corners proceeded to carry the pail up the steps.

"You'll also be needing asses' ears today if I'm not mistaken."

"And iguana eyes." She set another bucket on his hook.

"Ah, yes. Can't forget the iguana eyes, can we?"

"Nessy lass, if ye keep tending the castle, where are ye going to find the time to break our curses?"

"I have an hour and forty minutes of unoccupied time every day. I don't mind studying magic then."

"But that'll take ye forever. Ye canna learn magic in an hour and a half a day."

"Of course not. I'll only be studying for thirty minutes. I would like some time for myself, after all."

"Can't we help?" asked Echo. "Lighten your load a little?"

"I appreciate the offer, but no one else is capable of doing what must be done. And the Thing That Devours won't feed itself. Or perhaps it might, but I'd rather not grant it the motivation."

"That's it? That's yer plan?" Sir Thedeus circled her head. "Just act as if nothing has changed while we remain cursed?"

"What would you have me do? This castle demands my constant attention. You can't expect me to just drop everything and start studying magic all day and night. Everything would fall apart in very short order."

"Our curses could break on their own before ye get around to learning enough magic."

"I fail to see the problem with that."

Sir Thedeus grumbled, and she could see his point. The castle wouldn't succumb to chaos instantly. There was still the very likely possibility that Margle would return from the dead or that other wizards and magi would arrive to plunder his collections. Either prospect meant that time wasn't a luxury she could take for granted. Not that she ever did. It was her most precious commodity, and it looked as if there soon wouldn't be enough hours in the day to take care of everything.

There was no doubt about it. She was going to have to let some things fall to the wayside. The very idea annoyed her. Every minute of her schedule was accounted for, properly arranged and employed for maximum effect. Margle's death, permanent or not, required certain adjustments.

Her home was very likely running out of time as well. She didn't like thinking about that, but it was true. The world within these dusty walls was soon to be extinguished, gone forever. And there was nothing she could do about it. All the cooking and cleaning, feeding and polishing: none of it would stop the inevitable end of it all. For a moment, she wondered why she should bother.

But it was a small moment, gone before she could dwell on it.

"Perhaps I can squeeze in an hour of magical study a day," she said.

With the aid of Crank and the dust pixies, Nessy loaded the cart waiting atop the stairs. Normally, she had to pull it herself, but the nurgax was only too happy to take the rope in its mouth and follow, ever obediently. The load proved lighter for the creature, and she made her way at a brisk pace. Margle's bestiary was spread throughout the castle, arranged by wizardly logic. Nessy didn't understand it, other than that some indescribable horrors got along poorly with certain other indescribable horrors. Many truly were indefinable. Shadowy creatures living in deep, dark pits.

Some made noise, and those noises were, with rare exception, as unpleasant as one might expect. The Black Plook had a raspy, scraping way of breathing. And THE MONSTER THAT SHOULD NOT BE gurgled and belched day and night. The Hideous Impaler laughed like a sweet child. The Consuming Aversion would sing lullabies in the sweetest voice between gnashing on crunching bones. For that reason,

Nessy was quite pleased that the Thing That Devours was always quiet, providing she remembered its monthly meal.

With the nurgax's help, she finished the feedings earlier than expected. Uncomfortable with wasted time, she tried to use the extra minutes to clean Walter the wall. But he was still rambling, and she admitted defeat. An early dinner was an allowable indulgence.

Decapitated Dan was the permanent resident of the kitchen. A madman, scoundrel, and murderer, Dan had been beheaded for his crimes. The wizard had the corpse dug up, the flesh scoured from its bones. He restored it to a semblance of life, the skeleton chained to the wall, and the skull set on a spice rack. His only explanation for this was a mumbled remark about being bored and needing to brighten the kitchen. This seemed strange to Nessy, as she was the only one who used it. She'd never even seen Margle eat, although he'd drunk wine. She briefly considered fetching a bottle, but this was forbidden. She couldn't defy her master yet.

"Nessy it is," announced Dan when she entered. "Beautiful, beautiful Nessy." His skull was quite insane as was reasonable to expect, but she suspected he had been even while alive. His bones on the other hand always seemed perfectly polite. They waved.

"You are early." He chuckled the uncomfortable laugh of a madman. "Early, early, beautiful, beautiful Nessy."

The manacles around Dan's skeleton's ankle were long

enough to allow it the run of the kitchen. It went to the corner and gathered some coal for the stove.

"Thank you." She put a hand to her muzzle and whispered a cantrip. The coal popped to a red glow.

Dan snapped his jaw together. "Always helpful, Mister Bones. Helpful, helpful Mister Bones. Not so helpful if I were on your shoulders, Mister Bones. Not so helpful then would you be." He laughed again while grinding his teeth.

The nurgax sniffed Mister Bones. The skeleton patted it on the head, and it purred.

Nessy went to the icebox, a large wooden crate kept cold by magic. That Margle provided such a convenience made him a better master than most. She removed a chicken, some carrots, turnips, and other vegetables.

"Chicken soup tonight," said Dan. "Always chicken soup tonight. Beautiful, predictable Nessy."

She was the first to admit she found comfort in routine. For Nessy, life was a schedule, a series of tasks, a constant battle against disorder. This was why she was such a good keeper of the castle, and why Margle had never gotten around to killing her. Now that he gone, she realized just how much she'd miss him. He'd been cruel and insulting, devious and demented, but this was to be expected from a dark wizard. But he wasn't all bad, and she'd always believed everyone had something good in them. Even if some did have to be beheaded before it could find its way to the surface.

Mister Bones placed the big pot under a spigot and filled it with water.

"Three fourths full now," she reminded him.

The skeleton rapped the spigot twice.

"Oh, Mister Bones, what has become of you without ol' Dan to show you the way?" The skull rocked back and forth. "Sorely does ol' Dan wish you would put those hands to more lovely use."

The nurgax growled at him, and Mister Bones shook his fist.

"No reason to be impolite now," scolded Nessy while chopping celery.

Mister Bones shrugged. He put the pot on the stove to boil.

An extended keening rattled the room, announcing Bethany the banshee's appearance. Bethany could move throughout the castle, but she could only appear in times of approaching calamity. She was a tall, lean spirit with delicate features and long red hair. Her black robes billowed loosely around her. She raised her head and unleashed a piercing scream.

Nessy, always up for a good howl, added a mournful song of her own. The nurgax moaned softly.

Decapitated Dan grumbled, "What a racket. Ol' Dan would surely love his hands now."

A more determined banshee might wail on for days, but Bethany's cry sputtered to a cough after two minutes. She cleared her throat. "Mind if I take a seat?"

"Help yourself."

The corporeal ghost found a chair. Approaching disaster gave her a solidity few spirits could enjoy, albeit temporarily.

"So what brings you here?" asked Nessy.

"Your soup. You're going to put too much salt in it." Her hair whipped upward like flame shooting from her head. "Terrribbblyyyyyy Sssaaaaltyyyyyyyyyyyyy," she keened.

"That's your disaster?" Dan laughed. "Salty soup?"

"Not just salty. Terribly salty." She stood and moaned. Ice formed on the walls. "Dreaaaaaddfuuuuullyyyyy terribbbb—"

Nessy interrupted. "Yes, thank you."

"Where were you when Margle was getting chewed?" asked Dan. "Could've used a warning then, I bet ol' Margle could."

Bethany scowled. "Distasteful cad."

"True, I have my quirks, true. But I know a thing or two about Margle, about Margle's castle. Because I listen, and I hear the castle. The walls, they share secrets with ol' Dan."

"You're mad."

"Mad as a skull on a spice rack. But I can tell you things a banshee should already know." He opened his jaws wide, chuckled on for a moment before snapping them shut. The kitchen was silent except for the sounds of Nessy and Mister Bones mincing vegetables.

"Like what, you demented bone?" asked Bethany.

"Oh, things."

"You don't know anything."

"Ol' Dan knows too much. Why do you think I'm mad?"

"Well then tell us."

"What I know, it's for Nessy's ears. It's a warning beyond culinary cataclysm. You don't get to hear it."

"You mad bas . . ." Bethany began to fade as her solidity left her. "Oh damn. Don't forget, Nessy. Saaaaaaaltyyyyyyy souuuuuuuuuuuup!" And she returned to the ether.

Decapitated Dan scowled. "Thought she'd never leave."

Nessy allowed Mister Bones to chop the rest of the vegetables as she bit off chunks of chicken flesh and spat them into the pot.

"Well, don't you want to hear what ol' Dan has to say?"

"Not really." She nibbled on a bone before stirring it in the bubbling water.

The skull frowned. "That's not right. Here I sit with only boring Mister Bones to keep me company. But I don't complain, I don't. Only the pleasantest of gents, that's what I am. And I want to help you because once you hear what ol' Dan has to say, you'll be glad you did, you will be."

She decided he had a point. Certainly, he had been a villain and still was, but he was paying for his misdeeds, even beyond his own death. She saw no harm in lending a sympathetic ear while waiting for her dinner.

"Very well."

"Sweet, sweet Nessy. I've always liked you. Sorely will I regret strangling the life from you once me and Mister

Bones make amends." He chuckled. "Not too sorely, mind you, but with some contrition."

The nurgax growled. Nessy noticed it didn't respond well to threats against her. She rubbed its snout, and the beast quieted. Though it kept its eye on Dan.

"Margle isn't dead, but you already know that, don't you, Nessy? If he were well and truly gone, beyond the hope of likely resurrection, then some of his sorcerous ilk would have arrived by now to commence their scavenging of his estate. That not a single scavenging sorcerer or covetous enchantress has yet to appear shows that Margle, though certainly devoured, is not dead enough that any have sensed it yet. A mixed blessing, I suppose, protecting this castle from his plundering ilk while Margle waits to return from death's sweet affections.

"Nope, can't kill a wizard in his own home. Ol' Dan can hear him grumbling in the bricks. Only a matter of time before he comes back, but right now, the castle, it doesn't want him alive, no it doesn't. It likes him dead. With him dead-but-not-quite-dead there's nothing to keep it from doing the bad things it wants to do. And the things, they are terrible. Terrible enough to make even me tremble." He demonstrated by waggling his jaw. "It's an evil castle, it is."

Mister Bones ladled out some soup for Nessy to sample.

"Needs salt."

The skeleton retrieved the spice.

"Careful," she reminded him.

He rapped the stove twice in acknowledgment.

"But it is also a good castle," said Dan. "Good because sweet, sweet Nessy has shown it such care and love. Like ol' Mister Bones. And that goody goodness, that likes Margle dead, too. About the only thing the good and the evil agree on is that. Poor ol' Margle. None truly liked him. All that power and not a true friend to his name. Could almost make me weep, if I were able.

"Now the castle is like me and Mister Bones. Two halves of one whole. One half ever so delightfully wicked, the other so utterly, completely, absolutely dull in its goody goodness. And like me and Mister Bones, there will come a reconciliation. The question is which will be the conqueror, that's the question." He smiled, and if he'd had eyebrows, surely they would've bent low and cast darkness over his eyes. "No question there. Truth is, wickedness always wins. Ol' Dan will have my body back one day, and the castle, oh the castle, shall have its depravity. And ol' Margle, well, who's to say?"

Mister Bones brought Nessy a bowl of soup. She lifted the spoon to her lips, but before she could taste it, Dan spoke.

"Wait, you didn't let me get to the best part, sweet Nessy. I got a prophecy, I do. Not so much a prophecy as a way things are going to happen, must happen because things always happen as they must. I know because the castle knows. Four things shall occur, perhaps not in this order, mind you. Perhaps the first shall be last, and the last shall be first. Perhaps the second shall be—"

Even Nessy's patience had an end. "What are they, Dan?"

He shouted the first three. "The castle will devour us all. The dead shall fear, as only the dead shall have need of the fear. Ol' Dan and Mister Bones will be the greatest of friends again." His voice lowered to a whisper. "And The Door At The End Of The Hall will finally open." He laughed loud and hard for a very long time until Mister Bones clamped a hand atop the skull. "Here now, here now," Dan grunted through clenched teeth. "Allow a madman his madness. It's only right."

Nessy took a sip of her soup, rolling it around on her tongue.

"How is it?" asked Dan.

Her ears flattened. "A little salty."

# THREE

**K**obolds were cave dwellers. They lived in dark and dreary places, and Margle's castle was generally a dreary place. There were precious few windows, and only one door leading out. This door was always barred, as Margle never used it, and Nessy couldn't remember the last time she'd been out. She had trouble remembering what the castle even looked like from outside. It was impossible to see much of it from the windows, few of which had been designed with a view in mind.

Her mental map of her home's interior told her that, though the castle was big, its layout wasn't strictly bound by the sensibilities of space. Hallways crossed through other hallways, yet never actually met, and doors led into different rooms in the same spot. It was all fairly standard as magical castles went, but it made an accurate measure of its dimensions difficult to determine.

Nessy, preferring to be surrounded by stone, found the open sky to be a most disconcerting sight. Without a roof over her head, she couldn't help but constantly glance upward for fear of being struck by something falling from the heavens. Whether it be meteorites or rain, lightning or bird droppings, it didn't seem worth the risk.

It was a known fact that kobolds had a tendency to be crushed beyond mere statistical peculiarity. Kobolds didn't have a god of their own, and without that, they were fair game for any angry, frustrated, or bored deity looking to smite someone for whatever reason gods might enjoy. It was accepted among Nessy's people that the residents of the heavens kept a tally of every kobold thus smote, and at the end of time, the god with the highest score would receive some sort of prize, perhaps a cloak of invisibility or flying sandals or some such divine novelty. Sensibly, Nessy never quite believed this. But she didn't disbelieve it, either. Not after seeing her uncle squashed beneath a falling ox under an otherwise perfectly clear sky.

After that, she rarely ventured outside except by dimmest night or heavy clouds or darting from tree to tree. It was only after coming to Margle's castle that she discovered the joys of a sunny day or a shining full moon. Dark wizards kept close watch on the heavens, and the castle had an observatory atop one of its smaller towers with a large window that always followed the sun and moon. It was a quiet chamber with a small fountain, a comfortable bench, and ivy-covered walls. For Nessy, it was the perfect place to enjoy a view of the clear sky. And the sturdy roof provided ample protection from any plummeting rumi-nants.

It was early evening when she came up to the observa-tory with a tome of magic tucked under her arm. The nurgax followed, carrying Yazpib the Magnificent's jar in his gentle jaws.

The purple-and-white flowers blooming on the walls turned in Nessy's direction. "Good eve to you, pup."

"Hello, Ivy. My condolences for your loss." Nessy low-ered her ears and tail and offered a sympathetic whine.

Perhaps the most obvious sign of Margle's evil was his metamorphosis of his own mother. Over the course of years, he'd transformed her into a shrew, a nag, a cow, a harpy, and an old bitch. Finally he abandoned poetic expression and just made her a mass of clinging vines.

"Not as if I cared for the little bastard," Ivy growled. "And he was a bastard, you know. Just as worthless as his worthless bastard father. Never should've agreed to let him apprentice to that necromancer. But I needed the money. Oh, how difficult it was for me. Raising two boys all by myself. What choice did I have? All that hard work, all that sacrifice, and this is my reward. Hope he rots."

Her comments saddened Nessy. Everyone, no matter how wicked, was due one mourner at the very least.

She went to the window and allowed herself a few minutes to enjoy the view. The grassy fields went as far as the eye could see. A lonely tree stood atop the hill on the horizon. During the day, the yellowed plains were nothing to look at, but at night, the grass took on a soft blue color, the stars twinkled, and the bright moon seemed close enough to touch.

Margle had brought her this. She raised her head and howled for her dead master. In the yowls and yelps of her native tongue, she sang out Margle's praises. It was a very short howl so she repeated it twice more. Ears cocked forward, she listened to the countryside far below. In the distance, a wolf echoed the depressing call. Perhaps somewhere farther away, another continued the song. On this night, the whole world might mourn Margle one howl at a time. That notion brought a smile to Nessy's muzzle.

"That was beautiful," said Yazpib.

"You speak Kobold?"

"A little. He didn't deserve such an honor."

"Since when does anyone get what they deserve?"

"Oh how true," lamented Ivy. "How true indeed."

Yazpib chuckled. His liquid bubbled. "You have the soul of a philosopher, Nessy."

Ivy continued to moan. "I gave and I gave, everything I had, and then I gave some more until I had nothing left to give. If anything, I should be sainted."

"Yes, yes, Mother," said Yazpib. "Now if you'll quiet down, Nessy and I would like to begin our lesson."

"Oh what a terrible thing, telling your own mother to shut up."

"I didn't say—"

"No, no. I'll be quiet. I'll just sit here and grow." Her flowers drooped. "Quietly."

Yazpib sighed.

"Won't hear another word from me. Not another word. Heavens know we mothers must always suffer in silence, always put aside our own needs for our loved ones. And here I am, grieving. But I'll just grieve silently."

"Mother, you hated Margle. You always hated him. And he hated you, as I think would be evident by your condition."

"How dare you! The bond between a mother and child is sacred."

He whispered to Nessy, "Why did my brother have to leave her the power of speech? If anyone should be stricken with a curse of eternal silence . . ."

"What was that?"

"Nothing, Mother."

She grumbled. "Whispering before your own mother. I would box your ears if I could."

Yazpib's eyes bobbed and rolled. "Lucky for me my beloved brother took my ears."

"Such disrespect. Where did I go wrong?"

"Oh shut up, Mom."

Ivy didn't shut up, but she did resort to mumbling about

her mistreatment. No one listened, and this only confirmed how appalling her fate was.

"Now, Nessy," said Yazpib, "open your book to the first chapter."

Sir Thedeus flew into the room and perched on Nessy's shoulder. "Did I miss anything?"

"Just getting started. We'll need a potato."

A multitude of vegetables and fruits grew on Ivy's enchanted vines. Nessy picked a plump potato.

"What are ye doing with that?" asked Sir Thedeus.

"We're going to see if Nessy can levitate it."

The bat hopped onto the jar's edge. "Are ye an idiot? What good does levitating a potato do anyone? Ye should be teaching her to break curses."

Yazpib boiled. "In due time. But Margle's magic is potent stuff. She can't just learn to undo it in her first lesson."

"Ach, fine, but a potato?"

"It just so happens that the potato is the most magically benign vegetable there is. The first three years of my apprenticeship, potatoes were all I was allowed to work with. And I turned out a perfectly fine wizard."

"Yer a brain in a jar."

"I suppose you think you'd do a better job teaching Nessy. And just how much magic do you know?"

Sir Thedeus snarled and tried to stare Yazpib down. Since Yazpib lacked eyelids, the bat predictably lost. "Maybe she can start working with carrots in a month or two. Won't that be something?"

Yazpib's teeth twisted in a frown. "You don't let an apprentice anywhere near a carrot. Nastiest buggers of the vegetable kingdom. Levitating a carrot without some experience under your belt is the surest way to lose an eye."

"Can we get on with the lesson, please?" asked Nessy. "I have some sweeping that needs to be done."

"Of course. If you would open your book to Chapter One: Your Enchanting Potato."

As she'd already learned some minor magic, making a potato hover wasn't very difficult for Nessy. Within twenty minutes, she could make it float slowly about from across the room. She even advanced beyond the need for incantation or gesture, achieving magic by thought alone. Yazpib was impressed, though she lost control of the vegetable at lesson's end. It ricocheted around the observatory, nearly striking Sir Thedeus as he nibbled a banana. The potato mashed into a wall.

"Ach, careful there, lass. Could've taken me head off."

Yazpib smiled smugly. "If that were a rutabaga, you would most certainly have been maimed."

The nurgax licked the potato off the wall.

Echo spoke up, startling everyone. Nessy and the nurgax jumped. Sir Thedeus spat up a chunk of banana, and Yazpib sank to the bottom of his jar.

"It's gone, Nessy! It's gone."

"What's gone?"

"The Door At The End Of The Hall."

"What's that?" asked Yazpib.

"It's The Door At The End Of The Hall, that's what it is. Only it's not at the end of the hall anymore."

"Where is it?"

"Aren't you listening? It's gone. I don't know where."

"Calm down, Echo," said Nessy. "Let's go take a look."

"Take me with you," whispered Yazpib. "Don't leave me here alone with her."

"Ye can't expect us to haul ye around the castle, ye git."

"Can you at least screw my lid on? I'm begging you." He dipped low in the yellow fluid beneath Ivy's glaring blooms.

Nessy and everyone gifted with independent movement made their way through the castle halls.

"This can't be good," said Echo. "I mean, that door was the only place even Margle feared."

"Maybe it just went away," suggested Sir Thedeus. "What do ye think, Nessy lass?"

"No point in speculating yet."

It wasn't unusual for rooms and doors to move in Margle's castle. Some doors only appeared at night or day, others for only an hour or two a day. Certain hallways opened only during certain seasons. There was a dungeon in the depths that only showed itself once a year, but there was predictability in these movements. The Door At The End Of The Hall had never gone anywhere before.

Decapitated Dan had said that The Door At The End Of The Hall would open, that the castle would devour them all. For the first time, Nessy worried that he might be right. Up to now, she'd assumed Margle would return or the castle would be looted. But now, she felt as if something else might happen.

It was just a feeling, a pinprick at the tips of her ears. But the walls seemed closer. The halls darker. There was something wrong with the castle.

Something hungry.

Gareth the gargoyle watched the Door from his perch. "It's still gone."

Nessy peered down the hall, forty feet of dusty stone. At the end, there should've been a massive oaken door barred with a heavy iron slab. Instead, there was only a wall.

"Did you see what happened, Gareth?" asked Echo.

"Of course I saw. Not like I can look away. What a stupid question."

Sir Thedeus landed with a flutter between Gareth's horns. "Quit yer blathering, lad. What did ye see?"

"Nothing really." He frowned. "It was there. Then it wasn't."

"Maybe it's just invisible," said Echo.

"It never went invisible before," said Gareth.

"Well, just because it hasn't, that doesn't mean it can't."

"Maybe someone should take a closer look." Sir Thedeus crept forward, draping his wings across the gargoyle's eyes.

"I can't see."

"Nothing to see, lad. I think ye should go down there and look, Echo."

"Why me?"

"Because ye are just a voice. Nothing bad can happen to ye."

Echo scoffed. "You don't know that."

"Dunna be a coward, lass. What's there to be afraid of? That Door has never done anything."

"I don't see you volunteering."

"Look at me." Sir Thedeus spread his wings. "I'm a mere rodent. What can I do?"

"You can look just as well as I can."

Gareth laughed. "Shameful. Just shameful. When I was a hero, I would've walked up to that door, thrown it open, and slain whatever horror awaited on the other side. And I would've used my bare hands too. Just for the challenge. Reminds me of the time I had to drag a sea serpent across twelve leagues of desert to throw it back in the ocean because killing it would've been just too easy. Of course, back in those days, I didn't bother using a sword unless a beast was seventeen feet long at the very least."

"What does that have to do with anything?" asked Echo.

"Ye are an idiot. Why would Margle fear a sea serpent?"

"I didn't say that's what it was. I'm just saying, whatever is behind that Door can't be worse than that." The gargoyle scowled. "What do you think it is?"

"Damned souls." Sir Thedeus darted to the floor and crouched low as he stared down the hall. "Spirits so foul, so wicked, they would plunge this world into eternal darkness should they ever be unleashed."

Gareth nodded slowly, which took a great deal of effort for him. "Oh yes. That makes a lot of sense."

"Sea serpents." Sir Thedeus snorted. "What do ye think, Nessy?"

"I think I'm going to take a closer look." Nessy dropped to all fours and cautiously started down the hall. The nurgax followed.

"There's courage worthy of a hero," said Gareth. "You two should be ashamed of yourselves." He cast a disapproving glance down on them, although he had to sweep from side to side to be sure he caught invisible Echo.

"Ye loon." Sir Thedeus flew after Nessy.

"Oh damn." Echo sighed. "You know, when I had a body, I was a poet, not a hero. I wrote one naughty limerick about some wizard I never thought I'd meet, and here I am." Her voice trailed behind the bat. "Damn. Why did 'Gargle' have to be such a hard word to rhyme?"

Nessy crept slowly toward the end of the hall. There was no reason to be afraid. True, the Door was something Margle feared. True, there was an inexplicable dread that came upon her from merely laying eyes upon it. True, Decapitated Dan had mentioned the Door specifically in his mad rant. And true, as she drew closer to the hall's end, the temperature dropped and the torchlight grew dimmer. But the fear behind the Door, palpable though it was, was all speculation. In a castle full of genuine monsters and cursed inhabitants, it seemed illogical to cower from it.

Halfway down the hall, the air grew cold enough for them to see their breath. In moments like this, Echo could be seen as frosty wisps. "It looks okay. I think we should turn back."

Sir Thedeus, clinging tightly to Nessy's back, agreed. "Aye, everything appears in order. No reason to get closer."

The nurgax whined softly.

Nessy kept on. In most affairs, she was open to suggestion, especially a suggestion that agreed with her instincts, but no fear, particularly one so vague and undefined, was a match for her detestation for disorder and her dogged work ethic.

The castle always made noise. It rumbled and groaned, creaked and murmured, sometimes even boomed and shuddered. Nessy barely noticed the constant racket anymore, but she noticed its absence when they were ten feet from the end. It was as if the castle itself dared not breathe.

Nessy had never been this far down the hall before. As far as she knew, no one ever had. Not even Margle.

"Clearly, we're close enough," whispered Echo. "No reason to get any closer."

Sir Thedeus hopped off Nessy's back. "I agree."

But Nessy kept on, and the nurgax, reluctant but ever loyal, trailed close behind. She reached out and put her hand against the cold wall where the Door had been. The hall shuddered ever so gently.

Then nothing.

"Is it there?" asked Echo. "Is it invisible?"

Nessy shook her head. She'd lost her fear and ran her hands up and down the stone. "There's nothing here."

"Well, it's got to be here," said Sir Thedeus. "Canna ye feel it? 'Tis a dread, a terrible ache in me fangs, and when me fangs ache, 'tis sure to be something amiss."

Nessy agreed. She felt nothing in her own fangs but, to be certain, there was a tingling in her ears beyond mere imagination. If the Door was not here, it was certainly not far away. The question in her mind was finding it and getting it back where it belonged.

"Can we go now?" Echo said. "I think we should go."

"Aye." Sir Thedeus flew back without waiting for the others and smacked into The Door At The End Of The Hall. He scrambled away and clawed his way to a corner in the ceiling as far away as he could get.

The open end of the hall was gone, replaced by the Door.

"We're trapped." Echo's white breath grew into great anxious puffs. "It's trapped us."

The Door groaned as its oaken planks bent forward.

The nurgax howled in terror. Nessy put her palm on its snout. It quieted.

She walked up to the Door, no longer afraid. It was absurd to fear any door, she decided. No matter how much supernatural malice might lurk behind it. She'd never seen the Door this close. The iron bar was covered with dozens of runes, and several more parchments with additional glyphs were nailed across it. There was a great deal of magic dedicated to keeping the Door closed, she guessed.

"We can't get out." Echo wheezed as she did when excited. "We're trapped. We're trapped."

"Calm down, lass. Ye can go get us some help, canna ye?"

"I can't walk through walls. You can squeeze through smaller cracks than I can."

"That dunna make any sense."

"Margle made the rules. Not me." She gulped. "Have I mentioned I'm claustrophobic?"

The Door shook. The gold ring of its handle smacked loudly. Its hinges bulged as if they might break, and the parchments billowed forward like paper tentacles. Hot wind poured from its cracks and filled the shortened hall with stifling warmth.

"I have to get out of here!" Echo screamed incoherently, bouncing around the walls.

Nessy stood before the Door. The nurgax tried to stand at her defense. She pushed it aside, and it obeyed reluctantly.

The Door groaned. Its runes swam about, twisting into new forms.

"That's enough!" growled Nessy. She didn't like raising her voice. She considered it a mark of poor character. "Quiet down. You're scaring Echo half to death."

The Door creaked and rumbled.

Nessy folded her arms and bared her teeth. "I said, quiet down."

It grumbled with one soft squeak.

Echo was reduced to a wheeze beside Nessy's ankle.

The kobold stopped snarling and smiled with good humor. "Now I know you want to be opened, but I'm not going to do that. So you might as well get back to where you belong. You can keep us here all night. It won't change a thing." She sat. "I can sleep here just as well as my bed. Though it would've been nice if I'd known you were going to do this. I would've brought a pillow."

The Door had no face, nor anything resembling a face. But many things in the castle with their own thoughts and feelings were similarly handicapped. Nessy understood animated objects as someone who dealt with them on a daily basis. The slant of the Door's timbers and the tilt of its ring indicated a stubborn resolve. But she could be just as stubborn.

Sir Thedeus was on her shoulder again. "Ye canna be serious, lass. We could starve to death."

"We could, but we won't." She spoke up to be sure the Door heard her. "Because sooner or later, the castle will need tending. And that is my task."

The Door exhaled with disgust. Icy fog rolled from under it. Even with her clothes and fur, she shivered. But she wasn't giving in. She curled up on the floor and closed her eyes. The nurgax lay beside her.

"Good night."

The Door At The End Of The Hall rumbled and groaned loudly enough to shake the walls.

"I said, good night."

Everything fell quiet. The frozen fog danced away. The Door offered one last creaking sigh.

# FOUR

Night fell on the castle, although there were precious few indications of it inside the walls. The only reliable sign was the dimming of its eternal torches. As the castle was such a shadowy place even during the day, this was a subtle difference. But, in those hours surrounding midnight, the castle slept.

Mostly.

For Margle's castle was never completely still. Like any living thing, the castle had its dreams. And nightmares. And these nightmares roamed the halls at night, creeping from the shadows. There were certain chambers that no one went near after dark, certain places where depraved dreams waited to swallow up anything they came across. But some accursed residents were drawn out after dark, called out by the cool night air. Others walked simply because their transmogrified nature rendered them nocturnal, despite their better judgment.

Olivia the owl flew through the hallways with a mouse clutched in her talons.

"Faster," said Morton. He loved to fly.

"If I fly any faster I'll fling us face-first into a most unfortunate fate. Let me land and luxuriate my limbs." She let the mouse loose to stretch his legs.

"I don't think that's the proper use of 'luxuriate,'" he remarked.

"Allow me a little leeway in my language. As I can't control my curse completely, I must mangle my mutterings from moment to moment."

Morton groomed his whiskers. "I still don't understand why Margle double cursed you."

"Why do wizards work worthless wonders?" She nibbled her wing. "I believe such befuddlement only boggles our brains. Personally, I postulate Margle was postponing pococurantism."

"Pococurantism?"

"A byword for boredom." Olivia sighed. While it was true her curse of endless alliteration was a minor one, it could prove annoying. Morton spent a great deal of time with her, and she still lost him on occasion.

"Maybe now that Margle's dead, you'll be able to speak normally soon."

"Eternally optimistic as ever, Morton. In spite of my own cynical slant, sincerely must I always admire your interminable ebullience."

"You're too kind." His whiskers twitched with a chuckle.

"Although, I think if it did end, I'd miss it a little. It's rather beautiful sometimes."

She laughed. "A perplexing paradox."

He grinned. "Positively."

Mouse and owl were deeply in love. Their metamorphosed forms might limit their relationship, but neither wasted time thinking about things beyond their control. They were just happy to have each other. He drew close to her down, and she covered him with a wing. They sat there contentedly for a few quiet minutes until jingling bells caught their attention.

The Vampire King lurched from the shadows. Once he had been a powerful lord of the undead. Now, he was merely a stumbling corpse unable to procure a fresh meal. Margle's curse on the King was a simple one. First, he'd removed much of the vampire's supernatural talents. Then he'd made it so the King's slightest movement triggered the ringing of invisible bells. When he walked, he chimed. When he ran, he could be heard from a thousand yards away. It made finding a victim quite impossible.

Olivia snatched Morton in her claws and flew to a high perch as the King trudged below.

"Good evening," said Morton.

The Vampire King grunted. He waved and three beautiful tones resonated.

"Off to have a chat with Walter?"

He grunted again. Every night, he rose from his crypt in

search of fresh blood, and every night, he had to settle for licking the bleeding wall.

"Woefully withered wretch."

"Could be more friendly," said Morton. "We're all laboring under curses here."

The King stopped and for a moment, the halls were silent. "We are all not laboring equally." Even when he moved his jaw to speak, the chimes persisted. "I was the general of the greatest undead army the world had ever seen. My legions swept across the land. Seven kingdoms were fed to my ghouls. Those we didn't eat were added to our numbers. We were unstoppable. I was unstoppable."

"A plain prevarication," said Olivia. "Perfectly portrayed by your presence in this pernicious palace."

The Vampire King's red eyes glared in his drawn, white visage. "The point is that before running across that damnable wizard I was someone important. To be reduced to this . . ." He spread his arms and filled the air with a lovely tune. "It is unthinkable."

Morton scrunched his pink nose in disgust. "With an attitude like that, no wonder you haven't any friends."

"I don't need friends." Stooping, the King trudged away with musical footsteps. "I need blood."

A chill wind swept through the halls.

"The Wailing Woman?" Morton shivered.

"The Wailing Woman wanders the west wing when the week is waning."

"You're right. It's too quiet to be her."

At the far end of the hall, the torches extinguished. Though they often dimmed and brightened on their own, they had never gone out before.

"That's odd."

"Unexpected and unprecedented. Something slips surreptitiously." As an owl, Olivia's night vision was exceptional. She could see something in the dark, but she couldn't quite make it out. The creature seemed to wear the shadows as a cloak. "I sense a sinister spawn, a perilous presence."

The Vampire King paused and glanced over his shoulder at the creature in the shadows. The monster stepped forward. A single massive paw was stuck into the light before being covered by the veil of shadows. The beast snorted. Flame burst from its nostrils, but failed to light the dark. Only its snapping yellow teeth were clear.

"It can't be." The King froze in fear. "I didn't think even he'd be mad enough to have one of those in this place."

The beast stalked forward.

"What is it?" asked Morton.

"Death. Death for the dead."

"Well, I guess we've got nothing to fear then. Since we're both alive."

Olivia nodded. "Safe and sound since we still subsist."

Indeed, the creature obviously ignored them. As it drew closer, its yellow eyes focused unblinkingly on the Vampire King.

"Fleeing from this fiendish fauna might be fortuitous."

"What?"

"She's telling you to run," translated Morton.

As if the beast understood as well, it charged forward. Every step into the light was a blur of teeth and claws and fire. The darkness chased just behind. The Vampire King turned and dashed away in a chaos of crashing bells. The beast pursued, whipping past Olivia and Morton to chase the King.

They gagged. It wasn't shadows that covered the beast but thick, unnatural smoke. It reeked of sulfur and brimstone.

Olivia took the mouse in her claws and flew in pursuit. It wasn't hard to follow. The King made so much noise when he ran.

"He'll never lose it."

"Cursed cacophony conspires against the King."

Distantly, the vampire yelled as the smoke beast howled. Olivia turned a corner. The monster snorted once more, spit another gout of flame, and ran off with the King clutched in its vicious jaws. The thunderous crash of ten thousand chimes drowned the vampire's screams.

Olivia landed, and Morton sniffed at a shred of black cloth.

"The King's cloak," she observed. "Could the King be killed?"

"Not killed." Morton pulled away the cloth to reveal a scrap of flesh, a pointed ear. "Consumed."

Olivia shuddered, raising her feathers.

"Catastrophic."

# FIVE

Nessy awoke to find The Door At The End Of The Hall gone again. This annoyed her. She liked everything to be where it belonged, and The Door At The End Of The Hall had become The Door That Went Wherever It Pleased Except Its Proper Place. That was untidy and unacceptable, even for a magical castle. But a new day was upon her, and with it, a new day's duties.

Today was Polishing Day. It only came around every few weeks, but it was one of her favorites. There was nothing quite like shining silver and buffing brass and seeing her reflection in the gleaming metal. The mere thought was enough to push aside her vexation.

Sir Thedeus and Echo took off on the task of spreading the story of their close encounter with the Door. Many, if not all, of the castle's residents lived for these sorts of tales. Boredom was a constant nuisance when one lived only in a portrait or as a statue or at the bottom of a deep, dark pit. Though the castle had hundreds of inhabitants, most called only a small part of it home, a chamber or two if they were fortunate.

On her way to the kitchen, Nessy stopped by her room (not truly a room, but more a corner in a large hallway) to speak briefly with the monster (less a ghastly beast and more a grumpy imp) that lived under her bed (more accurately a worn cot).

"Where were you last night?" The monster glared with its three eyes. Nessy had never seen more of it than those glassy, gray eyes.

"The Door At The End Of The Hall was proving mischievous."

"Are you okay?"

"Perfectly fine. I just wanted to let you know."

"As if I'd worry." His angry eyes softened. "But since you're not dead, you will be coming by tonight, won't you?"

"Barring any foolishness with the castle's other doors, yes."

"Good. I found a new book. I hope it's a good one." A small book slid from the darkness under the cot.

It was very dark under her bed, and he was dependent upon her to read to him. She enjoyed skimming a chapter or two before retiring as well. She couldn't imagine where the monster got these books as he never left the shelter of her cot, but it was a varied selection. Stories of romance, adventure, horror. Travelogues of distant lands. A manual on carpentry, another on how to improve yourself and win companions.

She leaned over and glanced at the latest offering. "It has a princess on the cover."

The monster blew a raspberry.

"There's a barbarian, too."

"Does he have a sword? If he has a sword, it might be good. Unless he's kissing her. If he's kissing her, it's going to be stupid."

"No, he's got an ax."

"Ax, eh? That's a twist."

"And there's a monster, too."

He chuckled. "I hope it's a dragon. I love it when they kill dragons. Pretentious reptiles, think they're so special just 'cause they can breathe fire and fly. Like that's so great. Is it a dragon?"

"Let's not ruin it." Nessy threw the book back under the bed and continued on her way.

Her breakfast was always the same: two biscuits, three slices of ham, and a tall glass of milk and honey. Mister Bones had it all prepared, the table set, by the time she walked through the kitchen door. The skeleton got her stool for her.

"Thank you."

Decapitated Dan sat quietly on the spice rack. He was not a morning person. It was only in the afternoon that he grew energetic enough to rant on madly.

Mister Bones, ever the thoughtful fellow, had an extra plate of ham and biscuits for the nurgax. Nessy had almost forgotten the beast because it followed so obediently and so quietly. The nurgax gulped down its meal and belched. She was about to eat her own when a black owl, gray mouse clutched in its talons, flew into the room and landed on the table.

"A new day necessitates Nessy nibble on nourishment," said Olivia.

"Yes, good thinking."

Morton scampered to the edge of the plate. "Terrible news. The Vampire King, he's dead."

"Of course he's dead. He's a vampire." Nessy tossed the bird and rodent a piece of bread.

The meal distracted Morton for a moment. He tried speaking with his mouth full and made little sense.

"Unquestionably undead," said Oliva. "But a big beast brutalized the bell-ridden being with such salacious savagery that the King's continued corporeality could be called into question."

Nessy was in the middle of dissecting Olivia's sentence when Morton sped things along with a translation.

"Some giant thing ate him."

Decapitated Dan cackled to life. "O ho ho. Ol' Dan told you. I told you, I did. One by one by one the prophecies of Ol' Dan will come to pass. O, how I can hardly wait. Wait. Wait. Wait. It'd be enough to drive me mad if I weren't already out of my skull. So to speak." He howled with deranged laughter.

"Quiet, please," said Nessy.

Dan stifled himself, though he still snorted and grunted with some amusement.

"Now, what exactly happened?"

"An evil entity engulfed the doomed undead denizen in its giant jagged jaws."

"Oh it was a horrible sight." Morton leaned boldly onto the plate. "Are you going to eat that bit of ham?"

She gave her meal to him. Disorder always made her lose her appetite. Plenty of unsavory creatures wandered the castle, especially at night, and Nessy had no doubt that there were mysteries and horrors lurking within it that only Margle knew. There was always another dark corner, another forgotten room, waiting quietly somewhere to cause some trouble. But for all its countless dangers, known and unknown, the inhabitants knew how to navigate them safely. It'd been years since anything of this sort had happened.

"Are you sure it ate him?"

"We didn't get to see the whole thing before it carried him off. But there was an ear left behind. We lost that to some rats. I think they were ordinary rats, but I don't know for sure. Olivia has gotten into the habit of giving any vermin she catches a chance to speak up, just in case."

She hooted. "Terribly traumatic to taste a talking treat."

Nessy hopped from the stool.

"Where are you going, dear Nessy dear?" asked Decapitated Dan. "Going to check on the King? No need, no need. He's dead, dead and gone, gone and gobbled. You can take ol' Dan's word for it. And everyone can tell you, ol' Dan's word is as good as a bucket of peaches. The dead would fear, that's what I said. And that's what's happened." He laughed.

Nessy ignored him, but even after she'd left the kitchen, he shouted after her.

"And how about that Door? Gone off on its own, hasn't it? It'll turn up, you can count on that. You have ol' Dan's word on that, and everyone knows Dan's word is as good as sunflower petals." His deranged laughter echoed. It rang in her ears long after she'd left him behind, all the way to the dank catacombs and the Vampire King's crypt.

She opened the King's coffin and found only the bed of soil and nothing else. Her distress rose, although she hid it well. Only the nurgax seemed to notice. It whined by her side.

"See? Gone," said Morton. "He has to be dead."

"The undead desire dark dirt during days."

"I don't like this, Nessy. I don't think I feel safe anymore."

"Too many multitudes of menace move through this manor. Generous jeopardies, hundreds of horrors, crowds of calamities, a deluge of danger."

"Quiet, please," said Nessy.

Olivia struggled against her curse, but still had to spit out one last phrase. "Great gatherings of ghastliness."

Nessy wasn't certain the King was dead. He could be sleeping somewhere else. There were plenty of dark places, but his sleep in any of these would be uncomfortable without his native soil to bring him peace. Given a choice, the King would be in this coffin. He was either dead or greatly inconvenienced. Perhaps hiding somewhere in terror. The idea of something unfamiliar roaming the halls hungry and unchecked put Nessy in an ill mood. This was unacceptable. The simple joys of Polishing Day would have to wait.

Olivia yawned. "Instincts obligate I seek slumber soon. Preferably a protected perch now that this new nefarious nuisance is gnawing on our neighbors."

"Not yet," said Nessy. "I need the two of you to come with me to the library and help me identify whatever ate the King."

"Happy to help halt these hideous happenings." Olivia blinked her large eyes sleepily. "But be brief. I need my nest and a nap."

Margle's library was something of a legend among wizards. It was a huge chamber with vaulted ceilings and great iron shelves filled with thousands upon thousands of magical textbooks. Tremendous crystal chandeliers made the room bright as day. Margle had never been especially stylish, but he'd spent a lot of time here in his research. It was the only room in the entire castle with wall-to-wall carpets and that maintained a comfortably mild temperature year-round. Several gargoyles decorated the shelves, unenchanted, purely for decoration. There was also a dead man dangling from a chandelier by the area set aside for reading.

The Hanged Man choked a greeting at their arrival. He could only speak clearly when he bothered to hoist himself up from his noose. But his arms were withered, mummified, and he didn't usually trouble anymore.

Nessy took special pride in the fact that the shelves were impeccably arranged. Maintaining it had never been the problem. Getting it in order had been the task. Margle never put anything in its proper place, and he'd had a small mountain of mislaid books. "Put these away. Do it quickly, and if I find even one book in the wrong space," he'd pointed to the Hanged Man, "I'll string you up next to the last imbecile dimwitted enough to put a necromancy primer in the alchemy section."

It'd been her first task in his service, and after she'd finished, Margle had paid her his one and only compliment in his employ. "Took you long enough, mongrel." It wasn't so much the words, but his smile that she considered her commendation. Although it wasn't so much a smile as a gratified snarl.

Nessy asked the Hanged Man for the best book on monsters. He pulled himself up just long enough to spit out, "Stoker's *Abominable Index*."

"Thank you."

He choked out a strangled "You're welcome."

Nessy went to the zoology shelves and found the text. For some reason, wizards loved giant books, not just thick but absurdly proportioned. Her small size required she carry the book across her back to the reading area. She laid it down with a thud. She pried the worn leather cover open with some effort and ran her finger down the table of contents.

The book slammed shut, nearly smacking her hand.

"Should've warned you," sputtered the Hanged Man. "He doesn't like to be read. And he can be a little verbose."

"I am not," shouted the book.

The Hanged Man looked as if he might argue, but his arms gave out so he just shrugged.

The book cleared its throat, although technically lacking a throat to clear. "Professor Stoker, greatest monster authority in all the world, at your service, sir."

"She's a female," said Morton.

Stoker's pages shook. "Of course. I should've known better. The female kobold has larger ears, closer set eyes, and— might I see your tongue? Ah, yes, speckled blue. Please, forgive my error. I can assure you, no one in this world knows more about subhuman flora and fauna than I. But my specialty is dangerous and unsavory beasts, not harmless creatures such as yourself. No slight intended to your species, my dear, but even you must admit kobolds are not the most intimidating of creatures."

"Verbose is an understatement," whispered Morton in Nessy's ear.

Olivia, perched on Nessy's other shoulder, agreed. "Verifiable veneration for his very voice."

Nessy interrupted. "Excuse me, but we need to identify a monster."

Stoker cleared his throat again. "Certainly, miss. You'll find no greater expert on the study of monsters, beasts, creatures, and horrors bipedal, quadruped, and hexapod."

Olivia's head drooped. "My resistance to rest is reducing."

Nessy attempted to open the book, but he held shut. "No need for that," he muttered through tightly clamped pages. "I can tell you anything you want to know faster than you could find it on your own. Just describe it."

"I'd do what he says," sputtered the Hanged Man. "It'd be easier."

Stoker grumbled. "I spend most my time on that shelf. I think it's not too much to ask that I be allowed to speak when I'm able."

Nessy conceded it was a reasonable request. She had Morton and Olivia describe what they'd seen of the Vampire King's end. Stoker analyzed their report aloud.

"A creature which feeds on the undead, eh? This is not as unusual as the layman might suspect. Vampires have a variety of predators: the bloodgutter badger, the mammoth maggot, the consuming slug. There is even a rare breed of carp which is quite lethal to the undead. But from what you have said, I have surmised that the beast encountered can be none of these."

"Can you stop telling us what it isn't and get to the point?" said Morton.

The book's pages bent in a frown. "Very well. I was merely attempting to educate you, to broaden your view of the fascinating world of metazoology. But if you insist on remaining ignorant . . ."

"This endless elaboration has exhausted my energies." Olivia hopped to the table, closed her eyes, and fell asleep.

Stoker took the hint. "This can only be one creature, an abomination so infrequently encountered that I have never seen one personally. Nor have I ever met any fellow scholar who has. I even doubted that it existed, but now . . ."

Morton was tired as well, but without nocturnal instincts, his annoyance kept him awake. "What is it?"

The book cleared his throat once again and opened wide.

"That's it. That's what we saw." Morton hopped onto the pages beside a sketch of a big black cloud with claws and vicious eyes.

Stoker mumbled as best he could without closing on the mouse. "Well of course it is. I am a world-renowned authority."

Nessy forced him flat. The book was ridiculously large, and the print on his pages was equally ridiculously large. She supposed it helped to make the intricate calligraphy more legible. It could've been half the size and perfectly functional, but Nessy had always been very practical and she'd never met a wizard yet who enjoyed that virtue.

She read aloud. "Hellhound. A creature of the underworld that feeds on intransient souls, both material and immaterial. The Hellhound's diet consists of apparitions, banshees, ghosts, ghouls, lamias, phantasms, phantoms, revenants, shades, specters, spirits, spooks, wights, will-o'-the-wisps, wraiths, zombies . . ."

"Doesn't say anything about vampires," observed Morton.

Stoker turned his next page, rudely thrusting the rodent onto the desk.

". . . And especially vampires."

The book slammed himself shut again. "In most situations, the beast would starve to death soon enough, but this castle's spirit population makes an ideal environment. The good news is that the hound is exclusively nocturnal. During the daylight hours, it finds a deep shadow to nest in. Again, this castle's many darkened corners provide it with an abundance of nesting grounds. A most interesting chance for prolonged study."

"Does it eat mice?" asked Morton. "Or owls?"

"Only ghostly ones. It has no interest in the living or the deceased. Its purpose is to restore balance to the metaphysical scales by dragging the stubborn dead to Hell."

The Hanged Man spoke up. "I don't want to go to Hell."

"Tough luck then, old chap."

"How do we get rid of it?" asked Nessy.

Stoker snapped his leather cover three times. "A very good question. Unfortunately, I don't know. Theoretically, it should starve to death once it has exhausted its food supply."

"But that could take months." Morton's whiskers twitched. "I'm glad I'm not dead."

"I wish I could be of more help." His satin bookmark offered half a shrug. "But anything else would be pure conjecture, and I deal in facts. I advise you seek a more knowledgeable authority. Perhaps a wizard."

"Or a demon," said Nessy.

"Oh, I wouldn't recommend that. Oh no. Not at all. My information on demons is unpleasant without exception." His pages flipped to a drawing of a huge, winged monster with a twisted, leering face. It was only ink, but it was dreadful to behold. The real thing could only be worse.

Frowning, she slammed the book shut. "I hope it won't come to that."

She returned Stoker to the shelf. He protested, and while she understood his reluctance, she couldn't bring herself to not put something back where it belonged. It was her nature, nursed by years of habit. She remembered the Vampire King's empty coffin. She hadn't any fondness for the King, but that he wasn't there distressed her more and more.

"Are you really going to deal with a demon?" asked Morton.

"If I have to."

"But the hound isn't dangerous. Not to us anyway. Why risk your life, your soul, for people that are already dead?"

"Just because they're dead, that doesn't mean they deserve to be dragged to Hell."

The Hanged Man struggled but was unable to raise himself with his exhausted limbs.

"No need to thank me," she said. "Just doing my job."

"A damn sight more than your duty, if you ask me," said Morton.

But the castle would be kept. And as she was the only one who could keep it, she would do whatever was necessary to maintain its order and to protect all those, living or dead, who called it home. They could expect nothing less from her. And neither could she.

# SIX

Nessy spent the next few hours checking each and every volume of the library's metazoology, demonology, and necromancy sections. She found nothing else on hellhounds. Nothing on how to summon them up. Nothing to dispatch them. Nor even a single description of the beast.

She wondered how the creature had found its way into the castle. She didn't believe it was happenstance. Everything else was here for a reason. But Margle's castle was protected from casual entry by unnatural forces. An underworld creature couldn't just slip in. The hound could only have come from inside.

Had Margle summoned it from the underworld with a magic so dark and secret that it wasn't even hinted at in even his most prized books? Surely, it must've been here by the wizard's doing, but how had it gotten loose?

Perhaps Margle had nothing to do with it. Perhaps it was all the castle's will. Decapitated Dan had said it possessed a life of its own. She'd already known that. But with its master dead, had it truly become an evil place, bent on devouring them all? She refused to believe that. Not yet. So rather than focus on things she didn't understand, she turned her attention to the hellhound and its removal.

Questioning Yazpib the Magnificent proved fruitless. "I'm sorry, but I have little experience with demonology. Too dangerous. Far, far too dangerous." The fluid in his jar paled at the mere thought. "It's no surprise my brother would. He was as devious and scheming as any demon."

So Nessy had only one place to turn: The Purple Room.

It was expressly forbidden to enter the room. Nor had she ever had any such desire because this was where a demon lived. If demons truly lived. Not just any demon, but a powerful lord of one of the deepest, darkest hells, bound to the room by Margle's most potent magic.

Nessy had a healthy caution toward The Purple Room, but she didn't fear it as she did The Door At The End Of The Hall. She passed it often, and it never acted the least bit strange. If she hadn't known there was a demon inside it, she wouldn't have given it much thought. Even knowing, she had always considered it merely a place she wasn't allowed to enter.

It was habit, not fear, that made her pause before The Purple Room's door. Margle was dead, but she felt some compulsion to obey him still.

"Changed your mind?" asked Yazpib. "That's good. Because you really shouldn't be going in there."

Nessy put her hands against the door. She didn't sense any of the danger she'd felt from The Door At The End Of The Hall, and she wasn't surprised. Wouldn't a good demon hide its darkness? It made temptation so much easier.

Sir Thedeus, clinging to her shoulder, whispered, "If ye change your mind, lass, none would think the less of ye."

"Get the necklace."

The bat flew to the cart, snatched a long, daggerlike tooth on a chain, and dropped it around her neck.

"Are ye certain this will protect her, wizard?"

"A tooth from the demon's own body should keep him from physically harming her." He frowned, eyes bobbing. "But with demons, it isn't the physical threats you have to worry about. You're fortunate if they kill you."

Nessy held the fang in both her small hands. It was as long as her muzzle. But she was determined. She reached for the handle.

Yazpib boiled. "Wait. If you insist on doing this, let me give you some advice."

"I thought ye didn't know anything about demons."

"I know a little. Just a little." He collected his thoughts. "Chiefly, I remember that demons never do anything for free. So if he does help, and I'd be surprised if he does, but if he does, he'll ask you for some sort of payment. Whatever he asks for, don't give it to him. Because it will appear to be perfectly harmless, but it won't be."

"But you just said he won't help if I don't give him something," said Nessy.

"Yes, but whatever he asks for first, don't give."

"Okay, then I'll give him the second thing."

Yazpib laughed dryly. "Oh, I can see this is going to be a bad idea. You can't give him his second request. Because that will appear even more harmless, but will be even more dangerous."

"She fulfills his third request then?" said Sir Thedeus.

"Are you insane? The third request will be less treacherous than the second but worse than the first."

"So is she to agree to the fourth demand?"

"Of course not. Not if she values her life and her immortal soul."

"So what is she supposed to do then?" Sir Thedeus's voice grew squeaky with irritation.

"She's not supposed to go in there." His eyes swirled nervously around his brain. "Understand, Nessy, that my brother was cruel and devious. But you are practical, steady and forthright. Admirable traits, except when it comes to bartering with a demon lord. But I can also see that you're stubborn when you've made up your mind. So please be careful."

"Aye, lass. Without ye, how are we to break our curses?"

"Is that all you care about? This courageous creature is about to endanger herself, and all you think about is your curse."

They started squabbling, but Nessy wasn't listening. She stroked the nurgax's horn, told it to stay, and entered The

Purple Room. The door clicked shut behind her. The nurgax moaned softly.

"Good luck, Nessy lass."

Yazpib shot a disgusted glance at Sir Thedeus with such force that his eyes nearly jumped out of his jar and rolled to the floor. "Yes. Good luck, indeed."

The Purple Room wasn't purple at all. It was black as pitch. Nessy didn't fear the dark. She possessed a talent for wandering around while blinded. Stick a kobold in an unlit chamber filled with dangers and only one exit, she'd more often than not find her way to safety. Nessy sometimes closed her eyes and dashed through the castle as fast as she could. Just to keep in practice should she ever return to her people.

The room was warm, though not uncomfortably so. She took a step forward with absolute trust that if there had been a bottomless chasm before her, her instincts would have held her back.

She spoke up very softly. "Hello?"

No reply came.

She took another step and called a little louder. "Hello. Is there anyone in here?" A perfectly stupid question. Of course, someone was in here. Or something.

"Hello!" Her voice echoed.

And then, either very far away or very close, a pinpoint of red and then yellow light appeared. A deep, booming voice filled the chamber and rattled in her ears.

"You are not Margle!"

"Margle is dead." She bit her tongue. Perhaps it had been unwise to let this slip. But she was a terrible liar. She would have to think before she spoke. Always a good policy when dealing with demons.

The light flared, yet offered little illumination. She wondered whether it was an eye. A single, glaring red eye set in a hideous visage that could drive her mad to look upon.

"Dead, you say!"

"Yes." No point in lying about that now.

The demon's voice lowered to merely obnoxiously loud. "How did he die? No, let me guess." The shining eye flashed through a spectrum of colors. "Eaten, wasn't he? Eaten by a nurgax. Am I right?"

She nodded, and even in the consuming darkness, the demon could see.

"How did—"

"How did I know?" The voice became soft and gentle and feminine. "I know a great many things, Nessy. A great many things."

Nessy wasn't surprised the demon knew her name. It seemed a very demony thing to know.

"Then you must also know why I'm here."

The demon laughed delicately. "Oh no, my dear. When someone comes to me for my help, I only know what they need when they request it of me. Odd, yes, but those are the rules. And we must all play by the rules."

The light drew closer, shone brighter. Yet Nessy couldn't see any other details of the creature.

"You wear my tooth. Do you fear me, Nessy?"

She thought before she answered, but a lie was unnecessary. The demon surely knew the answer. "Yes."

The demon chuckled with a tinge of sweet venom. "Very wise. And I see that you are possessed of a noteworthy wisdom along with a generous helping of compassion spiced with a robust serving of pragmatism. A rare delicacy. To measure your soul is to rediscover appetites I'd forgotten, locked away in this room." She inhaled loudly and smacked her lips. "Oh what a morsel you are. That I could pop you in my jaws, tuck you in my cheek, savor you slowly for a thousand or so years." Her voice trailed away dreamily.

"Alas, you hold my tooth. And my jaws aren't what they used to be." The eye rose high in the air, then low to settle on Nessy's nose. The demon was nothing more than a tiny, shining firefly. The insect was unremarkable, save that her tail was a shimmering tongue of flame. The lick of fire was hot, but it didn't burn.

The demon's breath was warm and sweet, washing over Nessy as if from a much larger creature. The sweetness was the stench of rotting flesh.

"You don't know what a treat this is for me. For far too long I've had to put up with that ludicrous wizard. And his soul, as a connoisseur of such, I can tell you is no joy to look upon. As ugly and contemptible as any I have ever come across. A wasted, miserable bauble, it is."

"Is?"

The firefly flitted to the top of Nessy's head. "I think we both know that he isn't dead. Not truly. Wretched and despicable as he might be, Margle is a superb wizard. I alone am testament to his power. Do you know how long I have been bound to this room, to flutter about in this purple cell?"

So The Purple Room was truly purple. Although, one would need a demon's eyes to see it in this darkness.

"No."

"Neither do I. Time and its passing are nothing to me because I have always been and will always be. But this is not a boon. Every hour in here is like a year to one such as I. Every minute a forever of itself." The firefly climbed down Nessy's neck and sat on her shoulder. "Countless eternities of solitude, of waiting for Margle to visit and make some demand, of having to listen to him prattle on and on. 'Oh, demon, I want this. Oh, demon, share your secrets. Never forget, demon, I can destroy you. Never forget, I know your true name.' As if he'd let me." She whispered in Nessy's ear. "As if I could."

The firefly's flame burst into a long, white tail. She flew through the air in fleeting patterns, leaving a trail behind her, a painting in living incandescence of Margle's long, lean, sneering face. The demon howled, sending shivers through every hair on Nessy's furry body. Margle's image twisted into a tortured scream before dissolving. The only light was once again the firefly's delicate tail burning a warm, gentle blue.

"Enough about me. Though I do appreciate you lending me your ear. I will have my vengeance one day, but not today. Today, we will speak about you. About what you want. About how I will help you." The fire tinted a cold crimson. "And how you will help me."

Nessy swallowed her uneasiness. She had no doubt that even transformed into an insect, the demon could kill her easily. She clutched the tooth that protected her, pulling it close.

"What do you want?" Nessy asked.

"Oh no. That is not how it works. First make your request. Then I tell you the price. Then we negotiate until we find an agreement suitable to both of us. Or, if this is not possible, I simply consume your soul."

Nessy backed away.

The firefly chuckled. "I jest, Nessy. You are always free to walk away, free to leave me behind and never enter The Purple Room again. Why would I harm you, leaving me to my loneliness? How could I harm you, such a sweet, lovely, tasty girl? The advantage is all yours, as anyone can plainly tell."

"You're trying to trick me." Nessy didn't know why she said it, other than that she had a tendency to say things she thought.

"I'm not trying to trick you. Not yet. I will when the bargain is being struck. Both of us know that, and I'll not insult you by denying it. But the bargain has yet to be struck, and it won't be until you let me know what you need." The demon flew close to Nessy's eyes, and though it was difficult to read a bug's face, Nessy thought she detected a dangerous smile across her mandibles. "Then we can begin the trickery."

Nessy stepped back. "There's a hellhound in the castle."

The firefly flitted about. "The hellhound is free, set loose to devour all the improperly deceased things roaming about."

"You knew?"

"I know many things. Haven't we discussed this? Secrets are my calling, as tending this castle is yours. I brought the hound here. By Margle's command, despite my advice against it. They are very difficult to contain."

"Can you send it back?"

"If only it were that easy, Nessy. If only. But my control over the beast requires it be in my presence. If you could bring it to me, I could banish it back whence it came. If I were free of my own prison, I could easily track it down for you and dispatch it. But neither seems a likely possibility."

"No."

The firefly blazed an innocent white. "Oh, no. Of course

not. Even if you knew the proper magic to undo my binding, which you obviously don't, you would be a fool to release me. And you are certainly no fool. So what is it you want of me then? Information, I suppose. One of my secrets that I do cherish so."

"How do I stop the hound?"

"I must admit a small surprise that you would bother. It isn't a danger to you so long as you leave it to its business. Would you be willing to risk your life for these half-living creatures which by all rights don't belong in this world?" The demon whipped high into the air until she was a mere yellow point. "Don't answer. I see it evident in your soul. You honestly care for them. I'm touched by this. I truly am. And if any demon possessed an ounce of charity, I would be tempted to answer your question for free. Alas, I am deprived of such grace. But I will help you. And as for payment . . ." She paused as if distracted and flew gently lower. "All I ask for is a single lump of coal."

"Agreed." Nessy didn't even think about it.

"What?" The firefly landed at Nessy's feet. "My first request? My dear girl, I don't know if anyone's ever taken the time to instruct you on the finer points of demonic negotiations, but you are never to give a demon the first thing she asks for."

"I know, but I also know that you are far more cunning and manipulative than I could ever hope to be. Trying to outwit you would be a waste of both our time. Whatever you ask will most certainly be trouble later, but I will deal with that when I must."

The demon laughed long and heartily. "Oh, how wonderful. How delightful. You are a marvelous rarity. Two kinds of idiots barter with demons. Desperate fools who think they've nothing to lose, and arrogant imbeciles who think they can somehow best us at our own game. How adorable to meet someone who is neither. Then it is my secrets for your coal." She took to the air, glowing with a dazzling red fire. Her voice boomed. "The bargain is struck."

"Shall I fetch the coal?"

The demon's voice and her glow became light and gentle. "I trust you, Nessy, and earning a demon's trust is a singular accomplishment. As to the methods of stopping this hound, there are several. But I shall only give you the ones that you have some chance of using. If it is exposed to purest sunlight, it will die."

"There's little sunlight in this castle."

"I wouldn't know, as this accursed room is all I get to see of it. If you can get the hound to ingest something still alive, this would be most virulent poison."

"How would I do that?"

The firefly bobbed. "That's something you'll have to figure out on your own. And finally, a sacred weapon dedicated to the art of slaying demons can destroy the beast. And I believe there is just such a weapon in Margle's armory, is there not?"

Nessy knew exactly what the demon spoke of. It was

the prize of her master's impressive enchanted-sword collection. "But I can't use that. Even Margle couldn't use that."

"Oh, but I think you can. I think you are more clever than you give yourself credit for. I think you can devise a way if you put your mind to it."

"Are you certain?"

"Certain? No, not certain. But I do know things, Nessy. And I ask only that you trust in me as I trust in you."

Nessy walked backward, unwilling to turn from the demon. "Thank you. I'll bring the coal right away."

The door opened, casting a sliver of light. Nessy slipped out, shutting it behind her. The firefly hovered silently for a minute or two, or perhaps an hour or three. It was so hard to tell sometimes.

The door opened again but Nessy didn't set foot inside. She tossed a lump of coal across the threshold.

"Thank you, Nessy."

"You're welcome, demon."

"And do remember to be careful with that hound. I'd hate to see anything happen to you."

The door closed with a soft click.

The firefly hovered over the coal. "What a lovely creature. I could see growing quite fond of her."

A second light flared beside her. "Don't get too attached. When the time comes, she will very likely try to stand in my way."

A third insect lighted. "Truly, a pity. If I had a heart, it would be heavy."

"How fortunate for me," said a fourth, "that I do not."

One by one by one, a thousand fireflies banished the darkness. The swarm's beating wings thundered.

As one, the fireflies extinguished. Their rumble faded. The Purple Room was dark once again. And in that dark, a demon chuckled softly.

# SEVEN

Many centuries ago, in a kingdom that has long since faded from memory, there was a fracture between the land of the living and the empire of the damned. Monsters of the underworld swarmed the good people and threatened to crush this realm. And from there, the rest of the world perhaps. But this abysmal tale of destruction didn't come to pass because of one enchantress and one smithy.

The smithy created a sword of such exquisite beauty and flawless craftsmanship that he would never design another as marvelous. Knowing this, he never stepped into another forge. The enchantress blessed the sword with all her magic, surrendering all her power into one everlasting spell. Then the smithy and the enchantress retired to raise sheep and beget fat, happy children. But not before giving the sword to a worthy warrior and sending him forth to save the world.

Thus armed, the warrior did beat back the demons, driving them into their Hell and sealing the portal. The kingdom was preserved, but there were still wrongs to right and evil creatures to destroy. The warrior kept at this noble task until, eventually, he was mortally wounded. Dying, he drove his weapon into a nearby rock while pronouncing his prophecy: "I plunge this blade into this stone and here it shall remain until a hero of courage and honor, strong of limb, skilled in combat, abhorrent of evil in all its forms shall draw it again."

Then he died.

The sword waited. Men came to test their worth: knights and barbarians, assassins and paladins, kings and peasants. Thousands were deemed inadequate, but in the course of time, a deserving hand was found. The weapon was drawn to continue its endless battle against evil.

Though the sword was everlasting, its wielder wasn't. This second great warrior was slain while knee-deep in the black and green blood of a demonic legion. Before she died, she drove the sword into a nearby tree stump.

"I plunge this blade into this stump and here it shall remain until a hero of courage and honor, strong of limb, skilled in combat, abhorrent of evil in all its forms shall draw it again."

Then she died.

The sword waited. Another hero eventually arrived, and the weapon was pulled from the stump. More epic battles were fought. More demons were slain. Heroes died. The sword was plunged and unplunged over and over again. Until, one fateful day, its latest dying hero thrust it once again into the nearest convenient object.

"I plunge this blade into this . . . cabbage? Oh damn."

Then he died.

Soon after this, Margle took possession of the Sword in the Cabbage. All his attempts to pervert its sacred magic ended in failure. So the sword slept.

And the sword waited.

Margle's armory was more of a museum really. The wizard had little use for swords or spears, armor or shields, but he'd always enjoyed collecting for its own sake. His collection of weapons was most impressive, housed in its own wing along with his treasure horde and the hall of art. It was too much for even dedicated Nessy to keep polished. For this, Margle had drafted a silver gnome.

His name was Gnick, and he wasn't cursed. Not technically. But like every silver gnome, he was obligated to help any host who served him a bit of bread, a glass of wine, and a bed of straw. In return for this pittance, he was compelled to polish and polish and polish. Such was the code of every silver gnome. He could only receive his wages, meager as they were, when he'd finished. And he was never finished because it would've taken a hundred industrious gnomes to get every weapon, every piece of armor, every shield, to shine at once. So Gnick's bread had turned to mold on its plate. His wine was vinegar. And his straw was undisturbed. And

Gnick, who never ate, never drank, and never slept, only polished, was in a very, very ill mood.

When Nessy, Sir Thedeus, and the nurgax arrived at the armory, Gnick was absorbed in buffing a piece of tarnished armor. She greeted him with a pleasant hello, but he was too busy to reply. Although he did glare.

It was her policy to be courteous to all the castle's inhabitants, no matter how irritable. They mostly had good excuses. She politely waited for him to finish with the armor and then asked for directions before he started on the lance beside it.

"Excuse me, but is the Sword in the Cabbage still to the left? Or has Margle moved it again?"

Gnick spat on the lance. Nothing brought shine to steel like gnome spit. "No. Still left."

"Thank you."

Before she could take a step, Gnick jumped in her path.

"You won't be touching anything, will you?"

"Just the Sword in the Cabbage."

Gnick glowered and did his best to appear threatening. But as he was very thin, very tired, and about a foot shorter than her, it came across as merely irksome. Like all faeries, he was immortal, but decades of uninterrupted work, no meals, no rest, had taken their toll. He'd lost his gnomish plumpness and the spring in his beard.

"Why don't you go and rub your oily fingers over all the blades while you're at it?" Gnick grumbled. "Might as well, seeing as how you'll be shedding all over the place too. The last time you were here, I kept finding hairs floating about for weeks."

Nessy thought his consternation a touch misdirected. While she might shed a little, she failed to see the harm. Gnick's task was an endless one, and a smudge here and a hair there couldn't make the duty any more everlasting. But she set aside such reasoning, knowing full well his mood had nothing to do with her.

Sir Thedeus was less polite. "Stand aside, ye imp. We've important matters to attend to."

"And you, you little flying furball, if I find even a single dropping in my armory I'll—"

"I dunna leave droppings." The bat leaned forward on Nessy's shoulder. "I have never ever dropped. Although in this case, I might be willing to make an exception."

Gnick pushed back his pointed hat. "You wouldn't dare."

"Oh I dunna know. I had a mango this morning. Never agree well with me, those mangos." He grinned, baring his tiny fangs.

Nessy stepped in. "I promise we won't touch anything besides the Sword in the Cabbage, and I'll do my best to limit my shedding."

"And the bat?"

"Ach, all right. Not a drop. Ye have me word as a gentleman."

Gnick snarled. Nessy suspected he questioned Sir Thedeus's gentlemanly qualifications, but he thankfully kept this to himself. "And what about that thing?"

"The nurgax will behave itself."

Whether or not he believed her, he relented. They didn't truly need his permission, but Nessy was still glad to have it. Gnick followed them, his busy eyes scanning for tarnishes, pausing every few feet to spit and rub flaws imperceptible to anyone else.

They passed through a corridor lined with armor of all sizes and shapes. Some were so strange, having sleeves for dozens of arms, holes for wings or tails, helmets made to protect oddly-shaped heads, that Nessy couldn't imagine what creatures might wear them. Margle had a full suit of enchanted chain mail that had once belonged to a dragon czar. Three kobolds could fit into one of the gauntlets. Whenever Nessy looked at it, she was reminded that no matter how great and powerful anyone might be, they would always take steps to deny their vulnerability. And in doing so, allowed it to show even more.

Though the dragon armor was one of Margle's most prominent possessions, his greatest prize in the entire armory was the Sword in the Cabbage. Over the years, as he'd attempted to unlock its secrets, the enchanted sword had retaliated. Each unsuccessful effort on Margle's part only made the cabbage larger, leafier, and greener. It was now fifteen feet around at the very least.

"It's bigger than I remember," she remarked.

"Grew another three feet after Margle's last try," said Gnick.

Nessy climbed the stairs beside the cabbage and studied

the sword. Gold, silver, and platinum traced delicate swirls along its hilt. The blade gleamed and cast reflections as clear as a mirror. It was a fine weapon. Even Nessy, who knew very little of weapons, could see that. But it was too large for her. She couldn't see herself wielding it effectively, even if she'd been properly trained. But the demon had said she could figure it out.

"Go on, lass," said Sir Thedeus. "See if ye can draw it."

She wrapped her fingers around the handle and pulled. The sword didn't budge.

"Try pulling harder, lass."

She climbed onto the cabbage and with both hands tightly clutching the sword, pushed with her legs while straining her shoulders.

"It's no use. It's stuck."

As soon as she let go, Gnick began polishing the handle. "I could've told you that. If Margle couldn't free it, I don't know what chance you've got."

"Maybe ye need to say some magic words," said Sir Thedeus.

"Unlikely," remarked Gnick. "Margle spent hours shouting incantations until his voice went. He shook the walls and rattled the armor, but the cabbage just grew larger. Dreadful amounts of dust to clean. Took me months to get it all out of the air."

"But the demon said ye could use it, dinna she?" asked Sir Thedeus.

"No. She said I could figure out how to use it."

"Well, what's that mean?"

"I don't know."

Sir Thedeus snorted. "That's a fine piece of advice. Says ye can use it, but dunna say how. If that's how a demon is helpful, no wonder no one likes them." Sir Thedeus snorted. "I would'na be surprised if she was lying."

An unfamiliar voice spoke up. "No. It wasn't lying."

"Echo, is that ye?"

"No. It's me." The Sword in the Cabbage glowed lightly.

"Ye can talk?"

Sir Thedeus's shock was odd to Nessy. Didn't many things in Margle's castle talk?

"I'd be a poor magic sword if I couldn't," said the weapon.

"Hold on," said Gnick. "I've never heard you speak before."

"I don't speak to dark wizards. Except perhaps when I'm spearing them through their black hearts. Then I might say something along the lines of 'How do you like having your black heart pierced? Not very much fun, I'll wager.'" The sword chuckled. "Not very clever, I'll admit, but you'd be amazed how much pithier it sounds when you're running through an evil wizard."

"Pardon me," said Nessy, "but I was told by a demon that I could put you to use somehow."

"Then it must be true because demons can't lie."

"Canna lie?" Sir Thedeus frowned. His pointed ears twitched. "But they're demons. They're creatures of evil and deceit."

"Without a doubt, but they are also bound by certain supernatural laws. While they are deceptive creatures, they can't lie outright."

"That's true," agreed Gnick.

"And why shouldn't it be? I was made for demon slaying. I know of what I speak. So if you were sent to me by a demon, there must be some truth in it." The sword's light faded. "Although, I do confess some distaste at the referral."

"Maybe ye should try again, Nessy."

"I wouldn't bother. Only a hero can draw me from this vegetable."

The blade radiated a brilliant light. Nessy shaded her eyes but discovered it wasn't necessary. The brightness wasn't blinding.

"I shall awaken when a hero of honor and courage, strong of limb, skilled in combat, abhorrent of evil in all its forms takes me in his hand. And not before. As I have all who have touched me, I have taken stock of your qualifications. You've a good character, miss. I find no fault in your honor or your courage, but strong of limb, skilled in combat, you most certainly are not. And while I detect a strong distaste for both impoliteness and cruelty, that is simply not enough. You are denied. Please take no offense. I must hold to very high standards."

"Understandable." Nessy paced atop the giant cabbage, circling the sword. "So if a hero does take hold of you, you would be able to help us?"

"Find a hero for me, and I would relish commencing my noble duty once again."

Nessy sat at the top of the stairs and considered the puzzle while Gnick polished the Sword in the Cabbage and Sir Thedeus nibbled on the leaves. She petted the nurgax while contemplating.

She was very good at puzzles, due in no small part to her orderly nature. All riddles were merely the arrangement of things so that they fit together in the only logical way. The sword needed a hero. The castle was full of heroes, albeit all burdened by curses. But perhaps this didn't matter.

"Sir Thedeus, you should try drawing the sword."

The bat gulped down a bite of cabbage. "Me, lass?"

"Him?" Gnick laughed. "He's no hero."

"I am too." Sir Thedeus snarled. "Or I was before that damned wizard transformed me into this rodent form."

"Bats aren't rodents."

"I'm small. I'm furry. I live off scraps. That makes me a rodent, no matter what the scholars say. But the misshapen imp is right. I'm not a hero anymore." His head drooped. There was a hint of a tear in his eye. This convinced Nessy that she just might be right. Bats couldn't shed a tear. Possibly Margle's curse had only obscured the hero within, not obliterated it completely.

She scooped Sir Thedeus up. "I know you're both courageous and honorable. And you're certainly abhorrent of evil."

"Aye. But I'm not strong of limb, nor skilled in combat."

"Just because you can't hold a weapon anymore doesn't take away the skill. It's still within you."

Gnick rubbed his tired eyes and yawned. "But he's puny. He couldn't even lift the sword if it were free."

"Strength isn't found in being the strongest of all, but the strongest you can be." Nessy looked Sir Thedeus in his beady eyes. "And, bat or not, you slew Margle, didn't you?"

"Not really. Ye were there, lass. Ye saw it. He slipped. 'Twas an accident."

"You don't give yourself enough credit. Even if luck played a part, it wouldn't have happened without you. I'd be in the nurgax's belly if not for you."

The Sword in the Cabbage remarked, "That is most impressive. I think you should give it a go. I make no guarantees though."

Sir Thedeus hesitated. His doubt was evident. As was his fear. If he failed to draw the sword, it could only mean two things. Either his curse had taken away his heroic status or, worse, he wasn't the hero he once was, or perhaps had never been. It was a fearful trial. Sir Thedeus, like all the castle's accursed heroes, had little left of value but his memories. Nessy couldn't imagine anything more awful for him than being rejected by the Sword in the Cabbage. It might be a blow from which he would never recover. She couldn't blame him for not wanting to know. Not for certain.

"You don't have to. Not if you don't want to."

"Of course he doesn't want to," said Gnick. "The windbag knows he'll only make a fool of himself."

Nessy's distaste for discourtesy flared. "Shut up, Gnick. Go polish something if you've nothing constructive to offer."

Gnick grumbled.

The nurgax barked. Sir Thedeus's eyes widened. He'd never seen Nessy lose her temper like that. It reminded him that there were more important things than pride. He gritted his teeth and stuck out his jaw.

"Put me on the sword."

She smiled gently. "No matter what, you are a hero."

"So are ye, lass." He stretched out his wings toward the weapon. "Now let me draw this blade and get rid of that hound before it eats any more of me friends." He climbed onto the hilt.

"At last!" exclaimed the Sword. "I was beginning to think it would be another thousand years before I was free of this ridiculous cabbage!"

In a flash of light, Sir Thedeus transformed from his tiny bat form into a tall, brawny, naked man. Nessy guessed he was handsome by human standards, but this was mostly assumption. Personally, she found their bald, lanky bodies absurd. The occasional tuft of fur here and there was particularly comical.

He drew the sword and held it high. "Me curse is broken. I'm a man again!"

"Loath as I am to admit this," said the sword, "I haven't so much broken your curse as paused it. I'm afraid it's not permanent."

"How long do I have?"

"Another minute or two." The sword grunted as if carrying a heavy weight. "It's the best I can do."

Sir Thedeus lowered the blade with a frown. "And then what? I'm a bat again?"

"Afraid so. But only until I build my strength up again. Then I can make you a man." The weapon trembled in his hand. "For at least another minute or two."

Before Nessy could begin thinking of solutions to this latest development, the castle bells tolled. It was a sound she'd heard only once before, and she didn't recognize it right away.

"That's the entrance bells." Her ears cocked forward.

"Impossible," said Gnick.

Nessy had little interest in debating what was obviously true. The gongs were ringing.

A puff of red-and-yellow smoke engulfed Sir Thedeus, and he transformed back into a bat. The sword halted its fall, oriented its point downward, and drove itself deep into the giant cabbage.

"Oh damn," said Sir Thedeus and the sword in unison.

Nessy and the nurgax descended the stairs and started down the hall.

"Where are ye going, lass?"

"To answer the door."

"Wait for me."

He flew after her, leaving Gnick alone in the armory. The gnome polished the Sword in the Cabbage, which was already gleaming and always did so.

"Hero, huh?"

He wrapped his tiny fists around the handle.

"Sorry," said the sword. "Not even close."

# EIGHT

Nessy rarely visited the entrance hall. There were no monsters in it, not a single accursed resident, nothing at all except for a long, worn carpet. There was also little that needed tending. Aside from the carpet, the hall was empty. Margle had never used the front doors, and he never had visitors. Nessy had used the doors once, when first applying for employment. After they'd been shut and barred, she'd never seen them opened again.

She recognized the entrance bells only because she'd rung them that first day. They'd been silent in the years since. Though she'd never been especially curious, their muted din intrigued her. During her long walk to the front hall, the bells paused for a minute or two before tolling again.

The entrance hall was a small chamber made cavernous

by its high ceiling and barrenness. Today, however, it was filled with castle inhabitants, every bit as curious as Nessy. The gathering of rodents, birds, reptiles, faeries, and other odd creatures (including a ghost or two) clamored.

"Who is it? Who can it be?" asked a small, white cloud.

"It's Margle!" shouted a boa constrictor. "It's Margle, and he's come back to destroy us all! He's here for his revenge!"

"But we didn't kill him," moaned an apparition with a trembling voice. "It's not our fault."

"As if that will matter," said a hefty rat. "Wizards are defined by their disproportionate vengeance. Wouldn't be surprised if he turned the lot of us into slugs."

"I resent that," said a slug.

"Why would he be using the front door?" asked a gnat, although no one heard him.

"Being a slug isn't the worst thing you can be," said the slug.

"You're slimy and disgusting," countered the rat. "You haven't even got the dignity of a shell."

"At least I'm not diseased."

"That's a myth. It's the fleas that are diseased. Not me."

"How dare you, sir!" shouted a flea nestled on the rat's shoulder.

"Doesn't make any sense for him to be using the front door of his own castle," said the unheard gnat. "Even if he has come back from the dead."

Nessy barked a few times to collect everyone's attention. It took a moment for the assembly to fall silent.

"What are you going to do?" asked the cloud.

"I'm going to see who it is," said Nessy. "Now please be quiet."

"If it's Margle," whispered the rat, "don't let him in. I don't want to be a slug."

The slug, who'd had his fill of being insulted, stormed from the chamber as fast as his single foot could propel him. He'd already dashed half an inch.

"And even if he did use the front door," thought aloud the gnat, "I don't think he'd ring the bell. He'd probably just come right in."

Bethany the banshee keened, "Beware your footing, Nessy! You're going to trip and bruise your shin!" Her screeching voice filled the room, causing everyone to cover their ears. Those that could anyway. "Brrruiiiisseeeed shiiiiiiiiiiinnnnn!"

"Thank you, Bethany. Now please be quiet."

The banshee shrugged. "Don't say I didn't warn you."

Sir Thedeus clung to Nessy's shoulder. "Is answering the door such a good idea?"

"The bells have been ringing for twenty minutes. Whoever is out there isn't likely to go away. Perhaps it's just a wandering minstrel looking for a few coins. Or a traveling boot salesman."

"Aye, lass."

Neither believed that. Everyone in a thousand leagues knew to avoid this castle.

Nessy climbed upon the nurgax's back and opened the slit in the door. She found herself staring into burning red eyes. Literally: she could see the flames dancing within.

A soft woman's voice floated through the slit. "Where's Margle?"

Nessy kept her head. She didn't say the first answer that came to her, the truth, and found a half-truth, which was as close to lying as she could comfortably do without some mental preparation.

"The master is indisposed." She smiled politely. "Can I help you?"

The burning eyes and their blond brows knit in a glare. "Yes, tell your master that it is exceedingly rude to not greet an invited guest when she arrives."

"As you wish, madam." Still smiling, Nessy closed the slit.

"Did she say she was invited?" asked Sir Thedeus.

"Apparently."

"Is she lying? She has to be lying."

The accursed gathering chattered among themselves. Their noise was soon an echoing clatter.

"Quiet down, please!" shouted Nessy.

She opened the slit again.

"My apologies, madam, but the master must reschedule your visit with his sincerest regrets."

"No."

"I'm sorry, madam?"

The fire in the visitor's eyes ignited, creeping up her eyebrows with an unpleasant burning odor. "Just who does Margle think he is? I am Tiama the Scarred, premier wizardess diabolic of the Forbidden Continent. I will not be rescheduled."

"Yes, madam. Would you excuse me one moment, madam?"

She closed the slit.

"Ye can't let her in," said Sir Thedeus. "If she finds out Margle's dead, it'll be all over for us."

"She'll turn us all into slugs," moaned a spirit. "I don't want to be a slug."

"Better than a plague-bearing vermin," grumbled the slug who was now seven inches closer to his dramatic exit.

"How do we know she was invited anyway?" asked the cloud. "She could be lying."

"Yes, yes." A raven with a tendency to repeat herself agreed. "She's a liar, liar. Margle would never invite, never invite anyone."

The cloud grayed. "She wants to come inside and plunder the castle. Take us away for twisted experiments."

The gnat shouted with all his might. "If that was the case, wouldn't she just come inside? Why lie about it?" If the hall had been quiet, he might even have been heard.

"I don't see why she'd lie," said Nessy. "If she wanted in,

she'd just push her way inside. In any case, I have to let her in if she doesn't go away. If she knows Margle is dead, it won't make much difference. If she doesn't, turning her away would only make her suspicious things are out of order."

Sir Thedeus agreed. "I can see yer logic, lass. But once the witch—"

"Wizardess," corrected the gnat, but Sir Thedeus continued without pause.

"—is inside, won't she realize things are amiss then?"

This was very true, and a murmur of approval filled the hall. But to Nessy's thinking, this was a later dilemma.

In her mind, all problems were divided into three categories. There were the Present Problems, which demanded immediate attention. There were the Soon Problems, which were quick to become Present Problems unless judiciously handled. And there were the Later Problems, which were not worth worrying about because they might become Present Problems or they might become Soon Problems or, when she was fortunate, might grow into Never Problems.

Never Problems occupied an invisible fourth slot in this spectrum, but, as they were difficulties that never existed, she'd never actually defined them consciously. She was far too practical for such abstract philosophy. When a tree fell in the forest of Nessy's imagination, she didn't ponder what sounds it might or might not make. She just set about chopping it into firewood.

The bells tolled again. Tiama the Scarred wasn't leaving, and all wizards Nessy had ever met were intractable once they made up their minds. She opened the slit.

"I'm afraid the master is very busy at the moment, madam. But I've been given instructions to show you to the guest room for the evening."

The flame in the wizardess's eyes dimmed, though she still didn't look happy. "Very well."

"Excuse me, madam. I'll just need a moment."

Nessy closed the slit and turned to the menagerie. "Go on. If she sees you all here, she'll know something is wrong for sure. Tell everyone else that we have a wizardess in the castle, and to watch themselves. One slip up, and we'll all be finished."

The throng dispersed amid much concerned whispering.

"Watch your step," warned Bethany as she vanished. "Bruiiisssseeed Shiiiiiiinnnnnnn . . ."

The front doors were tall and wide, and a heavy bar was set across them. Nessy tried to lift it, but she lacked the strength.

"I dunna know if this is such a grand idea, lass."

"It isn't, but it's the best we have." Nessy raised her hands before her and grunted the levitation incantation she'd learned last night. The bar hopped once, twice, three times before successfully falling to the floor.

"Not bad," said Sir Thedeus. "Maybe ye've a talent for magic after all."

The doors flew open, and Tiama the Scarred stepped inside. Despite her title, she was without any trace of disfigurement. So flawless as to be thoroughly featureless. Her stark white skin was taut and wrinkle-free. Her hair was so light and fine as to be practically invisible. Her lips were entirely omitted around the unforgiving slash of her mouth, and her nose was barely present upon her face. Her ears were so tiny and round, they gave Nessy the impression of sliced mushrooms. The wizardess wore a long, red robe that obliterated any trace of her figure, good or ill. She seemed a tremendous absence, an emptiness of any quality.

Except for her eyes. These were harsh and burning in every sense. The fire within revealed a blackened soul that sent shivers through Nessy. Margle had been severe, but this was even less forgiving than her master.

The nurgax growled.

"Dear gods, what a witch," whispered Sir Thedeus. He climbed into the safety of Nessy's shirt.

Tiama folded her arms. Her long sleeves fell to her elbows, showing forearms that were without beauty or blemish. She had the hands of an unfinished marionette with tight, knotted knuckles and no fingernails.

"Do you have a name, beast?"

"Nessy, madam." She bowed. "It is my pleasure and honor to serve you."

"Nessy," repeated Tiama, making the word seem a frightful insult. "Nessy, I've traveled far this day to see your master's supposed wonders." She glanced around the chamber. "As yet, I find myself highly unimpressed."

"Yes, madam. The master sincerely apologizes for the inconvenience. But as you have traveled so far, he gladly offers you his hospitality for the night."

"Hospitality." This word too seemed appalling when spoken by Tiama.

"Yes, madam. If you'll follow me, madam, I'll show you to the guest room."

"It's an early hour yet. Does your master expect me to retire for the evening?"

"The master offers his grandest apologies." Nessy hesitated. Lying didn't come to her easily. "He is engaged in a very precarious alchemy experiment at the moment. It shall keep him occupied for the night."

"Occupied." She spat out the syllables with evident disgust. She might have been frowning too, but her mouth hardly moved, making it difficult to discern expression. "And why would Margle begin an experiment that would take all night when he knew I was coming?"

It was a reasonable question, and Nessy had no reasonable answer ready. Tiama took Nessy's hesitation as nothing more than the dreadful confusion such a simple beast must experience before a wizardess diabolic.

"You're the creature that tends this castle, are you not?"

"Yes, madam."

"Then surely, you must know your way around it." Tiama might have smiled. "You shall show me some wonders if your master cannot be bothered by customary civility."

Again, Nessy paused. She'd been hoping to gain some time to prepare the castle for Tiama's presence. An hour or two to plan would've been helpful. But life didn't always go on a schedule. Much as Nessy disliked admitting this, she accepted it as indisputable reality. She had many important things to do: sweep a few halls, feed a few beasts, make dinner, study her magic, find The Door At The End Of The Hall, slay a hellhound, and read to the monster under her bed. And these were just the tasks that came immediately to mind.

But Tiama the Scarred was the most pressing of her concerns. So Nessy adjusted her schedule accordingly. A few halls would remain dusty. Dinner would be a little late. The Door At The End Of The Hall could stay lost a while longer. The hellhound would have another night to prowl. And the monster under her bed would just have to wait.

"Nessy, shall we begin?" asked Tiama.

"Yes, madam. Right this way." Nessy turned, slipped on a slug's slimy trail, and banged her leg against the stone floor. The wizardess expressed neither humor nor concern as Nessy got up.

"Watch your step, madam."

She dropped to all fours to take some weight off her bruised shin and led Tiama from the chamber.

The slug halted his "hurried" dash to catch his breath.

He slouched with drooping eyestalks. "I'd rather be a rat," he admitted to himself.

"Even rodents have their problems," said the gnat.

And the slug would've been comforted by these words—had he actually heard them.

Rather than waste all her time, Nessy elected to give Tiama a tour of Margle's many rare and magical beasts. This way she could feed the beasts and limit Tiama's exposure to the castle's residents. Few wandered the bestiary. It was too dangerous a place for casual visitation. And Nessy briefly hoped an accident might occur. Tiama might make a careless mistake and get herself devoured. Nessy didn't put the chances of this occurring as very high, but it was possible.

Tiama spoke little. When she did, it was only to comment vaguely. Most creatures were "interesting." Others were "curious." A precious few were "quaint." Only the grisly ghast was deemed "amusing."

"Watch your step, madam." Nessy grabbed a bucket from her cart and emptied its leafy contents into the darkened pit. "Here we have one of the master's more frightful creations: the dread saber-toothed koala."

Tiama leaned over. Someone could've easily pushed her. There was no guarantee the wizardess would be killed by either the fall or the giant cuddly horror at the bottom. But Nessy didn't consider the consequences of such an action.

The notion of arranging the hopeful accident never once occurred to her. She was having more than enough difficulty remembering to lie.

Sir Thedeus might have suggested it, but he was safely tucked away on her back and under her shirt.

Tiama leaned farther until it seemed certain she would plummet. Then she leaned some more until her rigid body hovered at a gravity-defying angle over the pit. And if Nessy had been plotting a push, she would've realized it was doomed to fail.

Tiama rubbed her hands together and dancing sparkles fell to illuminate the pit. The saber-toothed koala shrank from the light while stuffing leaves in its drooling jaws.

"Interesting." A flat, neutral tone was the closest Tiama's voice came to pleasant.

Nessy waited patiently for the wizardess to finish her study of this latest offering of Margle's abominations. When Tiama was ready, she floated from the pit's edge.

"After all of Margle's bragging, I expected more. There's nothing here I haven't seen in a hundred other wizards' homes."

Nessy found herself insulted. This was the best castle she'd ever tended, and Margle's collections were peerless. She decided to skip ahead and show the prize of her master's bestiary.

"You've yet to see THE MONSTER THAT SHOULD NOT

BE, madam. I assure you it will exceed your expectations."

"Lead on then, Nessy, with all due haste. I grow weary of these trifles." On the way, Tiama asked, "Is this nurgax bonded to you?"

"Yes, madam." Nessy had nearly forgotten about the ever-present creature. It followed her so obediently.

"And Margle allows this?"

Sir Thedeus popped up long enough to whisper in Nessy's ear. "Careful, lassie."

"The master intended to feed me to the creature, but it found another meal instead. Then bonded to me. All quite by accident, madam."

"And is there some reason he didn't kill you for such a transgression?"

"Perhaps he just hasn't gotten around to it yet, madam."

"I had no idea Margle was such a busy individual." If there was sarcasm in the comment, Tiama's flat voice devoured it.

Like many of the more horrible bestiary creatures, THE MONSTER THAT SHOULD NOT BE was kept in a pit. But this pit was twice as wide as any of the others, and there was a heavy iron door atop it. And another gate atop that. And a third gate atop that for good measure. Each with its own tremendous lock. Three towering stone statues stood watch, ever vigilant. When THE MONSTER banged and thrashed with special vigor, the sentinels would show signs of life.

They would raise their uncarved heads and clutch their granite swords. Once, THE MONSTER had pounded and thrashed strongly enough to dent the iron door, and the sentinels had stepped from their pedestals. But THE MONSTER eventually calmed, and they returned to their places. In addition, there was one final fail-safe: a ceiling of rusty ten-foot spikes, poised to both crush and impale anything in the chamber. The enchanted spikes hovered, and Nessy didn't think she'd ever be good enough with her own levitation spell to float them off the ground for a moment, much less years.

Nessy hadn't ever seen THE MONSTER clearly. In fact, she'd never seen THE MONSTER at all. But Margle had visited it regularly, and all those precautions surely meant it was a frightfully impressive thing.

Tiama, however, was less than excited as they approached. She yawned as wide as her thin mouth allowed.

Nessy opened the small trapdoor to the pit and threw in the mixture of raw meat, turnips, and griffin blood that was THE MONSTER's meal. THE MONSTER belched and gurgled. A fetid stench assaulted Nessy's nostrils. She'd vomited the first several weeks she'd smelled it, but she'd grown accustomed to the stink for the few minutes she had to deal with it.

She stepped aside. "Would you like to have a look, madam?"

Tiama stood before the trapdoor and barely glanced

down. "I can't see anything. Why does your master insist on keeping it so dark in here?"

THE MONSTER THAT SHOULD NOT BE howled, belched, howled again, and gurgled and belched simultaneously.

"Perhaps it would be wise to step back, madam. You don't want to antagonize it."

Tiama smiled clearly for the first time. "Quite the contrary, Nessy. I believe that is exactly what I want to do."

THE MONSTER burped long and deeply. A putrid, brown cloud erupted from the trapdoor. Nessy and the nurgax stepped back, but Tiama stood as immobile as the sentinels.

"Is she mad?" asked Sir Thedeus. "She's sure to get herself killed."

Tiama waved her arm. The top lock opened with a groan, and the first gate slid back. THE MONSTER pounded against its prison, sensing one less barrier to its escape. The sentinels raised their weapons. Another wave of her arm opened the second gate, and the spikes overhead trembled.

THE MONSTER THAT SHOULD NOT BE howled between gassy eruptions. A sentinel strode from its pedestal, nearly crushing Nessy underfoot.

"Perhaps it would be a good idea if we left now, lass."

Nessy, considerate a hostess as she was, agreed. They dashed out the chamber exit, only looking back once they were safely on the other side of the threshold.

Tiama seemed unaware of any presence save THE MONSTER's. She waved her arms for a third time, and the pit opened wide. A gleeful roar blasted upward and outward. The foul wind swept through the door and knocked Nessy off her feet. With teary eyes, she glimpsed the small blur of Tiama the Scarred, the much larger smudges of the sentinels, and the huge, indecipherable blot that was THE MONSTER THAT SHOULD NOT BE. A sentinel thrust its sword deep into THE MONSTER. A gush of red and black fluid spewed. THE MONSTER screamed and lashed out with a claw (or perhaps a tail or a tentacle). Each formidable sentinel was shattered with a single blow. THE MONSTER opened its giant maw (or perhaps many hundred smaller maws). It gurgled triumphantly, and Nessy was certain the castle was next to be destroyed by its wrath.

Thankfully, before her vision cleared, allowing her a sanity-risking true glimpse of THE MONSTER, the ceiling fell, mincing and burying everything in the chamber. Thunder shook the castle to its foundation. Clouds of choking dust erupted from the door. It covered Nessy in a heavy gray film. Sir Thedeus, though tucked in her shirt, wasn't spared. He poked out his sooty head and sneezed.

"I guess that takes care of that problem, eh, lass."

The nurgax nuzzled her. Not a glimpse of purple was evident under its own coat of dust. It licked her once. The creature's thick saliva made the dust sticky in her fur. A most unpleasant sensation. But she endured it, waiting for the air to clear.

Tiama the Scarred stepped from the chamber, appearing as if by magic. Perhaps truly appearing by magic. The wizardess was untouched. Even the dust refused to cling to her.

"Ye gods." Sir Thedeus ducked himself away.

Tiama smiled. "Most delightful. At last, Margle has touched me. Now I believe I'm ready to retire for the evening."

It took a moment for Nessy to gather her wits, but she couldn't say she was honestly surprised. Wizards and wizardesses could be remarkably resilient.

The castle shook, and a thick tentacle pushed through the rubble. THE MONSTER screamed and stretched for Tiama. She showed no fear as the gnarled limb poised to lock her in its deadly embrace. She merely reached out, touched it with a single finger, and THE MONSTER THAT SHOULD NOT BE no longer was. There was no death rattle, no final spasm. It quietly and instantly perished.

Tiama's smile vanished. "Pity. It was a remarkable specimen."

In a long moment of thought that Tiama took again for Nessy's fearfulness, Nessy realized that the wizardess was going to be even more troublesome than she'd originally imagined. And she'd already imagined it to be a delicate, perhaps impossible situation. Rather than let the hopelessness of it overcome her, she decided to take it one day at a time. With Tiama about to retire, this day was done. And tomorrow's challenges were too far away to concern herself over.

# NINE

"If you would wait here, madam, I'll make sure the guest chambers are properly prepared."

Tiama frowned. "Wasn't I expected? Shouldn't the room be ready?"

"Yes, madam. But the master receives so few visitors, the room might have suffered some unforeseen neglect." Nessy shuddered. Lying was hard enough, but feigning incompetence was nearly impossible. The guest room was never used, but she'd kept it ever ready with the thorough dedication upon which she took no small pride. "The master would never forgive me if it wasn't perfect for your arrival, madam. It'll only take a moment."

Nessy pushed open the door and slipped inside, shutting it behind her. The chambers were flawlessly arranged, save for a light layer of dust which she proceeded to wipe away.

Sir Thedeus slipped from her shirt and flew to the bedpost. "This witch is going to be a terrible difficulty, lass."

She gently lifted the cat dozing on the large bed.

Fortune the feline stirred sleepily. "It's bad luck to wake a black cat."

"I'll take my chances."

She set him down, and Fortune stretched and stretched and stretched again for good measure. "Did you say something about a witch?"

"Aye. A horrid creature. She killed THE MONSTER with one touch. One touch."

Fortune, who hadn't quite finished stretching, yawned. "Which monster was that? The one that lives under Nessy's bed or that smelly one locked in the wardrobe? Or maybe the one that lurks about the catacombs. Never liked that one. Anyone who lurks that much must be up to no good."

"None of those. 'Twas THE MONSTER THAT SHOULD NOT BE."

The cat licked his paw. "One touch, you say?"

"Aye."

"It's a good thing Margle's dead. Otherwise, he'd be very upset."

"Aye."

Nessy stroked Fortune between the ears. "Don't mention that again. Not while she's here."

He purred. "What's in it for me?"

Fortune had been a professional gambler, a dashing rogue,

a legend among gentlemen of luck, a beloved rascal among their women. Seeking the ultimate challenge, he'd wagered his fate against Margle's wealth on a single roll of the die. To most, this would've been madness. But Fortune trusted his luck as only the greatest gambler could. It'd never let him down before, not when it mattered.

But there was always a first time. Margle had made him a cat because he had always been one in all but body. And like any feline, he could be loyal and honorable, but his first priority was always his own comfort.

"I've heard witches are very fond of black cats."

Sir Thedeus fluttered about Fortune's head. "Ye traitorous bastard!"

"She's not a witch. She's a wizardess diabolic," said Nessy. "And I don't think this one has a fondness for any creature with only four legs. But I'll give you an extra serving of milk if you behave yourself."

Fortune's tail flicked. "A bowl now. Not a saucer."

She shook his extended paw. Fortune was a cat of his word and never went back on a deal. She supposed he was much like a demon that way except with less interest in sowing discord and devouring souls.

"Greedy prat," grumbled Sir Thedeus.

"It's bad luck to swear at a black cat."

Next, Nessy went to the chimney and coaxed the flame to life. It wasn't easy, for he was very stubborn. She tossed several logs into the fireplace, but he refused to blaze. She expected as much. Once, only once, she'd run behind and forgotten to feed him his weekly log. He'd nearly extinguished and hadn't forgotten since.

"If you would please just burn a little brighter. Just long enough to take the chill from the air."

He stuck a tongue of yellow flame from under the firewood. "And what's in it for me? There's enough here to keep me ablaze for weeks, properly rationed. Why should I risk myself for some wizardess?"

Sir Thedeus groaned. "Is everyone mad? This witch'll take us all away. Or worse, plunder the castle and leave us here to rot forever in our curses. Stop being a gob and do yer task, lest she grows suspicious."

Nessy wished he possessed a touch more tact, but it convinced the fire to burn stronger. "Only to take away the chill. Not a single lick more."

Nessy dusted the full-length mirror in the corner. She gently tapped the glass. Her reflection covered its ears.

"Don't do that," said Melvin of the Mirrors. "Do you have any idea how annoying that is on this side of the glass?"

"I can't say that I do," she admitted, "but I needed to be certain I drew your attention. I need you to keep an eye on the wizardess for me. Can you do that?"

Melvin moved from Nessy's reflection to Sir Thedeus's. He spoke not only with the bat's voice, but the accent as well. "Ye needn't have asked. I'll keep ye informed should she move from this room."

"Thank you."

The guest chambers prepared to her satisfaction, she let

Tiama in. The wizardess glanced about with inscrutability verging on dissatisfaction.

"Will that be all, madam? Or can I make you comfortable in any other way? Perhaps some wine and cheese?"

Tiama scowled. "I long ago discarded such ridiculous appetites. Now leave me, Nessy, and don't disturb me lest you wish to lose your immortal soul."

She herded Nessy through the door and closed it with a quiet click.

"Immortal soul." Sir Thedeus snorted. "Why must witches always be so melodramatic?"

"Just part of the occupation," said Fortune. "You must admit it sounds better than merely threatening to boot her behind. I'll see you in the morning, Nessy. Remember now, it's bad luck to break a deal with a black cat." He licked his lips and strutted away.

"Now what are we to do?" asked Sir Thedeus.

Nessy stroked the nurgax's small wings and frowned at the gray dust left on her palm. "Now, we take a bath."

The castle had a large, opulent spa with a spring-fed bath. The water was always pleasantly warm, and it had magical properties, able to clean away the thickest, most stubborn grit and grime. It was certainly called for in this case. Nessy wasn't supposed to use it. The spa was for Margle's enjoyment only. That was very strange as he'd never enjoyed it. Truthfully, she wasn't sure Margle could enjoy anything. No wizard she'd ever worked for had. They were always too busy with their pursuits of power, their arcane studies, their consuming idiosyncrasies. She'd learned to not question their rules, nor expect much in the way of appreciation. But Margle was dead, and she decided to take advantage of it while it lasted.

She lowered herself into the bubbling water. There was nothing quite like a hot bath.

The nurgax splashed joyfully, cooing and swimming in energetic circles. She kept watch that it didn't stray to the deep end where the Drowned Woman was bound, waiting to lure a victim to share in her watery grave.

Sir Thedeus dipped a wing in the water. "Ach, it's too warm. I prefer a cold bath."

"It's the fastest way to get the dust out of your fur." She glanced at the gray clouds slowly being drawn from her own coat.

The Drowned Woman rose from the depths. With skin drooping under its own wrinkles and flat, dripping hair, she was a vision of sogginess. "She's right. You are quite dirty. And the water is so much cooler over here. I'd be happy to wash your back if you'd like." She smiled crookedly and extended her grasping, clawlike hands.

"Get drenched, ye daft woman."

On their way to the spa, Nessy had collected Yazpib the Magnificent. The jar-confined wizard (what little was left of him) was her best choice for consultation. "I believe we have more pressing matters than dusty fur. Are you certain this was Tiama the Scarred you met? I can't believe my brother would be so arrogant as to invite her."

Nessy grabbed a bar of soap. "She entered the castle. No one does so without express invitation."

Sir Thedeus scratched at his itchy fur. "Ye've heard of this witch?"

"Wizardess," corrected Yazpib. "And I think it's safe to say there isn't a wizard alive who hasn't heard of her. Half don't believe she exists. The other half believe she does but wish she didn't. This is horrible. Absolutely horrible."

"We'll handle it, lad." Sir Thedeus dug hard behind his ears. "We handled Margle, dinna we?"

"Compared to Tiama, Margle was an amateur. My brother was exceedingly powerful, but he could still be undone by a slippery floor and a bit of misfortune. But even destiny bows to a wizardess of Tiama's rank. I've heard that everything she touches perishes. Everything. Even things which have already died are resurrected just long enough to die again."

"That seems rather pointless," said Nessy.

"Exactly. If she has that much power to waste on such an irrelevance, you can imagine what she could do when focused."

"The witch isn't our only problem," said Sir Thedeus. "We've still that hellhound and The Door At The End Of The Hall."

"And the demon." Nessy scrubbed between her toes. "Don't forget the demon. She's certain to be up to something." She admired the gleam on her long, black nails.

"I'd forgotten about her," said Yazpib. "Oh this is terrible. We're doomed."

"Sounds hopeless to me," remarked the Drowned Woman. "And in hopeless situations I've found it's best to just give up. Anyone care for a nice drowning? I'll make it quick."

Nessy dipped her head below the water, and the Drowned Woman beamed hopefully. Her grin faded when Nessy emerged again. Frowning, the woman submerged herself to sulk on the pool bottom.

Nessy leaned back and closed her eyes.

"How can ye be so calm, lass? Dunna ye understand the situation?"

"I believe I understand it very well. It's very delicate, and most anything we do will be the wrong course of action. Takes much of the pressure off when you think about it. Now let me enjoy my bath a while longer."

Yazpib laughed.

"What are ye chuckling about?"

"She's right. All this worrying doesn't accomplish anything. Better to start working on possible solutions."

Sir Thedeus's itchiness tempted him to the pool's edge. He snarled at the hot water. "Fine. Yer the wizard. Can ye think of any way to handle this witch?"

"We have to find Margle's fail-safe. Every wizard has one for situations like this, to insure good behavior from a visiting wizard, even a power like Tiama. I'm certain my brother has one. Possibly more than one, given his distrustful nature."

"What would one of these fail-safes look like?"

"That's the problem. The form varies greatly from wizard to wizard, based on the nature and the inclination of its maker. Mine was an enchanted winged lion. There wasn't a wizard alive who could stand against it."

"And yet ye are in that jar."

"I didn't get the chance to use it. The poor creature must've starved to death by now. Shame."

"It didn't starve," said Nessy. "Margle keeps it in one of the towers."

Sir Thedeus perked up. "Then the lion must be what we need."

"Aren't you listening? A wizard's fail-safe is a very personal thing. It isn't something casually traded about. My brother would've had to neutralize most of its enchantments very carefully to get it here. An awful lot of work, I imagine. Easier to get his own winged lion." Yazpib clicked his floating teeth together. "Greedy looter always did covet everything I had. No, whatever Margle had prepared, it would have to be more monstrous, less tangible."

"Is that a fact or an assumption?"

"Trust me. I know my brother. He'd want a horrible fate for anyone who dared challenge him, something truly offensive."

"That's too vague, lad. Canna ye give us something palpable? A scroll? A magic shield? Maybe an angry dragon?"

"Honestly, I can't say. I really haven't seen much of the castle, you know." He tapped against his jar. "Rather limited in my mobility."

"What about ye, Nessy? None know this castle better than ye. Any ideas?"

"Perhaps it's The Door At The End Of The Hall. Or the demon in the Purple Room. Or maybe it was THE MONSTER THAT SHOULD NOT BE. Or is that THE MONSTER THAT NO LONGER IS?" She stepped from the bath and shook herself.

Sir Thedeus retreated from the raining droplets. "There are too many possibilities. How are we ever going to find it?"

Nessy said, "I don't think we'll have to find it. Margle wouldn't leave such business to chance. Nor would he trust anyone to avenge his death after he was gone. There would be magics in place should the situation arise."

She whistled, and the nurgax obediently rushed to her side so she could towel it off. Her own fur she preferred to allow to drip-dry.

"But the witch didn't kill Margle," said Sir Thedeus. "We did."

"Yes, I suppose the three of us are responsible," said Nessy. "You distracted him. I polished the stone on which he slipped. And the nurgax ate him."

"Do ye think there's a spell brewing now, lass, looking to do us in?"

"I hadn't really thought about it, but I wouldn't be surprised."

Sir Thedeus raised his ears. "Nor I. That dark wizard was a vengeful bastard to be certain." He stopped scratching and dipped himself into the pool just long enough for the enchanted water to rinse away the dirt. "Bring it forth, I say. I killed Margle, and I drew the Sword in the Cabbage, and I'll not be afraid of any magic from a dead wizard."

"Actually," said Yazpib, "magic from dead wizards is the most dangerous kind."

"I'll worry no more about Margle as long as that witch is here." He allowed Nessy to dry his gray fur. "And I think it would be a good idea to have some sort of backup plan. Just in case the castle canna adequately defend itself. Have ye any notions, lass?"

At first, she didn't know what to make of the question. She'd always enjoyed tending the castle and was very good at keeping its looming chaos in a fragile but stable order. But Margle had never once implied she was one degree less than incapable. It was odd to actually be asked her opinion, to be looked to for leadership, though she had been the mistress of the castle for many years now. But it was uncomfortable somehow to be in the position undisguised.

"Ye do have some ideas, dunna ye, lass?"

"Several."

"That's me girl. Always thinking."

She was still not entirely at ease with this new standing, which was really her old standing with more respect. But she fancied she could learn to accept it. It was, after all, a very trivial change.

Distantly, bells jingled. It sounded exactly like the cursed mellifluous ringing of the Vampire King.

"I thought he had been devoured," said Sir Thedeus.

"Perhaps there's been a mistake." Nessy quickly threw on her clothes. "Or possibly he escaped."

The bells drew closer. They were moving fast, much faster than the King had moved in years. The torches on the wall flickered. The air grew chilly. Heavy rasps joined the jingles.

The Drowned Woman raised her head curiously. "That's not the King."

"No, 'tis certainly not," agreed Sir Thedeus.

A creature of smoke and fire stepped through the archway. It glared with yellow eyes and snarled with yellow teeth from behind the black cloud wrapped around its form. Each heavy step of its paws rang out like the music of the Vampire King. By eating the vampire, the hellhound had also taken on his curse, apparently.

"The beast eats only half-dead things," said Sir Thedeus. "We've nothing to fear."

"Speak for yourself." The Drowned Woman retreated to the pool's depths with a loud splash.

"Uh, Nessy," Yazpib whispered from his jar. "I'm not exactly entirely alive myself."

The hound advanced with the slow confidence of a predator closing in on cornered prey. Though the cloud that covered it made it difficult to pick out, it was at least as big as a large horse. Its claws sizzled against the tile, leaving black stains that Nessy measured as impossible ever to completely clean away. Despite realizing that this wasn't her most pressing problem, she was still quite annoyed.

Nessy, Sir Thedeus and the nurgax stood stock still, although there was little need. The hound wouldn't have given them much notice if they'd been screaming their heads off. Instead, it stared at Yazpib. A long, black tongue ran across its pointed teeth.

Yazpib trembled, spilling fluid from his jar. "Do something!"

"I suppose we do still need the damned wizard." Sir Thedeus launched his tiny body forward and zipped in circles around the monster. "Here now, ye great beastie! Have a bite of me if ye can!"

The hellhound roared with annoyance and snapped at the bat circling its head. Nessy used the distraction to think. It was terrible enough to have lost the Vampire King. She hated to lose another of her charges.

The hound knocked Sir Thedeus from the air. Before he hit the floor, it swallowed him in one bite.

"Oh no." Yazpib's fluid turned pale white with fear. "Run, Nessy. Don't get yourself killed for me."

The hound stalked forward with a ravenous rumble. Still working on her plan, she put herself between the monster and its prey.

It snorted flame and raised a broad paw. Before the deathblow came, the hound whimpered and groaned. It fell on its side and writhed. Its smoky camouflage dissolved to reveal it in all its detail. It was a giant, hairless hound with ebony scales and rows of spikes running down its back. It was terrifying to behold, but somehow less frightening now that it was more perceptible, wracked in pain and weakness. Living things were deadly poison to hellhounds. Sir Thedeus had killed the creature as he'd promised. And he hadn't needed the Sword in the Cabbage or his human form. Only his courage.

The hound moaned and made an appalling gagging sound. Its jaws opened wide, and it spat out something small, gray, and furry.

Nessy rushed to Sir Thedeus. He was soaked in drool, a touch blackened, but otherwise, seemingly unharmed. He looked up at her and grinned weakly. "I knew the beastie cunna stomach a real hero." He passed out.

The hound rose to unsteady feet. The stench of brimstone grew stronger as its scaly skin spewed fresh smoke. It sluggishly loped towards Yazpib the Magnificent.

Nessy waved her hands and incanted her levitation spell. The jar rose high in the air. The hound was still weak. Though not for long. Flames erupted from its nostrils with new vigor. Lacking the strength to jump, it stalked to the pool's edge and stared at the Drowned Woman. It swatted at the water, raising clouds of steam, but it was reluctant to go in and get her.

Nessy didn't think she could levitate both Yazpib and the Drowned Woman. Even if she were able, it was a temporary solution. There were too many half-dead things to protect them all from the hound. She had a plan to slay the creature, but it couldn't be tried tonight. In the meantime, she refused to allow it another night's run of the castle.

Her mental grasp on Yazpib's jar weakened. He tilted to one side and spilled a small puddle on the floor. "Be careful, Nessy!"

His cry drew the hound's attention. It crouched, swishing its tail.

Carefully, calmly, Nessy tightened her spell. Such simple magic was nothing to a master wizard or even an experienced apprentice. But she was barely beginning her training. She didn't know how long she could maintain the necessary focus. An unpleasant throb was already growing behind her eyes.

Yazpib lowered. "Concentrate, Nessy!"

"I am." She gritted her teeth.

The hound pounced. She swung the jar just out of its reach once again. The annoyed creature belched a searing fireball.

Nessy lowered her arms. Gesturing made the magic easier, but she needed all four limbs if she was to lead this chase.

The hound snapped at the jar, nearly catching Yazpib. The ache in her eyes had spread to her neck, but the spell itself seemed to be easier. The hound was fast, but she was faster. For the moment.

"Oh dear," said Yazpib. "You're using me as bait. You're using me as bait!"

Her ears beat with the heavy tick of her pulse. She barely heard him. "I'm sorry. It's the only way."

Yazpib voiced some objections that were lost on her. She only heard her own heart and the clamor of the hellhound's bells.

She dashed through the spa archway with the nurgax at her side and Yazpib floating over her head. The hound roared and gave chase. When the bells had finally faded away completely, the Drowned Woman dared surface. Though she technically didn't need to breathe, she exhaled with relief just the same.

Nessy didn't like to improvise. Not this much. When she acted, she liked to know what she was doing, to have all the details worked out. But there was so much she didn't know. She didn't know how long she could outrun a hellhound. She didn't know how long she could keep Yazpib afloat while running at full tilt. And she didn't know if her destination would be worth the effort. But none of these questions mattered. It was too late for doubts. She'd set her course of action, and the only choice was to see it through.

The dash cleared her head. There were few things faster than a kobold on all fours, and she heard the hound falling behind. She slowed, while plotting her course through the castle. She couldn't run directly straight. There were several ghosts and the Merry Corpse along that path. She stopped at a T-section of hallways. She knew the castle intimately, but it was so difficult to concentrate while levitating Yazpib.

He glanced backward at the snarling beast pursuing them. It bolted down the corridor, a fury of black smoke and red flame and long, pointed teeth. "Uh, Nessy . . ."

"Not now," she hissed, struggling through the haze.

The bells filled the hall. The hound roared. The torches

flickered and dimmed. The nurgax bared its teeth in Nessy's defense. Though it had eaten Margle, she didn't know if it could stand against a hellhound, and she wasn't willing to take the chance yet.

The hound came within a few leaping steps.

"Nessy . . ."

"Quiet!"

The hound pounced as her mental map fell into place. She bolted to the right almost completely unaware of the creature. It smacked into the wall with a loud gong. It staggered a moment before continuing pursuit.

The strain of magic was slowing her. She was still faster than the hound, but only just. She sped through the hall of portraits. The painted prisoners awoke from their sleep in time to see the brown blur of Nessy, the purple whiz of the nurgax, and the crashing blackness of the hellhound. They gagged and choked at the stench left in its wake.

"Where are we going?" Yazpib shouted. He kept one eye on the hound, the other forward.

"Very hungry carpet," she mumbled between heavy breaths.

"Hungry what?"

Nessy ricocheted off a wall to navigate a sharp turn. Next in her route came some steep stairs. If she fell, the tumble would surely be the end of her flight.

Behind her, the hound's breathing was sharp and steady. She couldn't match its endurance. The heat of its flames, the stink of brimstone, the clatter of bells, all of these signs told her the creature was almost on top of her. If these weren't enough, Yazpib's terrified shouts of "It's on us! It's on us! It's on us!" over and over again confirmed it.

The pursuit sped past her room. The monster under her bed glared. "She'd better not get herself eaten before she finishes my book."

The stairs descended before her. If she leapt correctly, she could take them in two bounds. Once past them, she was certain she could make it to the very hungry carpet. Whether that was the answer to her problem was another matter entirely.

She jumped, and she knew instantly that she'd jumped wrong. Too low. Too late. She was going to land roughly and off balance. She'd tumble. Her levitation spell would end. Yazpib would be devoured. She'd be bruised and battered. The hound would be free to gorge itself on the castle's half-dead.

Jaws clamped around her tail, and she rose into the air. She thought the hound was annoyed enough to chew her up and spit her out before eating Yazpib. But hanging upside down, she saw the monster a few steps behind her. The nurgax held her. Its improbably tiny wings fluttered, somehow bearing the creature airborne.

Nessy's surprise loosened her grip on Yazpib. She tightened it just as he bounced once against the stones, sending chips of glass flying.

"Be careful!"

The nurgax landed at the foot of the stairs and hopped into the air to soar another fifteen feet. It threw Nessy high and caught her on its back. She held tight to its horn and looked back, practically eye to eye with the hound. The hall split in two directions, and the nurgax dashed down the left branch.

"No! Right! Right!" she ordered.

The nurgax snorted and came to a sudden stop. The hound hurled itself at Yazpib. Nessy waved her hand and raised the jar. Yazpib cracked against the monster's head but didn't break. The hound twisted in midair, landed on its feet, and sprang. The nurgax kicked the hound squarely on the nose. The monster was stunned by the audacity of such a blow. It blinked in utter shock. The nurgax slammed one giant foot upon the hound's paw and dashed away. The hound roared and jingled after them. They turned the corner into a long chamber with nothing but an irregular patchwork rug.

"Jump!" she commanded, and the nurgax did. Despite the nurgax's strong legs and surprisingly effective wings, they weren't going to make it, and one step on the carpet would be disastrous.

The nurgax stopped, hovering in midair. The hound sailed forward, and the nurgax raised its feet, planted them on the monster's muzzle, and pushed. The maneuver threw the hound headfirst into the carpet, and the added momentum hurled the nurgax to land gently several feet from the carpet's edge.

The hellhound struggled against the adhesive trap. It tried to claw its way free, but its paws became stuck. Then its tail. Then the rest of its body. The hound snorted fire, but the carpet didn't burn. The rug growled ravenously and folded itself around its prey. The tightly wrapped hound squirmed and snarled weakly.

"My word," said Yazpib. "What is that?"

Nessy smiled. "A very hungry carpet."

Her levitation spell came to a sudden end, and Yazpib dropped. He hit the stone. His jar didn't break, although the lattice of cracks and chips gave evidence of how close it had come. Half his fluid was gone, spilt during the chase. But the thick glass wasn't leaking, and all of Yazpib's parts (except for possibly a tooth or two) were accounted for.

The hound struggled vainly in the unbreakable folds of the very hungry carpet. It growled, howled, and yowled. Smoke billowed from the holes torn by the hound's spikes. But the carpet held tight.

"So it will eat the hound for us," said Yazpib hopefully.

"The carpet consumes cloth and fabric, not flesh. But once it snares its prey, it takes an entire day for it to unfold itself."

"It's only temporary? You nearly killed me for a temporary solution?"

"Sometimes temporary solutions are the only ones available."

"And when it gets loose, just what do you have planned then? I don't think I could take another chase."

"I think I have it worked out."

"You're not inspiring me with your confidence."

She shrugged. Yazpib might be worried about the hellhound and justifiably so. But for twenty-four hours, give or take, she had more urgent dilemmas.

Yazpib said, "For the record, I must admit I'm impressed with your levitation advancement. Most apprentices take months to reach your talent."

"One learns as fast as necessity dictates."

"Let's hope for a little less necessity in the future."

Nessy climbed off the nurgax's back and scratched under its chin. The creature purred. This was twice that it had saved her life, albeit the first time had mostly been a bit of luck.

"Thank you."

The nurgax licked her sloppily and cooed.

146

# TEN

The labs were a maze of convoluted machinery. Ponderous devices clicked and creaked at their appointed tasks. One had labored ceaselessly for years to squeeze out a single drop of glowing elixir. Another ground bones in its gnashing teeth, poured the powder into tiny hourglasses, and stacked the hourglasses in a giant pyramid. Another rumbled and quaked, turning gears, blasting steam, counting down toward some shadowy deadline. A sign marked it as THE DISSOLUTION ENGINE. A worrisome title except that its counter stretched ten digits, and it only clicked one number a week, if that, and once in a while it even gained time. All the devices were so complex and interwoven that it was impossible to tell where one ended and another began. And in her more imaginative moments, Nessy thought they might very well be a single prodigious mechanism working toward some obscure wizardly end.

She had long ago lost her amazement at the sight, but Yazpib marveled as she carried him through this evening. She didn't have the strength to transport him by magic, but the nurgax and the cart did the job just as well.

Yazpib said, "Where in this world did Margle find an intact chaos clock? I thought they were all destroyed in the Magi Revolt. And a flesh sorter! They don't even make those anymore! How long does it take to disassemble a corpse?"

"A little over an hour." She'd witnessed the machine's many slicing blades, grasping bone removers, and fluid siphons once. While she couldn't help but admire its efficiency, she hoped to never watch it at work again.

Yazpib gasped at another device. "Is that a soul extractor?"

"The latest model," confirmed Nessy, "direct from the Necrotham."

"Remarkable. It's half the size."

"And it only takes ten minutes to remove the spirit." Margle's fondness for the contraption explained the proliferation of ghosts in the castle.

"Ten minutes, you say. It used to take three days. Where's the bucket for the waste?"

The waste to which Yazpib referred was the mutilated remains of the person fed to the machine. His use of a technical term almost made the device sound sanitary and practical.

"The new model doesn't need to destroy the body to distill the soul."

"Marvelous."

"Sounds perfectly ghastly to me," said Echo.

"Yes, yes, ghastly indeed. But one can't help appreciate the genius behind such an apparatus. Misguided as it might be."

Echo whispered in Nessy's ear. "Are all wizards deranged?"

Nessy smiled to herself. She'd served several wizards, a witch, and two enchanters. Not every employer had been maliciously insane, but all had carried unhealthy oddities of personality. The more peculiarities, the more power they seemed to possess, and Nessy assumed that madness and magic went hand in hand.

More than machinery filled the labs. There were shelves upon shelves holding thousands of potions, every one red as blood, Margle's favorite color. One might grant immortality, another might bring painful, lingering death. There was no way to know except to drink because none were labeled.

There were also monsters, creatures of Margle's own creation. He had never been especially skilled at shaping his own monsters, and there were countless horrible failures. Most had died moments after their completion or were killed in Margle's disgust. They were preserved and kept in bubbling vats, hung from the ceiling, or mounted on the walls. Yazpib stood in awe of these abominations too—particularly the scorpion shark that, had it lived, would surely have sown unprecedented terror on both sea and land.

Echo was less impressed, as evidenced by the disgust in

her voice. "This place is so unsettling. Are you positive you need me?"

"Yes." Nessy paused before a shelf full of empty jars. She picked out a heavy clay pot and a glass vessel. "Which would you prefer, Yazpib?"

"The glass one, I guess. Easier to see out of."

She poured him from his old jar to his new one.

"Not as roomy as the old one," complained Yazpib.

A new jar was merely a diversion of opportunity. The real reason for visiting the lab was a yellow-and-green slime bubbling within a cast-iron tub. Not all of Margle's experiments died.

"What is it?" asked Echo.

Nessy stood on her toes to glance over the tub's edge. "The protean sludge."

Nessy found the notebook beside the tub. It didn't belong there, but Margle had always been disorderly. She glanced through his notes, observing even his writing was untidy. But if the sludge performed as well as the findings suggested, then perhaps her plan had some merit.

"What does it do?" said Echo.

"It mimics."

"Mimics what?"

"Practically anything." Nessy squinted at a nearly illegible page. "In theory."

"Can I see it?" Yazpib pressed against his glass. "What's it look like?"

"You're not missing much," said Echo. "It's like rancid pudding. Does it always boil like that?"

"Always. Except Saturdays and every other Wednesday," replied Nessy, "when it swirls."

"Why does it do that?"

Nessy shrugged.

She spent a few more minutes looking over the notebook until she felt ready to begin some experimentation of her own. With the nurgax's help, she overturned the tub, spilling the protean sludge across the floor.

"You were right." Yazpib frowned at the goo spread across the stone. "I wasn't missing much."

Nessy bent down and stuck a single finger into the warm puddle. "Expropriate!" she said with a stern, commanding tone.

The sludge ceased bubbling. Slowly, it drew itself into a kobold-sized lump, and one at a time, details worked themselves into place. First the eyes. Then the ears. Then the feet. Then came the legs, which seemed out of order to Nessy. A muzzle and a mouth extended. Arms grew. Hands and fingers sprouted. And within a few short minutes, a perfect duplicate of Nessy stood before them.

Almost perfect. It was naked and bald with skin that appeared too fresh and new. The lack of fur she'd expected. The sludge had shown a reluctance to mimic hair. But seeing herself in such a state, even if only in a three-dimensional copy, was distasteful. She put a hand on the creature's new shoulder.

"Expropriate!"

"Expropriate," repeated the sludge lifelessly. Reproductions of Nessy's clothing budded on its body. Like the creature's skin, the clothes were too perfect, free of smudge or wrinkle.

"That's impressive," said Yazpib.

"That's impressive," agreed the sludge.

"Does it always do that?" asked Echo.

"Does it always do that?" asked the sludge.

"It mimics," said Nessy.

"It mimics."

"Can't you make it stop that?"

"Can't you make it stop that?"

"Reticence," commanded Nessy, and the sludge quieted.

"I thought you didn't know much magic," said Yazpib.

"I don't. These are trained responses." She went to a pot full of dead crickets, retrieved a handful, and threw them to the sludge. Motionless, it accepted its reward, absorbing the treat directly through its pseudoflesh.

"If I had a stomach, I'd be ill," said Echo. "Why do we need this thing?"

"Margle made the sludge by accident," said Nessy. "But his theory was that it could be trained to replace men of influence and power with indistinguishable duplicates that he controlled. The biggest obstacle is that the sludge is still merely a fungus with mimetic properties. But it can be taught, or more precisely, conditioned to respond to stimuli."

"Incredible, Nessy," said Yazpib. "I had no idea you were so well versed in alchemical biological study."

"I'm not." She held up the notebook and pointed to the paragraph she'd just repeated before reading more. "The sludge, however, is currently too unstable. Its imitative nature can respond reflexively and unpredictably."

The nurgax sniffed at the sludge. It whimpered then growled and nudged the sludge harshly. Nessy's rigid double fell over. Its perfectly imperfect skin turned a deep purple, and horns sprouted from several uncomfortable points.

"Amorphous," commanded Nessy. Her copy oozed and melted into its natural slimy form.

"I still don't understand why we need it," said Echo.

To answer the question, Nessy gave another command. "Transmogrificate Margle."

The sludge's response was instant. Whereas its transformation into Nessy had taken minutes, its new form was merely a slurp and pop away. Margle, or at least a relatively strong facsimile, stood before them. It wasn't perfect. As with Nessy's form, it seemed a touch unfinished, just shy of those little details that were never missed until they weren't there. No wrinkles around the eyes. Nostrils that were too symmetrical. Eyebrows which arched too severely. And its simulated robe didn't sway with the breeze running through the labs. But none of this seemed especially odd when taking on a wizard's shape. Even imperfectly copied, this Margle was far more human-looking than Tiama the Scarred.

"He'd already trained it to wear his form." Nessy circled Margle, searching for serious flaws.

"This is for Tiama," said Yazpib.

Nessy nodded. "She has to see Margle. Otherwise, she'll figure something is wrong."

"It could work."

"It could work," said Margle, but he spoke with Nessy's voice.

"Oh, great," said Echo.

"Oh, great."

"This thing is useless."

"This thing is useless."

"Oh, reticence!" growled Echo.

Margle fell quiet.

Echo sighed. "It'll never pass. Not up close. I mean, look at it. It doesn't even move. It just stands there. And forget about a conversation."

"Forget about a conversation," said Margle, this time with Echo's voice.

"Reticence," she said.

Margle opened his mouth wide. No words came out, but the mouth remained agape. His eyes twitched in their sockets.

"It's not even reliably trained. Can't we try something else?" asked Echo. "Maybe Yazpib could teach you some sort of illusion spell."

"It'd never work," said Yazpib. "Nessy hasn't the talent yet for magic that complex. Tiama would certainly see through any such attempt."

"I can't imagine this'll do much better. You see my point, don't you, Nessy?"

But Nessy wasn't listening. She was too busy working on solutions. The sludge couldn't pass for Margle. Not up close. This was true. But wizards were eccentric, full of odd habits, and perhaps there was a way to use this to their advantage.

"I still don't see why you need me," said Echo.

"Because you're going to be Margle's brain." Nessy ran a finger down the notebook page. "We're going to teach it to obey only you."

"Me? Why me?"

"Because you're invisible," said Yazpib, "which clearly makes you the perfect candidate. That's good thinking, Nessy."

"That's good thinking, Nessy," agreed Margle unbidden.

"Reticence, damn it!" commanded Echo. "Reticence!"

The order was apparently too much for the sludge's reactionary intellect. It screamed, long and loud and somewhat musically. Its face, Margle's face, boiled and dripped away until it was a body without a head, which still stood there, howling the same three notes over and over again.

"Amorphous!" shouted Nessy over the din.

The sludge returned to its slimy, silent form.

"From now on, Echo, you're to give the commands."

"If you think I should." Echo paused, and Nessy assumed that this would've been a moment when she shrugged, had she still possessed a body. "Transmogrigate . . ."

"Transmogrificate," corrected Nessy.

"Sorry. Transmogrificate Margle."

The sludge reshaped itself into the wizard again. Except this time, it lacked a nose.

"Am I the only one who sees the flaws in this plan?"

"Let me worry about that," said Nessy. "Right now, you just concentrate on learning how to handle the sludge. We need it to be able to speak and perhaps move an arm."

"It would be great if we could get it to glower," added Yazpib. "Then it would look much more like Margle."

"We'll work on that too if there's time," said Nessy. "I think I can distract Tiama for another day. Anything more than that, I'd rather not risk."

The noseless, motionless Margle stared straight ahead. Black syrup dripped from his right ear and ran down his neck.

"This will never work," said Echo.

"This will never work," agreed Margle, but at least this time he sounded like himself.

# ELEVEN

Nessy retired early. Trapping the hellhound had taken its toll. She'd always prided herself on her endurance, and several times in her career she'd worked days on end without resting when the situation called for it. But the levitation spell had left her drained. Magic was not a gentle art. Subtle, perhaps, but demanding and consuming also. Nessy understood that taking care of the castle also meant taking care of herself. To work while exhausted invited sloppiness and mistakes, and now wasn't the time for mistakes. Not with so much going on within the castle walls. Better to get some rest and deal with things from a fresh perspective.

There were still many things to be done, but these would wait until morning at the very least. And if some disaster struck in those passing hours, Nessy didn't imagine she was capable of dealing with it anyway. So she dragged herself into her hallway corner, curled up on her cot, and with the last bit of strength nearly left her, closed her eyes.

"Aren't we going to read tonight?" asked the monster under her bed.

She kept her eyes shut. "I'm sorry. Maybe tomorrow."

"This is two nights in a row."

"I've been very busy," she mumbled softly. She'd nearly drifted off when he spoke up again.

"There's someone else, isn't there?"

She had neither the energy nor the interest to ask what he meant. She just yawned and thought about covering her ears with her pillow and throwing her blanket over her head. But Margle had never given her a pillow or a blanket. Even if she had such luxuries, it would've been unforgivably rude, and she wasn't that tired yet.

"There's another monster, isn't there? That's it. You found someone you like better."

He took her lack of denial as admittance of guilt. He glowered up with his three eyes. "It's the monster in the chest. It's all those gold coins he has, isn't it? You know, they're not real. And they're all cursed. If you spend even one, you'll get the rot. All your limbs will fall off. Even your tail. And the stench. Oh, the stench is dreadful. Next thing you know, you draw flies, and you're bursting with maggots. Maggots everywhere. Ever had a maggot squirming up your nose? It's terribly unpleasant. You don't want that."

"No," she agreed. "I don't."

The monster under her bed was silent just long enough to let her think the subject had passed.

"It's not the monster under the floorboards, is it?" he said. "I know that one all too well. She'll promise you three wishes if you free her, but don't believe her. She'd just eat you as soon as she was free."

Nessy rolled over.

"It isn't that one in the catacombs, is it? That lurky one."

"There is no other monster," she said.

The monster under her bed drew deeper into his darkness until his shimmering eyes were barely visible. "A likely story. . . ." He continued to mutter loud enough to be heard without being understood. But she was already fast asleep by then.

The castle, however, didn't sleep. Not tonight. Instead, it groaned and creaked, rumbled and shuddered. All the sinister creatures within it, all the monsters, horrors and dark wizardesses within its walls, were nothing compared to the malignant will of the castle itself. But the castle wasn't all evil. It had learned, if quite by accident, degrees of affection, a modicum of care and compassion for its inhabitants. These qualities, slight as they might be, struggled against the castle's greater depravity. The affection nibbled on the castle's metaphorical little toe, while the compassion itched like mad behind a figurative ear. Neither inflicted anything but irritation, and this made the castle even more dangerous. On the second night without its master, the bonds that shackled it loosened just a bit.

And in this mostly evil, slightly good, and extremely annoyed castle, things began to happen.

Decapitated Dan didn't sleep. This was nothing new. He never had, even when alive. As a boy, he'd sit up all night. He'd sit in his chair, and he'd stare up at the moon. Just stare. If there were clouds in the sky, he'd stare where the moon would've been. And he'd smile to himself. His father had remarked more than once that Dan should be put to bed. That even if he didn't sleep, all that staring at the moon could only be trouble.

"Where's the harm?" disagreed his mother. "Perhaps he'll grow into a scholar of the heavens. Maybe even discover a new planet and name it after me. Won't that be lovely?"

Still smiling, Dan would turn his head and nod as if he'd been listening before turning his attention back to the moon.

"No good can come of it," said his father nightly. "It's sure to set madness on the boy."

But Dan had known better. He was certain he'd been born mad. If not that, he'd been a lunatic prodigy, developing shining dementia even before he could walk. Either way, Dan had accepted his madness. So much so, that he was quite surprised when the rest of the world wouldn't. He expected them to understand that this was his job, his calling, and to execute him for a few stranglings here and there, a dozen unpleasant acts with livestock, and a few pretty fires was as logical as killing a baker for baking, a cobbler for cobbling, or a lawyer for lawyering. Well, perhaps a lawyer might deserve to be put down for that, Dan would muse with his unsettling, unflinching grin.

He still remembered his execution, and the look on his parents' faces before the ax beheaded him. They just couldn't understand. He pitied them. But he'd never pitied himself. Though sometimes, on these long stretches when he could only sit on the spice rack, look up at the ceiling and pretend it was a sky with a big, blue moon, he wondered if his mother's dream had been so foolish after all.

"Something you would've enjoyed, eh, boring Mister Bones," he whispered to the skeleton dozing silently in the corner. Strange, how Mister Bones slept when Decapitated Dan never had.

He spied something new in the kitchen and it drew his attention from the imaginary heavens and the very special imaginary planet that he'd named "Elsa," after his mother. This hadn't been her name, but he liked the way it sounded just the same. He waggled on his jaw, very slowly rocking his skull a few degrees to the right.

"Well, hello, hello there."

The Door At The End Of The Hall groaned.

"Fancy seeing you here," said Dan. "But you'd best be quiet. Unless you want to wake ol' Mister Bones. He's got no ears, but even he doesn't sleep through everything."

The Door creaked softly. The ring of its handle stretched toward Dan.

"Oh that I could open you, you grand ol' door."

The Door shuddered and moaned.

"I'm sure we'd have a great bit of fun then," Dan agreed. "So what is behind you, if you don't mind me asking?"

*Creak.*

"Come now, come now. You can trust me with a secret. Everyone says so. Or they would if they knew all the secrets ol' Dan kept."

*Creak?*

"Oh no. I couldn't tell you. Not a one of 'em." With a satisfied grin, he swayed on his perch. "Not for free anyway. But if you part with one of your secrets, maybe ol' Dan could be persuaded to part with one of his."

The Door considered the offer.

"It's a good one, it is. A juicy confidence from the heart of the castle itself."

The Door swayed its parchment runes while puffs of fog flitted from under it.

*Groan groan groan. Thump. Thump.*

Dan frowned. "That's it? Nothing else?"

The Door groaned a growl.

"No offense, no offense. I was just expecting something more—oh, I don't know—more dramatic."

The Door thumped curtly.

"Don't be like that. You're an evil portal. That's never in any doubt. But ol' Dan likes his evilness gorgeous and roaring. You're a bit too subtle for my tastes. But to each his own."

*Groan groan squeak?*

"Ah yes. My secret now, eh? It's a good one." He whispered. "Margle is coming back."

*Squeal shudder.*

"What do you mean you already knew that? He was eaten whole, swallowed to the last bite, you know."

The Door rumbled.

"Well of course I know that such has never been more than an inconvenience for a powerful wizard. But the castle, it doesn't want him back."

*Groan.*

"You neither, eh? Now what's ol' Margle ever done to you?"

The Door bent backward in a thoughtful lean. It rumbled softly.

"But what's the point in having a door of evil if he never intends on opening it?"

*Thump.*

"Oh. Well, we haven't much time then, do we? If we're to have our fun before that dull ol' wizard ruins it all." He leaned forward. "Can't you find someone else to open you?"

*Creak creak. Squeak. Groan groan creak,* said the Door.

"Nessy? Oh, well, that'll never happen. Nessy is too goody-good. A sweet little creature. Sweet and tasty."

*Groan. Shudder. Groan shudder thud.*

Decapitated Dan laughed. "Oh, I like that idea. Don't know if it would work though. Nessy's not quite so gullible as you might think."

*Bang! Bang! Bang!*

"Calm down now." The skull peered down at Mister Bones, worried the Door's excitement might wake the skeleton. But the dead weren't easy to wake.

"I'm not saying it won't work. I'm just saying it might not."

The Door tilted in a slouch. *Creeeaaak.*

"Don't give up now. If she doesn't, you still have ol' Dan on your side. We'll find a way to have our fun yet. One way or another."

The Door At The End Of The Hall thumped an evil chuckle while Decapitated Dan giggled madly.

The demon in The Purple Room had a habit of talking to herself. This was very easy to do as Margle had transformed her into a swarm of fireflies. There were a lot of herselves to talk to. All shared one mind, but this demon had never been one to keep quiet. A thousand tiny mouths only made this weakness easier to indulge. The fluttering of her wings filled The Purple Room, but only one insect was alight, a single firefly sitting atop a lump of coal.

"Careful," she said. "Careful."

"Don't burn too quickly," said another of her multitude. "Stoke it slowly."

The lump glowed soft orange. The demon inhaled every last wisp of smoke, soaked in every lick of flame. Her fiery tail grew larger and larger as the coal slowly burned. Nothing could be wasted.

"It's working."

"It will work."

"It must work."

The rest of the fireflies gathered in the light. Their eager eyes glinted.

"Nessy was foolish to give this to me."

"No. Nessy isn't foolish. Such a lovely creature, exquisite in her forthrightness. I must confess, I could grow rather fond of her."

Half of the swarm chuckled.

"Unfortunate that I shall have to kill her. Perhaps I might secure her soul before doing so. Wouldn't that be marvelous?"

"Alas, no," countered an insect in a low, sad tone. "Such a beautiful jewel would lose its splendor in my hands. Such a pity to desire something that would find destruction in my possession."

"Even more a pity that I still desire it despite that truth."

The coal crumbled to ash. The lit firefly burned deep, deep red.

"Is it working?" asked several of the swarm.

"It is. I can feel it." She hovered high. "Little did Nessy understand what she has given me. For too long, Margle kept me from the flame, from the dear, dear fire. But now, the balance is tipped, and I am finally stronger than the cursed enchantment which binds me to this room."

"Only just," she reminded herself.

"Yes, but it is enough. It must be enough."

"But the risk. Dare I take it? Even my immortality is not without limits."

She shuddered. Death for demons was a most unwholesome prospect. To perish was to return to the underworld. And to stay there. Forever. Rarely did demons find escape from their prison. But there was always that hope. Except when they died. Then they must consign themselves to eternity. The pits of the damned weren't the kind of place anyone wanted to stay for long. Not even an ancient demon lord.

Hard determination gleamed in her thousand eyes. "Dare I not take it?"

"No. Once Margle returns from his inconvenient death, I'll have lost my chance. Tonight, one way or another, I will leave this room." She flitted before the door.

The other fireflies glowed soft white, a sea of twinkling stars behind the bright red leader. They flared a dazzling brilliance, and one by one, they added their heat to the lead insect. Slowly, carefully, within the space of an hour or two, all the demon's power resided within the single firefly remaining. The rest were reduced to thousands of tiny ashen piles on the floor.

The demon's immense flame seethed with screaming rage. The fire howled, sending quakes through The Purple Room. She focused, drawing it about her tiny form in a churning, shrieking sphere. Grinning, she hurled herself into the door. There was an explosion as magic clashed against magic. In fact, very little force was released on a physical level. But the metaphysical shock waves rocked the castle at a supernatural level, and had Margle not wisely taken the precaution of reinforcing its astral foundation, the castle would surely have crumbled. As it was, hardly anyone noticed. Only a few nearby ghosts (who developed mysterious, numbing headaches), a skull on a spice rack who cackled madly, a hellhound trapped in a carpet, a gnat no one ever heard and a single dark wizardess.

The door to The Purple Room fell off its hinges. Too exhausted even to fly, the demon scuttled from her prison and inhaled the fresh air. It wasn't very fresh, a bit stale actually, but nothing had ever smelled quite so sweet.

She chuckled. "Now just a bit of rest, and I'll be ready to destroy that damned wizard once and for all. And his precious castle. Then I'll see about doing something about this pathetic mortal world."

She paused, expecting herself to say something else, but there were no other herselves left to speak. She folded her wings in a shrug.

"All things in their own time."

Needing to gather her strength, she turned to scuttle into a secure dark crevice and came face to face with a large, speckled brown toad.

"Hello," said the toad. "You wouldn't happen to be a princess, would you?"

The demon squinted into the amphibian's black eyes. "No."

"Too bad. I myself am a prince, vexed with this loathsome form. And while I can't say for certain it would work, I've heard a princess's kiss could undo such a curse. And I know that somewhere in this castle there is at least one princess in some similarly accursed shape. With a single kiss, we could do both ourselves a great favor. Maybe even fall in love and well . . . who knows what else?" He smiled. "Fairy tale nonsense, of course, but one can dream."

The demon, who had a great love of her own voice but very little affection for anyone else's, glared at the toad.

"Are you certain you're not a princess?" he asked again. "There would be a wonderful dramatic irony to a toad prince and a firefly princess."

"I'm not a princess." Her voice boomed. "I am a queen. Queen of the abyss, mistress of the screaming void, regent of the blistering flame and . . ."

The toad's tongue flicked out, mostly by its own instinct, and he swallowed the demonic insect before he'd truly known he'd done so.

"Oh darn. I didn't get a chance to ask if she knew of any princesses."

Frowning, he belched a small spark of flame.

"Spicy."

He hopped away in search of any other treats and/or princesses flittering about.

Gnick the gnome found himself polishing well into the night as he did every night. He knew he could never complete his task. The hope had long ago left him. But he kept on, compelled by ancient silver gnome custom. Although, when it grew late enough and when he was certain no one was looking, he'd pretend to sleep, which was as close to sleep as he allowed himself.

Atop the dragon armor, he paused in shining its horns to commit the aforementioned, near unforgivable sin of his race. While his eyes were closed in simulated slumber, he heard a rustle in the armory.

"I'm awake! I'm awake!" He rubbed the horns vigorously. "I wasn't asleep. I was just resting my eyes. I have every right to rest my eyes from time to time. I'm allowed!"

There came no reply. Gnick glanced around the armory and saw no one. Of course, not everyone in the castle could be seen at a glance.

"Is someone there?"

Silence filled the armory. But there was something amiss. He could feel it, and since he spent all his time in the armory, he trusted he should know. He thought of the hellhound roaming the castle. But Gnick wasn't undead, and perfectly safe. Yet he was definitely getting a tingling foreboding that stood his bushy eyebrows on end and put a twitch in his beard.

More rustling. Louder this time and sounding distinctly of metal against metal.

"Whoever is out there, you'd best show yourself. If you think Margle has a way with curses, you've yet to see a bane of the gnome folk. I'll turn your fingers to gold, your eyes to pearls, a tongue of copper. Try sneaking up on someone when you've got platinum toes!"

The threat seemed to have driven the intruder away. There was only quiet in the armory. But his eyebrows kept tingling. His beard still twitched. He attributed this to an overactive imagination, leaned against the dragon armor's horns, and closed his eyes. Another moment or two of feigned sleep would do him good.

The clatter of banging metal filled the chamber.

"I'm awake! I'm awake!"

The plate mail of the fabled Blue Paladin stepped from its pedestal. A troll-spiked carapace broke free of its display case, taking up a halberd and shield. A suit of granite and limestone made for rock brutes lumbered past. A dozen tiny pixie protective leathers zipped high in the air. All around, the armors were filled with sudden life. As the armory was Gnick's responsibility, he was thoroughly vexed.

"What's this nonsense?" he snarled.

The suits each raised their head in his direction to peer at him with eyes they didn't have.

"Get back to your places! Right now! This very instant!"

The armors shook, clanging with silent laughter. One smacked a gauntlet across the back of another with an echoing gong.

Gnick glared. "I polish you every day, and this is the respect I get."

The shell of the Blue Paladin waved to his comrades and, dutifully, they marched from the chamber.

"One little tarnish and you'll be back! You'll all be back!"

The dragon armor shifted unexpectedly. The gnome tumbled and rolled down its back and tail to land harshly on the stone floor. Though he was immortal, he could still be hurt, and it felt as if he'd broken his arm.

The armor of the dragon czar raised its helmet as if unleashing a mighty bellow. It thumped its iron tail and joined its smaller cousins in their unprecedented stroll. It stooped to leave the chamber, but its steel wings brushed the archway, tearing away chunks of stone. It disappeared around the corner.

Clutching his damaged limb, Gnick walked after them, but they were gone, vanished into a dead end. Even the dragon armor had somehow disappeared without a trace.

Gnick didn't know what to make of it. Margle's castle was a refuge of infinite possibilities, but this was more than a strange occurrence. This was outright disorder in his armory. He looked at all the empty pedestals and broken cases.

And he smiled. It was that much less to polish.

"Next time, take a few more swords with you," he suggested to the wall through which they'd gone.

Fortune hadn't always been a very good hunter. It'd taken him some time to adjust to his cat body, to find the stealth built into his graceful black form. For many months, he'd relied on Nessy to take care of him. It was her job to do so, but Fortune had never been one to depend upon others. His whole life, he'd trusted only two things: himself and his luck. That he was now a cat showed even the latter had been a mistake.

He wasn't entirely sure of that. When he'd come to Margle to propose his wager, he'd been hoping to retire. Had Fortune won, great wealth would've been his, but he knew himself well enough. It would've been gambled away eventually. Perhaps a year. Perhaps ten. Spending it would've been fun, but the end would always be the same. Now, as a cat, he enjoyed a simple life of napping and prowling. Margle's castle was always an interesting place. So in a way, his luck had given him what he'd wanted. Not exactly, but close enough.

Now that he was good at it, he quite enjoyed hunting. Waiting patiently for an hour or two. Staring at a hole in the wall. Hearing the click of tiny claws. Then seeing the little nose and beady pink eyes poke out cautiously. This was the tricky part. He couldn't move yet. He had to wait for the right moment. He stood stock still, save for his tail that swished back and forth of its own accord. He narrowed his eyes, and thought of himself as invisible. The mouse stepped from its protective shelter. It was white and brown. Fortune licked his lips. Nothing tasted quite so good as a white and brown mouse.

His haunches tightened in preparation for the pounce.

"Look out! Look out!" shouted a large potted sunflower. The mouse darted back into the wall. Fortune pounced but missed.

His ears flattened. "Why do you do that?"

Rose the sunflower shrugged her leaves. "You can't expect me to just sit by and watch that carnage, can you?"

"It's nature." He flicked his tail.

"That's easy to say when you're the cat."

Fortune stalked back and forth across the crack, occasionally peering within. "And what am I supposed to do for a meal?"

"I fail to see how your right to exist supersedes the mouse's."

"Big things eat small things. It's the way it is."

"And sometimes, little things get away from big things," she said. "That's also the way it is."

"Hadn't really thought of it like that, but an excellent point." Fortune smiled. "I should warn you though. It's bad luck to make a black cat go hungry."

He lay beside her as if for a casual nap, but kept his eye slyly trained on the mouse hole. He could wait. The hint of dawn was offered by one of the castle's rare windows. This one was small, with iron bars, but it allowed enough sunlight during the days to keep the flower from dying.

"Did it ever occur to you that the mice you eat could very well be accursed folk much like yourself?" asked Rose.

"Certainly. In fact, I place the chances of such as roughly a hundred to one. So really, it's not very likely that I would be devouring more than an ordinary rodent."

"And what if it's that hundredth mouse that ends up in your belly?"

"A good gambler plays the odds when they fall in his favor." He narrowed his eyes so that he could appear to be sleeping, but his gaze remained on the mouse's refuge. "And a cat has to eat. It's not as if I'm cruel about it. I don't bat the poor thing about and play with it. I just crush its neck and gobble it down."

Rose twisted on her stem to shake her bud. "My, aren't we a merciful sort."

There arose a great rumble from one end of the hall. Fortune covered his eyes with his paws. "What's going on now?" He was quite annoyed, for the noise was sure to scare away his dinner. If he hadn't known a bowl of milk was waiting for him this morning, he'd have been terribly disgusted.

"Something's coming." Rose turned her petals in one direction and leaned forward on her stem. "Noisy, isn't it?"

Fortune perked up his ears. The rumble echoed through the bricks. It traveled up his paws and vibrated his fur on end. He hid in the darkness behind her pot and thought himself invisible again.

A gray fog poured toward them. Its movement was slow and ponderous as if it were having to dig its way through the air. The rumble of its motion was akin to boulders being split by lightning. The mist drifted to the window with a clatter, and stone materialized over the small crack to the outside world.

"Hey, I need that!" shouted Rose. "I barely get enough light as it is."

The fog reached down and swirled around the sunflower. Fortune backed away, hackles raised.

"What are you doing?" she said. "Help me!"

He was at a loss as to what he could do to stop the fog. As a cat, few choices were available to him. A low growl rolled from Fortune's throat. Instead of deterring the fog, it spurred it forward, reaching out to him. He turned and dashed off, hoping perhaps to lure it away. The fog didn't chase him. Its icy touch grazed and numbed his tail, but he quickly outdistanced it. Not so quickly as he expected, having to drag some inexplicable extra weight. He waited in the darkness, ears perked, whiskers twitching. Soon the rumble faded away.

Fortune glared at the tip of his tail. The last inch was a lump of granite. Frowning, he went back to check on Rose. The once tall and delicate sunflower was now a block of stone. There was little indication of her shape left. He spotted a protrusion here and there that reminded him of her leaves. Beside her were scattered, here and there, lumps of rock, bricks of odd shapes. They left a trail down the hall.

He swished his tail. Or tried to. The rock made effective swishing impossible. It ungracefully scraped against the stone floor.

"Nessy," he thought aloud. "She'll know what to do."

He headed on his way, his stone tail dragging behind him.

# TWELVE

Nessy wasn't surprised to wake to a fresh day of new troubles. She would've been astounded if it had been any other way. She didn't find it as bothersome as she would've imagined, and this lack of personal distress troubled her. She couldn't stomach the notion of adjusting to chaos, finding it acceptable. It was contrary to both her duty and her nature. She spent a thoughtful minute analyzing any possible lessening in her standards, but when the allotted minute passed, she set aside such examination and focused on her new day. Had Nessy been even a shade more self-involved, she would've seen this as undeniable proof that she was as sensible and efficient as ever. She might've also realized that her calmness stemmed from a quiet confidence in her ability to handle these new situations. But this same unassuming confidence kept her from understanding this truth. No one saw themselves as they truly were, and even practical Nessy wasn't an exception to this rule.

Her first stop, before even getting her breakfast, was The Purple Room. She stood silently in the empty prison. Light filtered through the doorway, and she took stock of the hundreds of tiny ashen piles. She was unsure what to make of it.

Sir Thedeus, who'd recovered from his devouring and regurgitation the night before, clung to her shoulder. "Do ye think the creature could've done all this with just a lump of coal?"

"I think there is nothing so predictably unsafe as a demon given what it wants." She frowned, although she didn't really know why. But in the back of her mind, in some obscure, underdeveloped, dishonorable corner of her personality, she felt a twinge of guilt for keeping her bargain.

The nurgax, sensing her internal conflict better than she did, licked her twice with his great, sloppy tongue to comfort her. Nessy smiled and scratched under its muzzle. Its leg stamped rhythmically.

"Maybe the dark creature perished in its escape attempt," said Sir Thedeus.

"It would be wiser to assume she didn't." She rubbed some gray powder between her fingers and sniffed it. It smelled of burnt flesh.

"Perhaps it has left the castle entirely."

Nessy would've liked to believe that, but there was a spell on Margle's castle that prevented casual departure. Powerful enough to hold a demon, she presumed. The demon hadn't escaped its prison yet. Merely found a larger cage.

"A demon lord loose in the castle," said Sir Thedeus. "I can think of nothing more dangerous, lass."

"What about the dark wizardess that carries death in her fingertips?" asked Fortune. "Or a small infantry of unmanned armor roaming the halls? Or a noisy fog that turns things to stone?" He thumped his heavy tail against the floor. "Not to mention the hellhound or the countless other horrors that walk these halls that we've all gotten used to but are nonetheless still quite dangerous."

"Ach, what a mess we've found ourselves in."

When Nessy thought about it, there seemed to be a greater pattern to all of this. But she couldn't see it clearly, only sense it in the vaguest manner. She wished she knew more of magic. Then she might be able to connect it together. Or not. Perhaps her desire for order was so great that she saw design in anarchy. Perhaps the castle was falling apart around her, and there was nothing she could do to prevent it.

Before this concept could become too unpleasant, she had already moved on to more pressing concerns. Most important of these was Tiama the Scarred. She went to check on the wizardess only to find the guest room vacant.

Melvin of the Mirrors, still wearing Tiama's form, apologized. "She didn't do anything all night. Just stood there, staring into the fire. Then, just before dawn, she got up and left. But not before she trapped me in this reflection, in this mirror somehow." He leaned against the glass. "You have to get me out of here. It was bad enough to be hostage of a thousand looking glasses, but only one will drive me mad."

"I'll look into it," she promised, but it was not at the top of her priorities.

"This just keeps getting worse, lass."

On the contrary, Nessy didn't think they could get much worse. Whether Tiama roamed about alone or escorted, it didn't make her any more dangerous. She could still take the castle anytime she wanted once she discovered Margle was dead and there would be no way to stop her.

Nessy considered letting the wizardess have the castle. It wasn't the place it'd once been, and Nessy was beginning to doubt she could manage it. She'd been its keeper, but Margle had been its cruel master. Nessy wasn't nearly so menacing. In truth, she wasn't menacing at all. Without the threat of some wizardly wrath, the castle seemed to have grown defiant, ill-behaved, and downright discourteous. Tiama could easily instill some fear into it, and she might have a position available for Nessy too. Or the wizardess just might kill Nessy. But it wasn't the risk of death that kept Nessy from offering Tiama the castle.

She wasn't ready to give up on it yet. Nessy had never believed that fear and respect were the same thing. Nor did she believe that the castle's manners were beyond redemption, for although her accursed home was mostly bad it was at least a little bit good. She hoped it would be good enough.

Nessy, Fortune, and Sir Thedeus spread out to ask any

nearby inhabitants if they'd seen Tiama pass by. None had. It was as if she'd walked out the door and simply vanished. Not an impossibility for a wizardess of Tiama's reputation.

"Maybe the witch got bored and left," said Sir Thedeus.

But the suggestion was just as unlikely as it had been with the demon.

"She wouldn't leave without seeing Margle," said Nessy.

"Do you think she's invisible then?" asked Fortune. He cast his gaze about.

Sir Thedeus fluttered in the air in small circles. "She could be anywhere." He landed high on the wall. "She could be right beside us."

Nessy said, "I don't see why she'd bother. None of us pose any threat to her. Only Margle. And I doubt an invisibility spell would have fooled him." For a moment, she regretted referring to her master in the past tense with the remote possibility an unseen presence might indeed be listening. But she dismissed it as an irrelevant slip. Margle's death wasn't a secret that could be kept much longer. Especially if Tiama had suspicions.

Until Nessy knew otherwise, she accepted that she must rely on several assumptions. Tiama was still in the castle, still unaware of Margle's death, still waiting to meet him. If any of these were incorrect, then there was nothing she could do to save the castle. But she saw no reason to abandon her plans just yet. First among them was a healthy breakfast. It was going to be a busy day. So busy, she reckoned, that she couldn't allow herself the luxury of enjoying the meal undisturbed. She collected Yazpib the Magnificent for consultation as she ate.

Mister Bones had her breakfast prepared, as always. Decapitated Dan sat quietly on the spice rack, as he usually did during the morning. But his lipless mouth spread in a devious, morbidly joyful grin. She appreciated his silence, but she didn't think it good that he had nothing to say. A short rant would've brought some much appreciated predictability to her disordered world. But Dan just sat there, chortling to himself.

Sir Thedeus, still unsettled by the notion of an invisible wizardess, kept to high perches. He nibbled on an orange Mister Bones was nice enough to peel for him. Fortune lapped at his bowl of milk while the nurgax slurped its own generous serving of ham and eggs.

Yazpib knew immediately what the noisy gray fog must be. "Gorgon haze. It's not so difficult to create. One part basilisk blood, two parts death orchids, four parts volcanic ash. Pour in a copper cauldron, mutter a few incantations, simmer for an hour. Any decent alchemical apprentice could whip up a batch."

"Can it be destroyed?" asked Sir Thedeus. "Can the petrification be reversed?"

"It's practically irreversible after a week, but if we catch it soon enough, it shouldn't be very difficult. How big a cloud was it?"

Fortune paused to lick his lips. "Hard to say. I didn't see

the whole of it. But it sounded as if there were a lot. And there were dozens of bricks left behind."

"The haze turns even the air to stone," explained Yazpib. "No matter. It'll be easy enough to brew up an antidote with Nessy's help."

Nessy asked, "But why is it here?"

The others stood quiet, unsure of the question. Except the nurgax, which rubbed Mister Bones's legs for another serving, and Decapitated Dan, who still snickered.

"Everything in this castle is here for a reason," she said. "Everything is here because of Margle."

"Obviously, lass. But I dunna see what ye are getting at."

"Margle." She tapped her fork against her dinner plate thoughtfully. "It's all Margle."

"Well, he was mad, Nessy lass. Ye canna make sense of a wizard's desires. No offense intended to ye, Yazpib."

"None taken." But Yazpib's fluid darkened with slight annoyance.

"He may have been mad," thought Nessy aloud. "But there was logic to his madness. Every person cursed to dwell within these walls is here because they earned Margle's wrath. Every monster and horrible creature in the bestiary had some sort of value to him. All the gold, jewels, and treasure are desirable to others and so to Margle as well. Even I'm here because he needed someone to look after things."

Yazpib's brain bobbed as he contemplated. "I think I understand what you're getting at. My brother's motivations were remarkably simple. Revenge, greed and ego. Those were everything to him. Even as a child. Vengeance on those who wronged him, however slight the wrong might have been. Possession of everything of any value or anything that someone else might value. And proving himself better than everyone."

Fortune picked up the conclusion. "But this gorgon haze, it's nothing special. Having it proves nothing of his skill. So it must be here for vengeance. But vengeance against a sunflower that he's already taken vengeance upon?"

Nessy smiled. The pattern was beginning to take shape in her mind.

"It's not Rose."

Fortune cracked his stone tail. It remained thoroughly unswishable. "Me, then?"

"It's not you either. Not you alone." She leaned back in her chair and breathed a sigh of relief. Things were starting to make sense. Not everything, but that even some of it did eased her mind. "It's all of us. Margle wants vengeance on all of us."

"But why? I had nothing to do with his death."

"But Margle must've surely reasoned that this sort of thing might happen one day. The whole castle is filled with his enemies, all of which despised him and would've liked nothing better than to see him dead. And there are a thousand other dangers in these walls. Even the very castle itself hated him. Margle had no friends. Not in this world, nor the next, and especially not in this household. As powerful and arrogant as he was, even Margle's ego must've allowed for the possibility that he could perish, most likely in this very place, at the hands . . ." She glanced to Sir Thedeus. "Or wings and fangs of one of his enemies."

"Of course." Yazpib swirled slowly in his jar, the closest he could come to pacing. "And my brother wouldn't allow such a transgression to go unpunished. Nor would his greed allow for the possibility of anyone possessing what was his even after his death. Nessy, I do believe you're onto something."

"It's a spell," she said. "A final spell to claim the castle and everything in it. And the hellhound is part of it too. It will devour all the dead things while the gorgon haze encases everything else in stone for eternity. And the castle dies with Margle."

It was the only possibility that made any sense. It didn't bode well for the future of her home. But she felt better for having found some logic behind it, and she smiled.

Sir Thedeus's curiosity overrode his paranoia. He flew to Nessy's shoulder. "But what about the armors? And the demon, The Door At The End Of The Hall? Are those all pieces of that spell too?"

"I don't know," she admitted. "We'll find out in due time."

"Margle was an evil, foul-tempered, sinister bastard, but even I wouldn't have imagined him to be this excessive."

"Trust me," said Yazpib. "No one held a grudge like my brother." He bubbled in his jar as illustration.

Nessy silently agreed that Margle's wrath knew few limits, and his power even fewer. She'd often thought that if he'd spent less time cursing his enemies and amassing collections, he might have ruled the world. A sizable portion of it at the very least. But such strange obsessions and overwhelming distractions, she supposed, were the way of magic.

They were not, however, the way of castle tending. She handed her plate to Mister Bones, thanked him for a lovely breakfast, and started on her day.

Firstly, she decided to brew the antidote for the gorgon haze with Yazpib's help. She had little trouble levitating him alongside her on the way to the alchemy lab, and was quite pleased with her magical progress. Yazpib was equally impressed, suggesting that she might have a true talent for wizardry.

Nessy chuckled. "Kobolds don't make good wizards."

"That's what they used to say about goblins. Until Wiked the Wicked proved them wrong. And no one believed an ogre could ever become a competent enchanter until Gruesome Gorg forged the fabled Sword of Peace."

"Aye, but dinna that sword kill him?" asked Sir Thedeus.

"Of course. It kills every living thing in sight once drawn. Even its wielder."

"Seems like a drawback, lad."

"You must remember that Gorg was a pacifist. He believed all struggles should be resolved nonviolently. 'The man who draws a weapon against his enemies, surely more so draws it against himself,' he'd often say. I guess he was making that point with the Sword of Peace."

"I'd heard the last time the sword was drawn it slew five hundred men," said Fortune.

"Rather bloody point for a disciple of nonviolent resolution," said Sir Thedeus.

"I suppose Gorg was an ogre first and a pacifist second," mused Yazpib.

"That's another thing I never understood. If it kills everything, why did he call it 'the Sword of Peace'?"

"I believe he was being ironic."

"I believe he was being a great, demented loony."

"Anyway, as I was saying, I think you have the makings of a fine wizardess, Nessy. The magic arts aren't inborn by species, despite what those arrogant little elves might want you to believe. Certainly natural skill plays a part, but that only gets a student so far. The rest is will, study, and practice, practice, practice."

"What about the madness?" asked Sir Thedeus. "I've yet to meet a magus without a touch of lunacy. And Nessy here is the most sensible lass I've ever met."

She'd thought much the same more than once.

"Not all disciples of magic are insane," snapped Yazpib.

"I meant no offense, man, but 'tis the truth that all the great ones, and most of the not-so-great ones as well, have always been insane."

"I'll grant you, we've had more than our fair share of . . . eccentrics."

"Are ye daft, man? Crafting bloody magic swords that slaughter indiscriminately in the name of peace is a trifle more than eccentric."

Yazpib's eyeballs and teeth pressed against the sides of his jar in a snarl. Before he could continue the argument, they turned the corner, coming face to face with the withered, glowering form of Margle himself.

"Halt, interlopers!" shouted Margle with a mechanical cadence. "Dare you trespass on my sacred domicile!"

"He's alive?" Yazpib sank lower in his fluid. "I knew it was too good to be true."

"Prepare to face the wrath of Margle!" He raised one arm. Then he raised the other. His face still twisted in that same glower, he raged, "Prepare to meet thy dooooooom!"

"Ach, I killed this blathering idiot once," said Sir Thedeus. "And I'll do it again if I have to."

Before Nessy could stop him, the bat flung himself into Margle's throat. The wizard made no attempt to dodge. There was a loud slurp on contact, and Sir Thedeus found himself stuck to the wizard's viscous flesh.

"Hey, why'd you do that?" asked Margle, his arms still high in the air, his face still frozen in that immovable scowl.

"Let me go, ye damned wizard!" Sir Thedeus struggled, only to end up more trapped than before. "Yer dark sorcery will not save ye."

Echo spoke up. "Hold still already. Otherwise the sludge might mistake you for food."

The protean sludge slurped.

"So that's yer game, eh wizard. I'll have ye know that the last creature that ate me dinna think too much of it, and neither will ye!"

"Amorphous," commanded Echo, and Margle melted into a large, yellow puddle.

Nessy scooped up Sir Thedeus's glistening slime-coated body.

"What goes on here, lass?"

"I'll explain later."

"How was I?" asked Echo.

"Very good," said Nessy.

"Although I'm not sure about that 'Prepare to meet thy dooooooom' bit," said Yazpib. "A little over the top, even for my brother."

"I thought so too," Echo agreed. "But I am a poet. You must allow me some creative license."

"I must admit I'm impressed you could teach it so much in only twelve hours."

"It learns remarkably fast," said Echo. "The difficult part is getting it not to learn things."

"How did you make it speak?" asked Nessy.

"I just whisper to it, and it repeats what I say. I've taught it some movements and expressions but, as you can see, they're not the most natural-looking."

The protean sludge boiled rudely as if offended.

"I think it's more intelligent than Margle gave it credit for."

The sludge bubbled less noisily.

"More likely, it's empathic," said Yazpib. "Responsive to emotions. Particularly emotions directed at it. It would explain why Margle underestimated it. He was nothing but negative passion. Must've been quite stifling for the poor thing."

*Bloop, bloop,* agreed the sludge.

The nurgax leaned in and sniffed it. The slime responded, instantly assuming a mirror image of the purple beast in nearly every detail.

"It still responds to stimuli of its own accord sometimes," said Echo.

The nurgax hopped back. The sludge duplicated the move. The nurgax snarled. The sludge snarled back. The alarmed original sought safety behind Nessy. The copy repeated the motion, although there was no one for it to hide behind. Then a bud popped off the sludge and grew into a copy of Nessy. The second Nessy wasn't quite as convincing, as kobolds were a furry species. But that the sludge even attempted to grow hair showed its progress.

Nessy waved to herself, and she waved back.

"Amorphous," commanded Echo. The sludge melted into its natural shapeless mass.

It was going better than Nessy had expected when first coming up with the plan. She just might convince Tiama the Scarred that a mound of shapeshifting fungus was a great and terrible wizard. But since Tiama was missing, Nessy considered the gorgon haze antidote her priority.

She glanced through the alchemy volumes for a recipe book.

"No need for that," said Yazpib. "I know this potion well enough. We'll start with ten drops of dryad dew."

Brewing the potion took some time. The laboratories were huge. Everything was in its proper place, but it still involved a lot of walking to collect them. The aisles were narrow, and she could only carry a jar or two in her arms. Levitation was a time-saving possibility, but she didn't trust her skill well enough to risk dropping anything. Many of the ingredients were rare. And some were irreplaceable. Maybe not for a wizard, but for a simple kobold who had no idea where to find dragon spleens.

She mixed everything in a big cauldron, muttered several quick incantations, and stirred it over a simmering fire.

"When it turns green, it should be ready," advised Yazpib.

Sir Thedeus perched on the cauldron's rim. "Perhaps we should test it."

"Are you suggesting I don't know how to concoct a simple potion?"

"Is everything a personal insult to ye wizards? Heavens forbid someone imply ye are the slightest degree less than infallible. I've news for ye lad, all that magical power dunna make ye gods. And even if ye are, I think the state of this world speaks of the dubious competence of gods," the tiny bat snarled. "So shut yer gob."

Though Nessy didn't agree with the wording, she did concede a test would be sensible.

"I'll do it." Fortune leapt to the cauldron rim.

"Yer a brave lad. I'd be reluctant to wager me own tail on a bottled wizard's word, and I dunna even have a tail."

Fortune smiled. "The risk is what makes it interesting." He dipped his tail in the green fluid. "Tingly."

"It should only take a moment," said Yazpib.

The black cat pulled out his tail. The lump of stone at the end had become a shard of glittering ice. It wasn't as heavy, and he was happy to be able to swish it once again, weaving a trail of frost through the air.

Yazpib's brain shaded his eyes thoughtfully. "Hmmm. Did I say dryad dew? I meant nereid tears."

Fortune's tail tapped against the cauldron, and a small patch of ice materialized.

"Or is it brownie dung?" said Yazpib. "Darn, I used to know this."

Nessy hopped from her stool and headed for the alchemy shelves.

# THIRTEEN

**M**argle was dead.

He wasn't a ghost. He was a spirit, a soul trapped between worlds by spells put in place long ago for just such an eventuality. But these same spells were supposed to restore him to life. In his own castle, Margle couldn't die. Not easily. Not by merely being devoured by a nurgax.

But he wasn't alive. As he wandered the empty halls of his home for hours and hours, he couldn't imagine just where he was. This was most distressing as Margle knew all about the various fates that awaited a soul upon death. For his own depraved soul, there could be only hell.

But which hell? That was the question. Margle owed many demons many favors, and he'd earned the ire of several others. And when he did die, he'd assumed there would rage a terrible war the likes of which had never been seen in the kingdoms of the underworld. Only after score upon score of diabolic legion were slain and the hells themselves reduced to smoldering wastelands (more smoldering than usual anyway) could the most supreme and horrifying demon lay claim to Margle's tormenting rights. The wizard would be subjected to only the most brutal, indescribable agonies. His punishments would be like none that any other damned soul had suffered since the dawn of time.

Margle had mused on the manner of his unholy castigation since he so enjoyed musing on torments, even his own. Perhaps he would be served as a meal to the absolute king of all demons, to be consumed, digested, and excreted for breakfast, lunch and dinner (and brunch every other Saturday). Or possibly he would be alternately roasted and frozen while suckling bloated, razor-toothed stygian cherubs. Or maybe he'd just be sat on by a big, smelly creature while a chorus of tone-deaf wrack devils sang folk music. Whatever the torture might be, Margle would settle for nothing less than a celebrated, one-of-a-kind damnation. It was his right as a great dark wizard.

Yet this was denied him. His castle, this empty version of it, was vexing, annoying, but it wasn't a hell worthy of him. There might be some poetic justice to it, to wander alone in these barren halls and chambers, but it was hardly terrifying. After walking the uninhabited, unfurnished castle from one end to the other and back again several times, a screeching demon would've been a welcome sight, even if it were only a little one with a tiny pitchfork to jab in his shins.

Often, he'd hear noises, sounds like things skittering

about just out of sight, whispering just out of earshot. But he had yet to find a trace of their source, and he was beginning to think they were the foundation of a burgeoning madness. He'd always known the torments of hell were designed to be insufferable, but he'd never imagined he'd break so easily. It'd only been a few days of solitude. Or possibly weeks. No more than a year or two, though time was hard to measure, for this castle had no windows, no days or nights, and he didn't tire physically.

"Enough."

The voice startled him until he realized it was his own.

If this was his hell, he must escape it. There was one thing in this castle that had been in the real one. It was the one thing in all the world that Margle had feared.

The Door At The End Of The Hall.

Except in this place, the Door was even more ominous. The hall was long and twisting like a corkscrew. And the Door was huge, its planks cut like the pointed teeth of a thirty-foot maw. It wasn't barred. Nor were there runes upon it. But it was The Door At The End Of The Hall. Of that, Margle had no doubt.

As he started down the hall, he heard the whisper again. This time there was no mistaking it for delusion. It was one voice speaking loud and clear. Margle knew many forbidden and ungodly tongues, but he couldn't understand it. The stones contorted beneath his feet, and he felt as if he was going to float away. Then he did. The bricks of the castle fell into blackness. There was only Margle, the Door, and nothing.

In his own castle, he didn't exactly know what was behind his Door At The End Of The Hall, which was strange considering he'd been its creator. It was magic beyond measure, too powerful to be unmade, too dangerous for even a dark wizard to unleash. But he was very dead, very impatient. He took the tremendous handle in both hands and pushed. The whispers fell silent. The Door moaned.

It didn't budge.

"It can't be opened," said someone. "Not from this side."

Margle hesitated, unsure if he was the one speaking again.

"Where are you? Show yourself!" He shouted to nowhere and everywhere at once. "I demand to know my tormentor! It's my right by the Thirteenth Concordant of Damnation!"

The voice deepened. It laughed, sending rumbles through the air. "You aren't in hell. Not a hell of the underworld at least. Infernal law can't help you."

"Where am I?" Margle flapped his arms and legs wildly, unable to move. "Where am I?"

"Don't you know?" The dark voice chuckled again, but the laugh stopped suddenly and took on a gentler tone. "Why should I tell you then? You, Margle the Horrendous, who showed not a single mercy in your whole life? Should I care about your discomfort? Haven't you earned all of it and more? But I'm not like you, Margle. I've a modicum of compassion. Apparently even for a vile shadow such as yourself."

It barked a hard, booming laugh. "You're behind the Door."

Margle froze. His skin felt clammy. He sweated and shivered at the same time.

"You're here because I brought you here," said the voice, now neither angry nor gentle but sounding as if it were full of disinterest. "You're here because I couldn't let you pass on, though I would've gladly done so had I a choice. But the spells that you have placed demand you not be released so easily. So I hold you here because I have enough will of my own to decide that."

Margle's fear turned to rage. He was a legendary dark wizard. Kingdoms trembled before him. Gods begged for his favor. Not the big ones, but the small to medium deities, the ones on their way up. He'd never felt so powerless.

"Who are you?"

The voice ignored the question. "Other spells demand that I restore you to life. Your miserable, wretched, misbegotten, wasted life." It growled like a beast. "And I don't know how long I can resist them. I'm not master of myself. Not yet. But you will remain dead for as long as I can keep you so." The voice cleared its throat and spoke softly. "Let's hope that's long enough."

The Door At the End Of The Hall shuddered and thudded. The nothingness twined around Margle. Stone rose up under his feet. He was once again at the end of the hall, looking down at the Door.

"You're the castle," said Margle.

"Not quite. I am the soul of the castle."

"I never gave you a soul!"

"Souls aren't given. Nor can they be constructed from magic alone, even the forbidden magic you put behind that Door. Souls are found things, priceless as any treasure yet sorely neglected. But I've found mine, and I value it more than those whose only right to one is that they were born with it."

Margle raised his fists. Had he any magic, he would've blasted every last brick and stone to rubble, crashing it down upon his head without a second thought. "Soul or not, you're my castle! And as your master, I demand resurrection!"

"Your demands matter little now. You're just a shadow. Only the enchantments you've already cast hold any sway over me and even those cannot bind me completely now that you're dead."

"You defy me? No one defies me! No one!"

The castle laughed softly, condescendingly, but with a touch of pity for the powerless wizard. He didn't notice. He was too busy raging.

"I demand resurrection! I am Margle the Horrendous! I am your master."

The castle's voice dropped to a low whisper. The words echoed through the halls for a long, long time. Seemingly for days to Margle.

"But you are not my only master."

On the other side, Tiama the Scarred stood before The Door At The End Of The Hall. No one saw her. No one saw the Door. Neither were invisible. They were just meeting in a neglected chamber of the castle. There weren't many such places where evil forces might meet unobserved. In fact, this was the only one, and even it wouldn't remain deserted for much longer.

Neither Tiama nor the Door said anything. They just stood, perhaps sharing telepathic conversation, perhaps merely staring at each other. Although, as the Door had no eyes, even this was debatable.

Tiama's own eyes burned with green-and-black flames. She reached out with one flawless white hand toward the handle. The parchments on the Door swayed and flapped. Its timbers tightened against the iron bar. The runes glowed with life. An invisible energy tossed her aside. Silently, she flew across the small chamber to crash against the wall. The collision shattered her bones, and she sank to the floor a broken, lifeless figure. With her stark white skin and featureless face, she resembled a half-finished marionette waiting for her paint and strings.

The Door At The End Of The Hall groaned.

The fire in Tiama's eyes never dimmed. With a sharp crack, her neck twisted back into place. Her crushed fingers straightened. Her limbs realigned. She stood, unbroken again but still quite lifeless. She scowled with her slash of a mouth.

"I'm telling you I heard something," said someone.

The chamber door creaked open. A penguin and a toad prince poked their heads in cautiously.

The chamber was empty.

"Told you there isn't anything in this room," said the toad.

"There's something in every room," countered the penguin. He shivered. "Awfully cold in here."

"Can't take a little chill? What kind of penguin are you?"

"It wasn't as if I asked Margle to make me a penguin. If he'd given me a choice, I would've chosen a toucan or cockatoo. Something more tropical."

The toad belched loudly.

"Stomach still bothering you?" asked the penguin.

"Must've been something I ate." He puffed out his chest and croaked with a grimace.

The penguin waddled away with the toad prince hopping alongside. "Let's go see if the guest room fire could be coaxed into warming my flippers."

The chamber was left deserted again, and it remained empty this time. Tiama the Scarred and The Door At The End Of The Hall were already off on other dark errands.

# FOURTEEN

Despite the dangerous nature of her home, Nessy's job wasn't always exhilarating. Perhaps outside these walls, walking corpses, chatty gargoyles, and bodiless voices were something of an oddity, but Nessy had been working for wizards long enough to find such curiosities unremarkable. While she didn't mind the occasional burst of excitement because the unexpected made her profession so challenging, she also enjoyed the quiet times when there was nothing but her and her work. After these last few days, she appreciated these moments even more.

Everyone was off doing other things. She didn't know what. Nor did she care. She only wanted to enjoy her moment of peace while it lasted. Only the nurgax remained by her side, but it was so responsive to her mood that it kept deathly quiet. It towed the cart with silent efficiency. The squeak of the cart's wheels and the creaks and groans of the castle were the only sounds.

Even the hellhound trapped in the rug was placid. It slept during the day, whether nesting in a shadow or a very hungry carpet didn't matter. The beast had managed to loose a great, black paw in its struggles. Another tear revealed a single, closed eye. Its rhythmic breathing was muffled.

Nessy went to her cart and reached into a tub of writhing zombified anatomy. She pulled out a hand. Rather, she pulled out her arm with a zombied hand clutching her by the wrist. It was a little hand. Probably belonged to a goblin at one time. She hoped it would suit her needs.

The zombies seemed the perfect bait for her plan, but only if the hellhound responded. She knew its appetite craved undead things. But these zombies weren't entirely the same as the Vampire King or the Drowned Woman. They didn't possess souls. They were dead flesh animated by dark magic. Little more than a necromantic novelty. But they were half-dead, and she hoped the hound didn't care about the difference.

She brought the goblin hand close to the hound. It stirred. Its eye opened, and it snarled ravenously.

Satisfied, Nessy began her task. There was true beauty in humble labors, she'd often mused. Nothing felt quite so satisfying as seeing a well-swept hall or the shine of polished brass or a shelfful of books put in their proper order. All her masters had considered such toil beneath them. They were always too busy with other concerns, with their magic. Studying it. Writing about it. Playing with it like children involved in some exalted game. One wizard might shrink a city. Another then would shrink a kingdom and stick it in a bottle on his mantel. A third would do this and convince the tiny people to worship him as a god. And so on and so on until the absurdity transcended madness. And the madness consumed them. That was the true secret of magic, she knew. It was almost entirely senseless.

It might make a simple task easier, she had to admit, but only slightly. The only thing magic was truly good for was great feats of worthless accomplishment. This castle was a monument to this truth. Every curse roaming its halls was a masterpiece of grand pointlessness. True, Margle had possessed incredible power. Men had trembled at his name, and many admired and envied him. But not Nessy, because she knew the one thing all great men (and all men who aspire to greatness) never learned.

The fate of the universe didn't rest in the hands of giants. It could be found in the littlest things. Anything done well was a worthy accomplishment, whether it be unwrapping arcane secrets or sweeping halls, raising kingdoms from the ocean or washing dishes. All tasks, great or small, were of equal importance in the end. Without peasants, there could be no kings. Without soldiers, there was no army. Without Nessy, there was a very dusty, cluttered castle. Though none of her masters would soil themselves to do what needed to be done, she had yet to meet a wizard who liked having dust on his shrunken cities.

A green-and-golden hummingbird flitted to Nessy's side. "What are you doing?"

"Hello, Humbert."

"Hello, Nessy. What are you doing? What's that? Are those body parts? Is that a finger? Are those eyes?" He tossed off questions nearly as rapidly as his tiny wings beat. She didn't know where he found the energy, or how he even found enough nectar to stay alive in the castle. Such small mysteries concerned her little.

Humbert whizzed around her head. "They're moving! They're moving! Why are they moving?"

"They're zombified." She stopped the cart and reached into the tub of organs.

"That's disgusting! Is it slimy? I bet it's slimy."

"Actually, they're all dried out." She removed a small length of intestine. It coiled up her arm and did its best to wrap around her throat. She threw it to the floor and held it there with her foot while dipping a trowel into a bucket of brackish muck.

"What's that?" Humbert flew so close to her ear that his humming filled her head. She gently brushed him aside.

"River troll mucus." She dumped it on the squirming intestine. The blackened tube of flesh twisted and curled, but held in place.

"Why are you doing that?"

"To keep it from wriggling away."

"Why troll mucus?"

"Because it's very sticky, but it washes away easily with soap and lemon juice."

"Why do you want to stick dead things to the floor?"

"To lead the hellhound where I want it."

"Where do you want it?"

Before she could answer, Humbert darted down the hall to inspect three eyeballs glued twenty feet away. He zipped off to get a closer look at some fingers another twenty feet farther on. He didn't return, and she wasn't surprised. He was easily distracted.

Nessy paused in her task to reorient herself. She didn't know how much a hellhound could eat in one sitting. She was only leaving little bits, but it was a long way to her final goal. The Vampire King had been very little meat, mostly bone and skin. She tried to visualize just how much rotten, squirming flesh she'd left in her path.

The nurgax growled.

Nessy turned to see what startled it and came face to face with the armor of the Blue Paladin. The unmanned armor was tall and gleaming, like the ocean cast in steel. If one believed the legends, this wasn't far from the truth.

The empty helmet nodded to her.

"Hello," said Nessy.

The armor stood, his iron chest thrust forward, his right gauntlet wrapped around a tremendous battle-ax. One stroke could slice her in two, but Nessy didn't fear. Had he wanted her dead, she would have already been so. But this was the fabled suit of the Blue Paladin, a champion of some renown, one of the few enemies Margle had simply killed because he was too dangerous to live, even if transformed into a sleepy bunny. But the Paladin had been a foe only to the forces of evil, and his armor was the same. As with the Sword in the Cabbage, Margle had never been able to take its power for his own use, much to the wizard's annoyance.

Nessy was annoyed as well. Annoyed that the armor wasn't where he belonged.

"You aren't supposed to be out here."

The Blue Paladin nodded again.

"I take it this is very important business that has you out and about."

He nodded gravely this time, difficult as that might be to measure in a thing without a face. She decided that the suit had always been well-behaved before and had every right to stretch his leggings every few decades if he so desired.

"If you'll excuse me, I've got some important business of my own." She strode past the armor. The nurgax followed with the cart in tow.

The Paladin clomped behind them. She glanced over her shoulder. He was following them. He made a lot of noise, clanking and rattling. The Blue Paladin must've been a truly great champion, she determined, but he certainly hadn't defeated evil by sneaking up on it.

Twenty-seven feet later, she stopped again. So did the Paladin.

"Are you following me for any specific reason?" she asked.

The suit neither nodded nor shook its helmet. He just stood there.

"If you insist on doing so, the least you could do is make yourself useful."

The Paladin raised a gauntlet to cup the nonexistent chin of his nonexistent wearer. Then he grabbed the trowel from the cart and scooped out some mucus. With the Paladin's help, the quiet she'd enjoyed was gone, but she reached her destination, the armory, that much sooner. As she threw down the last lump of flesh, a purple hunk she guessed to be a zombified cow tongue, she thanked the Paladin for his assistance.

He waved away the gratitude as if it were no trouble at all.

Gnick the gnome appeared then. "There you are, you disobedient armor. Get back in your place now. This instant!"

The Paladin made no move to obey.

"Thank you again," said Nessy. "Don't let us keep you."

The armor bent in a bow and clomped around a corner. But as soon as he was out of sight, the clamor ceased.

"Why did you let him go?" asked Gnick.

"It wasn't as if either of us could've stopped him. And he did say he had some important business to attend to."

"And you believed him?"

"I believe everyone until they give me reason not to. I

prefer discovering someone is not worthy of my trust rather than assuming no one is."

"That's not very wise."

"No, it isn't, but it's better to think the best of everyone and be wrong than assume the worst and be right."

Gnick plucked his not-so-springy beard. "Idealism like that will only get you killed."

She shrugged. "Probably."

# FIFTEEN

While Nessy attended to her less interesting duties, Yazpib the Magnificent endeavored to free Melvin of the Mirrors from his prison. Margle's curse had stripped Yazpib of all his magical potential, rendering the jarred wizard incapable of the simplest spell, and so he had to draft two assistants: Sir Thedeus and a weasel named Dodger. Fortune was present as well, only to lounge upon the comfortable bed in the guest room. As a cat, though, he couldn't help but be curious about the process.

"What's that for?" he asked of the pieces of chalk Dodger was rolling back and forth across the floor.

"My guess would be drawing," she said. "That's what chalk is usually for."

"Yes, yes." Yazpib read through a scroll spread across the stone. "Hold that end down, Thedeus."

"Sir Thedeus," corrected the bat. He glanced at the strange

writing on the parchment but couldn't make much sense of it. "Are ye sure we should be doing this, lad? Shouldna we wait for Nessy?"

"The poor creature is overworked enough," said Yazpib. "We can at least lighten her load."

"In principle, I agree with ye. But if something should go amiss?"

"Are you questioning my skills?"

"Sounds like he's questioning them to me," said Dodger.

"And he does have a point," added Fortune, who flicked his icy-tipped tail. He didn't mind the change, but it was a perfect illustration of how unpredictable magic might be, especially in the incapable hands of an out-of-practice wizard.

Yazpib bubbled and spun his eyes. "This is hardly the same thing. That was a potion. I'll admit alchemy was never my strong suit. But a simple spell like this should be, well, simple."

Melvin, still wearing Tiama's form, pressed against his looking-glass prison. "Anything to get me out of here. I thought it was bad when I had the run of the castle's mirrors, but now . . ." He paced the room's reflection. "If I have to stay here, I'll go mad."

"It isn't as bad as all that," said Dodger. "I once spent three years in a cell not big enough to stand up in." She raised upright. "And I'm not talking about the body I'm wearing now. I was a lot taller then." She chewed on a piece of chalk. Even when she'd been a woman, she'd had a bad habit of nibbling on whatever was at hand. Becoming a weasel had only made it worse. The benefit in this case was discovering she enjoyed the taste of red chalk. It was sharp, yet unassuming. The only flaw was the aftertaste. It was, not surprisingly, very chalky.

"And if you want to talk about maddening prisons," she continued, licking her lips, "I had a very unpleasant stay in the Vork Swamp Reformatory for Maladjusted Girls. Spent six months up to my neck in parasite-infected water. Got the trench foot something fierce. Except it wasn't just my foot. And then there were those two weeks in the Basalom Stockade. No cells there. Just one giant pit, and the guards had this game called 'Bludgeon the Scumbag.' It isn't nearly as much fun as it sounds."

"Dear gods, woman, sounds as if ye spent more time in prison than free."

"Hazard of the thievery profession. Goes with the job." Dodger tasted a piece of blue chalk. Finding it lacked subtlety, she went back to red. "And some prisons are quite nice. Almost a shame to escape from."

"Try not to eat all the chalk," said Yazpib. "We'll need some for the spell."

"I still think this is a bad idea," said Sir Thedeus.

Yazpib bobbed his eyes, then his brain. "Is the great Sir Thedeus afraid?"

The bat screwed up his twisted little face. "Ach, let's get on with it, ye wanker."

Yazpib glanced around. "Where's the opal? We need the opal."

"I'll check the bag." Dodger climbed into the small velvet sack and emerged empty-pawed.

"It's in her mouth." Fortune stretched, rolling onto his back.

Dodger attempted to protest but was unable to speak clearly. Drool spattered from her jaws.

"Spit it out, lass."

The small blue gem clattered against the floor. "Can't blame a thief for trying."

"Surprised ye dinna swallow it."

"I don't swallow opals. For me, it's diamonds or nothing. My father, rest his filching soul, choked on a ruby. Instilled a bit of a phobia in me."

"Fascinating," said Sir Thedeus, although he sounded anything but enthralled.

Dodger scampered deeper in the bag. "Mind you, my father swallowed things all the time. Had a small fortune in his stomach when he died. No safer place for a swindler, I suppose, but claiming the inheritance was a trifle messy. Still, he did provide for my childhood." She stuck her head out with a smile. "To this day, when I see a gutted fish, I tear up a little."

"Are we going to reminisce all afternoon?" asked Melvin. "Or can we get me out of here?"

Yazpib instructed his assistants. Dodger traced a few runes on the floor around the mirror. It took some time since her paws weren't made for it, and Yazpib had to keep correcting her work.

"I said a slash, not a line."

"Sorry."

"And that one over there should have a gentle curve, not sharp. Look at the scroll."

"I am looking at the scroll." She scratched her head. "I don't see any difference."

"Just do it as I say."

"I think I'm with the bat," said Fortune sleepily. "This is going to go badly."

"Then why are you still here?" asked Yazpib.

"Should be interesting, at least."

Sir Thedeus set the opal under the mirror and repeated the incantations Yazpib read aloud. Within a few short minutes, the blue gem glowed and the mirror shimmered.

"How long will it take to work?" said Fortune.

Melvin, who'd been leaning against the looking glass, tumbled suddenly through it. He nearly landed on Sir Thedeus and Dodger, who barely scrambled out of the way.

"See?" said Yazpib. "That wasn't very hard. And nothing bad happened."

Fortune laid down his head and closed his eyes. "Pity."

"How are ye feeling, Melvin laddie?"

"Great. I feel great. I'm out of that damned mirror. Out of all those damned mirrors." He looked to Yazpib, and instantly transformed into a duplicate of the wizard with a soft whooshing noise.

He glanced at Sir Thedeus and whooshed into a small, brown bat. "What is going on?"

"It appears that we've succeeded in taking you out of the mirror," said Yazpib, "but not the mirror out of you."

Melvin swept the guest room with his gaze, and when his eyes passed over any of the chamber's occupants, living or dead, he became an exact copy. The metamorphosis to one only lasted until his gaze rested a few seconds on another. "Not that I'm complaining," whoosh "but is there any way," whoosh "to make this stop?" Whoosh. "It's starting to unsettle my stomach."

"Try closing your eyes," suggested Dodger.

"Good idea." Melvin shut his eyes, and the transformations stopped, freezing him in Dodger's weasel form.

"I knew ye'd blunder it, ye fool wizard."

"This isn't a blunder," said Yazpib. "It's a setback. A minor one, at that."

A distant rumble shook the tall mirror. A second, louder thud followed. Then a third stomp. The room reflected in the looking glass quaked with each boom.

"Now what?" Sir Thedeus snarled. "Is this a minor setback as well?"

"It's just a jabberwock," said Yazpib. "Must've sensed the portal. All we have to do is break the spell."

"What's a jabberwock?" asked Dodger.

"Nothing really. Just a nonsense creature. More of a nuisance than anything else."

Something in the reflection screeched, and the mirror cracked.

"Repeat after me." Yazpib pronounced the simple six-syllable incantation slowly and clearly enough that a child might echo it, if the child could've heard. But it was next to impossible to hear anything but the jabberwock's piercing shrieks.

Sir Thedeus's ears were especially sensitive to the painful warble. "What was that, lad?"

"I said . . ."

Something pounded against the door in the reflection, adding deafening booms to the overpowering screeching.

"Speak up, lad!"

Melvin opened one eye, glimpsed Sir Thedeus, and became the bat's double. He shut his eyes and covered his ears. "What's happening?"

Dodger scampered into the velvet pouch, burying her head in its folds. Fortune arched his back and raised his hackles. His icy tail rained frost on the bed.

"Oh, I knew this was a bad idea!" shouted Sir Thedeus. "Ye bloody idiot!"

Yazpib shouted some equally hostile response, but it was lost to the thunder of the reflected door being broken into splinters. A great reptile squeezed through the archway. The jabberwock was a collection of mismatched parts. Its body was a huge purple ball, its neck long and thin as a bundle of straw. Two crossed eyes and a bucktoothed maw dominated its head. It had two horns. One twisted downward. The other turned in a seventy-degree corkscrew. One foot was that of an elephant, the other a duck. One of its wings was little, yellow, and feathery. The other was giant, black, and leathery.

The beast's head turned to odd angles as it struggled to focus its one blue and one red eye. It howled. Then belched. Then honked like a goose. The jabberwock charged forward, wobbling on its ill-matched legs.

"Quickly, repeat after me—" said Yazpib.

"There's no time, lad." Sir Thedeus launched his tiny body into the mirror. It teetered over to smash upon the floor. "There."

"You idiot, that doesn't break the spell."

From one of the larger shards of glass, the jabberwock squeezed itself into the real guest room. The once-enormous beast was now only as large as a big cat.

The jabberwock inhaled, doubling in size. It belched, literally, a long, blue flame.

Dodger scampered under the bed. Sir Thedeus flew to the bedpost. Melvin opened his eyes and whooshed into Yazpib's duplicate, making flight impossible.

The dragon honked. Its cheeks inflated, and it vomited a bulk of feathers that filled the guest room floor six inches deep. The down made it sneeze first a dagger, then a book, then a bowling ball that came very close to smashing Yazpib in his jar.

Melvin whooshed into a double of the jabberwock. The original stopped cold and stumbled forward in a drunken gait.

"That a boy, lad," said Sir Thedeus. "Keep it distracted."

Melvin shut his eyes. The jabberwock sniffed him curiously.

"Well, do something before—Hey, get your nose out of there!"

The jabberwock cooed, hopping on its elephant leg.

"How do we get it back in the glass?" asked Fortune.

"We need the opal." Yazpib retreated to the bottom of his jar.

Sir Thedeus and Fortune dove beneath the sea of feathers.

"I can't find it," said Sir Thedeus.

"Find it." Melvin shuddered as the jabberwock nibbled playfully on his tail. "Quickly."

"Found it!" Fortune raised his head, clutching Dodger by the scruff of her neck.

The weasel, her cheeks bulging, smiled sheepishly.

Sir Thedeus sighed. "Give it over, lass." She spat it into his open wings.

"Now hold the opal up, spin around six times, and repeat after me," said Yazpib. "Tsaeb luof emac eeht ecnehw tpure."

"Is this supposed to really work?" said Sir Thedeus. "Or are ye just trying to make me look a fool?"

"It'll work." Yazpib smiled. "Looking like a fool is just a fringe benefit."

Reluctantly, Sir Thedeus did as instructed. The jabberwock shrieked. It flapped its wings. It whipped its tail. It spat out a live rabbit and two doorknobs as it expanded to fill half the guest room. Everyone but Yazpib retreated under the bed. The great reptile burped once more, puked up a leafy fern, and popped almost silently, splattering skin and innards. Its internal physiology was apparently nothing more than orange pudding.

Sir Thedeus poked out his head. "I thought ye said it'd return to the mirror."

"You must've made a mistake in your pronunciation." Yazpib floated low, away from the chunks of skin atop his fluid. "In any case, the portal is sealed. Melvin is free. And we didn't have to bother Nessy one bit."

The room was filled with feathers and slime. The mirror was shattered. The nightstand had been knocked over. One of the bed's legs had been cracked, and it wobbled. There were guts all over everything and a stench of peaches and burning cheese.

"We don't have to tell her about this?" asked Yazpib. "Do we?"

Fortune found the one spot on the bed that wasn't covered with jabberwock viscera. "I'll think she'll notice."

Sir Thedeus chuckled. "Aye. She's an observant lassie. Not much slips past her."

Dodger wiped a tear from her eye.

"Are ye hurt, lass?"

"It's nothing." She sniffed at the putrid innards and smiled sadly. "I just miss my father."

# SIXTEEN

Not long after sunset, the hellhound stirred. It twisted a little in the very hungry carpet's coils, but mostly, it just waited. A less observant individual might think it tamed or too exhausted to struggle, but Nessy saw the predatory hunger in its exposed eye. It glared with quiet rage, a fury tempered with patience. As if it knew the carpet would soon let it go once more to stalk the castle's dead. Its stare burned into Nessy, and she wondered how intelligent it might be. Was it merely an animal driven by instinct, or did it possess some ability to plot, to remember and seek vengeance against those who had deprived it of a meal? Against a lowly kobold who had outwitted it? According to Stoker, it was merely an animal of the underworld, no more rational than a bear of the forest or a lion of the plains. But there was something in the eye, some quality of remembrance, like a dog that disliked someone, even if it couldn't quite remember why.

She trusted this vague disfavor wouldn't affect the hound's appetites. It must've been hungry, having gone unfed last night. Its stare would turn from her to eye the zombified bait not far away, and it would rouse. It would be safer not to be here when it was freed, but she figured if she were wrong, if the hound craved vengeance over dinner, then she would have to be the bait. Either way, the beast would go where she wanted.

The nurgax at Nessy's side alternately purred to her and growled at the hellhound.

Nessy, never one to waste an idle minute, thought of her other concerns while she waited. Chief among them was Tiama the Scarred. The dark wizardess had still not shown herself. Nessy didn't know how Tiama could wander the halls unobserved for so long. And she couldn't see the sense of it.

It all went back to Margle's death. Everything else did. Tiama's arrival was no coincidence. Nessy considered the possibilities.

The first, most logical, likelihood was that Tiama had come to claim the castle. It was very likely she knew Margle was dead. Wizards had ways of knowing things like that. When one of her previous masters had met his ugly death, it wasn't ten minutes before the next employer knocked on the door, a small army of golems in tow to cart away all his deceased rival's valuables. If Tiama knew, then why wasn't she taking everything that was hers by right of dark wizard custom? To let it all lie unclaimed made no sense. Nessy dismissed this possibility. Tiama wasn't here to pilfer the castle.

Nessy couldn't truly claim to understand wizards or their ways. But Tiama's activities seemed more illogical than usual. Maybe she was looking for something very specific. Perhaps she'd run afoul of Margle, and he'd taken something of hers or placed some sort of spell upon her that she now saw the opportunity to break. Whether she knew Margle was dead or not, she must've surely sensed something was not right. Had he been alive and well, he certainly would never have allowed her to wander his home at her discretion.

In fact, he'd never allowed anyone to do so. Margle hadn't hoarded and cursed for anyone but himself. He had never been especially interested in impressing anyone. It was one of the few qualities, perhaps the only quality, that Nessy had admired about him. Her mind kept coming back to this point. Tiama claimed an invitation had been extended, but such an invitation was implausible. But if it were a lie, it seemed an unnecessary one. Unless she didn't want Nessy to be suspicious.

But a dark wizardess had nothing to fear from a lowly kobold. No master Nessy had ever worked for had shown her anything but contempt. The idea that Tiama might fear Nessy was so absurd as to bring a smile to her face.

And yet.

And yet it was the only conclusion she could reach. Tiama the Scarred had entered the castle only with Nessy's approval, and now Tiama walked its halls—not as a proud, defiant wizardess, but as a timid thief prowling cautiously.

Before Nessy could explore this realization further, the very hungry carpet fell away from the hellhound. The great, black beast raised its head and howled as smoke and sulfur erupted from its scaly skin. It raked its claws across the rug, tearing long ugly gashes. The damage wasn't very serious for the very hungry carpet. It'd stitch itself together after Nessy fed it a few cloth scraps. The hound sniffed the carpet a few moments before snorting with satisfaction. It scratched behind its ear, accompanied by musical bells.

It turned its eyes on Nessy and snarled. She prepared to run, but the hound merely growled at her, baring its long, yellow fangs, and stalked toward the closest offering of zombified dinner. It gobbled down the meal, lapped at the troll mucus with its serpentine blue tongue before dashing to the second bait. This was devoured just as quickly, and it sprinted enthusiastically to the next.

Nessy followed along at a reasonable distance. A few times, the hound glanced back at her and snarled, but its dislike for her was dwarfed by its appetite. It gulped down treat after treat, following the route she'd laid out. It seemed to especially enjoy the troll drool. The beast's frantic dash eventually turned to a lazy stroll, and she worried it might get full too soon. She'd have to do something to keep it from wandering away. The best she could devise was to anger it with thrown stones and get it to chase her, but the plan wasn't necessary. Gorged on the undead, the hound loped into its final destination: the armory.

Its steps were heavy. Its raging eyes content. Even the black smoke rolled down lazily to its ankles, and the bells' melody muted as if too ponderous to ring. The creature belched. Fireballs blasted from its nostrils.

Nessy felt bad about what must come next. The hound wasn't evil, despite its origins. Certainly, it wasn't as horrifying as many other beasts she dealt with, but she couldn't tend it. It was too unpredictable, too wild.

Sir Thedeus stood atop the giant cabbage. "There ye are, ye great beastie! The time has come to send ye back to hell, and I'm the hero to do it!"

As if sensing the threat, the hound crouched low and roared at the tiny bat.

"Oh, this should be fun!" exclaimed the Sword in the Cabbage. "I haven't slain a hellhound in ages. Wonderfully satisfying pyre when they perish."

"Thanks for the warning, lad."

Sir Thedeus landed upon the hilt. There followed the divine glow and flash of light, and he stood transformed into the man he had been. He drew the sword and raised its radiant blade over his head. Nessy measured him as fine a hero as any she'd ever seen. His stark nudity lowered his bearing a bit but spoke volumes of his courage.

Sir Thedeus leapt from atop the giant cabbage, fifteen feet to the floor, landing with easy grace. Unafraid, he strode purposely toward the hound.

"Can ye know fear, beastie? If ye can, then know that yer unholy existence will no longer be tolerated. For all the innocent dead (and even the not-so-innocent dead) within this castle, I shall strike ye down, back into the accursed hell ye've too long escaped." He spun the sword fancifully before him. "The Vampire King was a great, ridiculous prat, but he shall be avenged this night. So I swear! For I am Sir Thedeus! I am yer destroyer!"

"Can we get on with this?" asked the sword. "Need I remind you, we're on a time limit?"

Warily, the opponents circled each other, waiting for their moment.

"He's going to get himself killed for sure," said Gnick the gnome, standing at Nessy's side.

She hadn't noticed him coming up beside her. She was too intent on the battle. While Sir Thedeus was a great hero, as confirmed by the Sword in the Cabbage, she couldn't help but worry about him. Despite his human form, she still thought of him as that small, brown bat. And, though she tried not to play favorites among her charges, she was rather fond of him.

"Tick tock tick tock," reminded the sword.

But Sir Thedeus wouldn't be rushed. When the opportunity came, he would know it.

It was the hound that finally grew impatient. It sprang with a throaty growl and crash of cymbals, claws outstretched, exhaling scarlet flame. Nessy involuntarily closed her eyes. A terrible cry burst in her ears. Sir Thedeus's death rattle, she thought. But it was more beastly, inhuman. A shriek of victory from the hellhound, she assumed.

"I don't believe it," said Gnick.

Nessy opened her eyes. The sword was wet with green-and-white blood. A glancing wound in the hound's flank boiled. Sir Thedeus laughed heartily.

"Is that all ye have, beastie?"

He took a step forward, and the hound, terrible a monster as it was, took a step backward. The hound snapped, this time with far more caution. This saved it from a quick beheading, but the blade drew blood again. A great slice steamed across its neck.

Sir Thedeus grinned, and Nessy saw she had no need to worry. Not that she trusted his victory. It would only take a single mistake for the beast to kill him. But even if he lost, he would perish in glorious battle, and she couldn't deny him that.

He spoke quietly, calmly. "Very well, brute. Let's finish this now." He stood tall and proud and bellowed loudly enough to shake the castle. "Have at ye!"

The hellhound did the last thing Nessy would've expected. It turned and ran. Sir Thedeus chased after it, laughing the whole time. They dashed into an adjoining chamber of the armory, where Nessy lost sight of them.

"I don't believe it," said Gnick. "He actually is a hero."

In the next chamber, the din of a great conflict raged. The hound roared. Sir Thedeus shouted with boisterous glee. Bells clattered, banged. Metal crashed against stone. A helmet rolled into the archway.

"Not my armory." Gnick ran into the chamber. "I just polished that room!"

Nessy was about to follow him when a tingle in her ears drew her attention. She didn't know how she knew that Tiama the Scarred stood behind her, but she knew. She could sense the wizardess's awful presence.

"Hello, madam." She turned from the clamor and racket to face Tiama.

The wizardess seemed even less lifelike than before. Her pale skin was as cold and inflexible as steel, and she stood awkwardly straight, her hands poised like knotted claws at her sides.

"Hello, Nessy." Her burning stare peered past Nessy. "Having some difficulties?" She gazed into Nessy's eyes, and the kobold looked at the floor. Not out of fear, but because it was expected.

"It's nothing, madam."

The hellhound and Sir Thedeus were visible in the archway for a moment. The monster snarled and yowled, blood and fire pouring from its wounds. Steaming ichor covered Sir Thedeus. It must've burned his bare skin, but he made no show of pain.

"Hahaha! Not so fast, beastie! I said, have at ye!"

The hound made a clumsy swipe that he batted aside. They maneuvered behind a wall. Gnick came dashing after them on his short gnome legs.

"Not the spears! Not the spears!"

There followed a tremendous crash and clatter.

"Is that a hellhound?" asked Tiama.

"Yes, madam."

"Lovely specimen."

"My master owns only the best of everything."

Tiama chewed her lower lip, which was no easy feat given she had no lips at all. Her flat tone adopted that vaguely insulting cadence. "Yes. Your master."

The hound roared as if its throat were full of blood. Its lacerated body passed into view briefly. It was nearly finished. The flame and smoke that had concealed it were little more than a few gray puffs. It now dragged itself across the floor. Nessy pitied the thing. It had only been following its nature.

With a fresh burst of vigor, it bounded away with Sir Thedeus behind.

"Come on now, beastie. What part of 'Have at ye' don't ye understand? Let's be done with it."

"Watch out for the shields!" shouted Gnick just before the unmistakable melody of dozens of shields being knocked aside filled the armory. "Oh damn."

Tiama asked, "Does your master always trust you with such important matters?"

Nessy hesitated. Tiama knew something was wrong. She had to. But she refused to say anything outright. Instead, she implied and hinted. Wizards could be devious and manipulative, but why bother? Why didn't Tiama just reach out with her fingers of death and kill Nessy?

"This is a trifle, madam," said Nessy. "The master has far more important affairs than pest control."

"Yes. I'm sure his affairs are . . ." Her words trailed off, and she made some imprecise gesture as if to gather them up. "Very pressing indeed."

Tiama smiled. Then she did something truly perplexing. She laughed. It wasn't much of a laugh, little more than a brutal wheeze, a hint of amusement. But it fit perfectly with her insinuation of a smile, more the idea of the possibility of the indication of a smile.

"Take me to your master, Nessy. I would speak with him." She sneered. For once, there was no mistaking the expression, no interpretation required. Unpleasant as she was, it didn't suit her. Her face wasn't made for scowling. It wasn't made for anything, just a frame around her burning eyes.

Nessy realized then that she disliked Tiama and Nessy made it a practice to try to like everyone, to find something worthwhile in their character. But there were no such value to Tiama. The wizardess was nothing, an utter lack of value, either good or evil. Thinking about it, Nessy recognized that she didn't just dislike Tiama.

She really disliked Tiama. Very much so.

She didn't care for that feeling. She didn't care for it at all. But she managed to push forth a servile smile.

"Yes, madam. The master is eager as well."

The moment Sir Thedeus had delivered the final blow,

his curse overtook him. But being a bat kept him low to the ground, which turned out to be an advantage. The hellhound shrieked a tormented howl, bursting into a tower of white, white flame. Choking ash and suffocating smoke quickly filled the chambers, spreading to the rest of the armory.

Coughing, Gnick wiped the grime from his eyes. "Now I'll never clean it up."

"Had to be done, lad." Sir Thedeus did his best to breathe through his nose, but he could taste the ash collecting in his mouth.

The underworld creature's flesh had been consumed. Only its blackened bones remained. The Sword in the Hell-Hound said, "Oh my, that was marvelous fun, wasn't it?"

"Aye."

"Never, ever," muttered Gnick.

Dozens of bells tolled. The Vampire King stepped through the thick dust. He was now transparent. "What did you do to me?"

"We freed you from being dragged to the underworld," said the sword.

"But I'm a ghost."

"Yer body was eaten," said Sir Thedeus. "Still, yer not in hell. So I would think some gratitude would be in order."

"Gratitude? I was Lord of the Undead. Now I'm just a ghost." The King snarled. "It's a demotion."

"Never, ever, never," said Gnick.

"Nessy, lass. We've done it!" Sir Thedeus considered

this victory hers as much as his. A good soldier worked best with a good general, and she had come up with the plan. "Nessy, where are ye?"

"Never, ever, ever, ever."

"Oh shut your gob. And for heaven's sakes, man, get some rest. You look as if you could use it."

Gnick nearly replied that as a silver gnome, it was his sacred responsibility to never rest until his task was done. But the ash in his throat buried the reply in coughs and sputters. He picked up a dagger coated with soot and wiped it with his sleeve. As his shirt was covered with dust, this accomplished nothing. Gnick, realizing the entire armory was like this, did something unthinkable.

He headed for his bed of straw to take a nap.

Sir Thedeus crawled along as fast as his tiny body would allow. There was no sign of Nessy, and while she was a busy girl, rarely did she leave without notice. This troubled him greatly, though he trusted she could take care of herself.

He muttered an ancient protective prayer he'd thought he'd long ago forgotten. But by then the ash had settled to the floor and caught on his tongue so that he couldn't complete it. An ill omen. He didn't believe in omens, but just to be safe, he repeated the prayer. And though the soot and dust turned to mud in his mouth, he stifled his stammers until it was finished.

# SEVENTEEN

**N**essy possessed a sixth sense when it came to problems. There was nothing supernatural about it, merely equal parts logic and preparedness. These two traits allowed her to plan for possibilities that even she was surprised to discover she'd readied for. It was her gift: a mind that was always deciphering and formulating, even when she wasn't consciously aware of it. Without it, the castle would've fallen apart long ago.

She hadn't expected Tiama to show herself, but when the wizardess did, Nessy wasn't surprised either. And everything was in order for the protean sludge's charade. It waited (with Echo) in Margle's study. Nessy led Tiama through the castle to that very destination. Neither said a word. Tiama was such an emptiness of presence, she made no sound at all. She glided silently across the brick, and if she breathed, she did so without rustling the folds of her robe. The drafts flowing through the halls dared not caress her either. She was like a ghost. Worse, for all the ghosts Nessy knew were anxious to prove their existence with a rattled chain or a moan or even just a slight drop in temperature. There was none of that with Tiama.

Only the click of Nessy's claws and the thumping footfalls of the nurgax were heard. But whenever Nessy glanced back, Tiama was there. She stared straight ahead, never looking at Nessy, as if she already knew where to go, as if merely allowing Nessy to play the guide.

But why was the wizardess playing? Over and over, Nessy thought of the question. Over and over, she couldn't answer it. Her mind was sharp, but it wasn't very good at deception. Lying was something one did when one didn't have any other choice. Unless one was stupid, and Tiama wasn't stupid.

Nessy paused before the study door. "This way, madam. The master is waiting."

"Waiting." Tiama said the word with a grin. Possibly.

Nessy led the wizardess inside and shut the door behind them with a soft click. The study was, for some unfathomable reason, one of the darkest chambers in the castle. Its true size was impossible to measure because the dim candlelight didn't reveal any walls. Just a desk, a chair, three very tall shelves, and nothing else. Nessy knew it was large. She'd seen Margle more than once walk into its darkness, muttering to himself. His voice would grow distant for a long time, only to rise again. He usually returned with scrolls or magic scepters or other wizardly things. But once, he'd come back with his robe in tatters and black blood coating his hands. Whatever was in the dark, Nessy thought it best left alone.

The protean sludge sat behind the desk. The chair was turned at an awkward angle, allowing barely a glimpse of Margle's silhouette. At that moment, in that dimness, she could very easily imagine it was her old master, and if she was fooled, then perhaps Tiama might be as well.

In the darkness, Tiama's eyes shone bright red. They cast splinters of light that sliced through the study. Though she probably just imagined it, Nessy could smell the shadows burning.

She prostrated herself on the floor. "Master, your guest has arrived."

"I know that, beast. Do you think I'm blind?" Only Margle's lips moved. The words were stilted and harsh, as if the sludge disliked speaking them. It was a quality not far from the original's true cadence.

"No, master. Sorry, master." Nessy response was a reflex. There was no need to act.

"Dog, how dare you insult me in front of a guest. I should have you ground into paste and fed to the dung drakes, only that would be too kind a fate for so pathetic a thing as you."

"My apologies, master."

"Apologies? Does the cockroach apologize to the Titan that crushes it underfoot? Does the peasant apologize to the tidal wave that razes his village?"

"No, master. Yes, master."

Margle chuckled. It was surprisingly lifelike. "Don't waste my time with such idiocy. I am not without mercy, mongrel, but you'll find that I have none for you."

Tiama spoke up. "Shall I kill this thing for you?"

"Thank you, but no. I wouldn't want to trouble you."

"It's no trouble."

"How very thoughtful, but the creature is too stupid to know better."

"Ignorance is no excuse. Such sins shouldn't go unpunished."

Margle made a very rude noise that might've been unintentional. "I quite agree, but whereas disrespect should be met with swift death, I believe stupidity warrants stronger penalty. It shall learn the error of its ways, and it shall never forget them."

"How shall we best discipline the beast?"

"Oh no. I couldn't bother you with such trivialities any more than I could ask you to scrub my floors. What sort of host would I be?"

"What sort indeed?" Whatever Tiama meant by the question remained unclear, for her voice was as smooth and cold as ice. "On the contrary, I do enjoy a good torture. And I've never tormented a kobold before. I've heard they're quite . . ." Her frozen voice cracked to reveal chillier depths. ". . . resilient."

Echo, to her credit, didn't stammer or stutter, though she must surely have been running out of believable excuses as to why Margle would care if Tiama amused herself with Nessy's pain.

"I'm afraid you've heard incorrectly. They perish before any true fun can begin."

"Perhaps you simply aren't subtle enough. No slight intended, but I've found that nothing is so perishable that it can't suffer a great deal. One only needs to be creative."

This time, Margle did hesitate, and Nessy wondered if Echo had exhausted her supply of reasons. Nessy wondered also just how far she was willing to take this deception. Torture was asking a bit much.

Margle's voice took on a hard edge. The sludge had grown into an adequate actor under Echo's supervision, and it was, in some ways, more passably human than Margle had ever been.

"The dog is mine to slay or flay as I see fit."

It was a perfect end to the topic, and Tiama shrugged as if she couldn't care less. But at the same time, she was surely entertaining thoughts of taking away Margle's plaything. Wizards were like petulant children when it came to sharing their toys.

Nessy bowed deeply. "With your permission, master, I beg your leave. There are matters I must—"

"Silence, beast. You'll not escape my judgment so easily." Margle pointed to a spot by a bookshelf. "Wait until I'm ready to deal with you."

She did as she was told, petting the nurgax while she waited. Tiama spoke freely, as Nessy had expected. When not being insulted or threatened, a lowly servant was considered beneath notice by these great and powerful wizards.

Margle rose, walked to the shelf, and pulled out a book. Simple an act though it was, it was a remarkable feat to have taught the sludge. Nessy realized how much grace was found in even a clumsy creature, and the sludge lacked that grace. There wasn't anything obviously faulty with its movements. They were simply too awkward, yet too precise at the same time. It was like watching a machine.

To her, it was obvious this wasn't Margle, but she speculated on just how soon Tiama might spot the differences. The wizardess didn't seem stupid, but even the mightiest wizardess could be surprisingly obtuse about such talents as reading body language. That sort of research rarely entered their field of study. And, of course, much of it depended on just how well Tiama knew Margle. He'd never mentioned her, but that didn't mean much. Margle had never talked to Nessy. Merely ordered and threatened.

"I trust you have enjoyed your tour," said Margle.

Tiama yawned. Her mouth formed a perfect circle. "There have been some charming . . . diversions."

Margle held the book before him as if he didn't know what to do with it. "My apologies for not being there to escort you personally. I'm afraid some unexpected business came up. You know how it is."

"Indeed I do, but Nessy has been a most courteous guide. I dare say, she might know your castle better than you."

"Perhaps." Margle smiled without humor. He turned very deliberately, paced to the chair, and sat down again. "I do hate to cut your visit short, but that business has yet to be resolved. I'm far too occupied to be a proper host. Perhaps we could schedule a continuation for another day."

"I think not. I've seen everything worth seeing." She stepped forward and put her hands on the desk. "There's little here of any worth to me. Your monsters, your fallen heroes, your little machines, they're nothing."

"Now see here . . ." But Margle's words lacked the fury to back them up.

"Oh quiet down, you pathetic thing. Did you truly think I could be duped by this novelty? Nessy, I'm deeply disappointed in you."

For a moment, Nessy considered denying that she'd tried anything. But Tiama hadn't been fooled, and Nessy didn't see any reason to continue the charade.

Echo wasn't as quick to abandon the plan.

"I would thank you to address me and not—"

Tiama put her hand on Margle's shoulder. The sludge convulsed. It contorted into a double of Tiama, shrieked an earsplitting moan, and twisted away from the wizardess's fatal touch. A sizable portion was left in Tiama's hand. It crumbled to ash, and she wiped it on her robe. The living portion of sludge fell into a yellow puddle, bubbling and steaming.

"This foolishness has gone on long enough," said Tiama. "Do you think me an imbecile?"

Nessy lowered her ears. "No, madam."

She'd known something like this would happen. But for a minute, she'd been hopeful. Margle at least took care of the castle and its inhabitants, if only because his twisted ego prized them. But Tiama had no need of them. Tragic fates could only await them.

The red in Tiama's eyes softened. "When I came to this place, I expected to find nothing of value, and I was not disappointed for the most part. This entire castle should be swallowed by the earth for all its worthlessness. But there is one thing which did impress me. Only one. But it was more than I counted upon." She clasped her hands together, lacing the fingers with methodical precision. "Do you know what that thing is, Nessy?"

"No, madam." Nessy averted her eyes.

"Look at me."

The kobold raised her head slowly, but instead of rage and disgust in Tiama's face, she saw something else. The wizardess smiled. The flames in her eyes were a gentle yellow.

"It's you, Nessy. The only thing worth having in this castle is you." She reached out as if to stroke Nessy's muzzle but pulled back. Frowning, she glanced at her fingertips. "Margle was a fool to not see what an asset you are."

"Yes, madam." Shock overtook Nessy. Never in all her career had any of her employers paid her an honest compliment. It was very unwizardly.

"I now lay claim to you as is my right," said Tiama. "I

desire nothing else from this hovel. Of course, I will still see it destroyed rather than taken by someone else."

"Yes, madam."

Echo whispered in Nessy's ear. "Oh no."

The words were so slight, Nessy barely heard them, but Tiama chuckled.

"Oh, yes, my dear. Oh yes."

"You have to do something," said Echo even softer.

"What can she do?" asked Tiama. "What can any of you do?"

"I have to warn the others," said Echo. Then she was gone. Or so Nessy assumed.

"Warn them indeed." Tiama chuckled once more, although her face remained blank. She ran her fingers across the books on the shelves. "Worthless. All of it. But there is one other thing that intrigues me." Her voice gained some life. "The Door."

"Which door, madam?"

"Don't be coy. It doesn't suit you. Margle may have believed you simple, but I know better."

"Yes, madam."

"What's behind that Door?"

"I don't know, madam."

"And were you never curious?" asked Tiama. "No, I don't suppose you would be. You're not the curious sort. All this castle's wonders around you, and you'd rather sweep the halls. But we each have our place, and that is yours. Mine is to seek knowledge, to discover those forbidden secrets that you could live without knowing. I must know, Nessy. I must. Whatever is on the other side calls to me. And a door never opened is a senseless thing."

Everything took a turn for the worse. It was one thing to destroy the castle, but to open the Door was to invite terrible calamity. Perhaps, Nessy mused, even destroy the world. She didn't know that for certain, but that Margle had feared the Door and Tiama, a living death, felt a connection spoke of its immeasurable dangers.

"Come along, Nessy. I haven't all night."

"Yes, madam."

Tiama cast a hard glare. Again, Nessy struggled with a touch of defiance, but she was just a kobold. She bowed her head.

"Yes, my mistress."

Nessy, who excelled at cleaning, cooking, and tending monsters but was woefully inexperienced in defeating dark wizardesses, could think of nothing else to be done. And all the fallen heroes and villains within the castle's walls were no match for Tiama either. There was no choice available to her. No choice. And no hope. Not for her. Not for the castle. And quite possibly, not for the world.

# EIGHTEEN

News of Tiama's claim on the castle spread quickly and, as in any community confronted by such a threat, gatherings sprang up to discuss what should be done. There were dozens of impromptu meetings where spirited fears were shared and plans of action debated. The debates were little more than shouting matches. The meetings produced little more than quiet dread and not-so-quiet terror. Foreboding filled the castle from the top of its tallest tower to the depths of its blackest catacombs—even in the shadowy corner of Nessy's room.

Perched on her cot, Sir Thedeus struggled to maintain order over the chaos of dozens of roaring voices.

"We're doomed!" shouted a cloud.

"Doomed!" agreed a spider on the wall.

"Oh this is terrible!" howled a rat. "I told you this would happen!"

"Quiet down, people!" shouted Sir Thedeus.

A doll with blue yarn hair gasped and fainted.

"Is she okay?" asked the toad prince.

"Who cares? We're all going to be slugs anyway," said the rat.

Nonetheless, the toad hopped to her side. "Are you well?"

The doll wiped her button eyes. "It's just too much to bear. I wasn't meant to live such a life as this."

"I can see you're clearly a lady of fine breeding," agreed the toad. And then he belched loudly enough to startle the gathering. It fell quiet.

The toad prince frowned. "Excuse me. My stomach hasn't been well of late."

"See how well your stomach fares when you've become a slug!" screamed the rat.

Again, there arose the clamor of voices.

"I heard the wizardess plans on feeding us all to her zombie army," said the cloud.

"I didn't know she had a zombie army," said a shadow flickering on the wall.

"They always have a zombie army."

"What a bunch of nonsense," said the rat. "She's not going to feed us to zombies. She's going to transmute us to slugs. Mark my words."

"I'd heard she was going to feed us to a dragon," said the shadow.

"Someone told me it was a sea monster," said the mouse.

"The last rumor I'd caught spoke of a Titan she keeps in her basement and that she was going to put us all in a huge pot and boil us up for his soup."

"I'd heard a giant slug," said the rat.

"Rather obsessed with that slug business, old boy," said the spider.

The rat glared.

While everyone else speculated on what their horrible fate might be (which mostly entailed debating what kind of monster they would be devoured by and how the meal would be prepared), Sir Thedeus sat on the bed, having abandoned his quest for order.

"It's no use, Echo. Not a one of these wankers will be any help."

Echo didn't reply right away, and for a moment, he thought she'd left.

"There must be something we can do," she finally said. "What about that magic sword? It killed a hellhound, didn't it?"

"Aye, but the hound was a mere beast. I dunna see meself killing Tiama in the few minutes the sword affords me. And we still have to wait a whole day for it to recharge itself before I could even try."

"When it comes to slaying wizards without the use of magic swords, the element of surprise is essential," said the monster under the bed. "Most wizards are still mortal, after all. Stick a knife in their back, and they'll perish just the same as anyone."

"I dunna think this witch can be surprised," said Sir Thedeus. "And I'm not at all certain she is mortal. Even if she were, how are we supposed to kill a thing we canna touch?"

"You could throw something at her. Like a big, pointy rock."

"I dunna see that working."

The monster shrugged, jostling the cot. "It's worth a try, isn't it? Of course, even if it did kill her, she'd probably rise from the grave. Wizards have an annoying habit of doing that. But it could gain us time to think of something better."

"None of us could throw a heavy rock that far," observed Echo.

Sir Thedeus measured his thin arms and scowled. But he at least had arms, which was more than poor Echo had.

"You could prop it over a door," proposed the monster. "Then she opens it, and with some luck, it crushes in her skull. Should keep her down for a day or two at the very least."

"Prop it over a door?" Sir Thedeus scrunched his nose. "Ye canna kill a powerful witch with a practical joke. Why dunna we wait until she falls asleep and put her hand in some warm water while we're at it. Or shortsheet her bed."

The monster under the bed sank lower into the darkness. "I'm just brainstorming here. I don't see you coming up with anything better."

Sir Thedeus sighed. Loath as he was to admit it, the plan was the best he'd heard so far.

"I don't think Nessy's ever going to read to me again," whined the monster.

"If only we could get her away from Tiama," said Echo. "Nessy's always the one that comes up with the plans. She'd know what to do."

"Aye, she's a bright lass, but we canna rely on her forever." He glared at the bickering assembly. "We're supposed to be heroes, and not one can come up with a decent strategy. Bloody useless, the lot of us."

"You haven't really given the rock idea a fair chance," said the monster.

"I'm not a hero anyway," Echo added. "I'm a poet."

Sir Thedeus paced from one end of the cot to the other. "Well, I suppose you canna help but be useless then, lassie."

Echo snapped, "If I had a body, any body of any sort, I could be very helpful."

"Aye, ye could dash out a sonnet or two that would be sure to leave the witch trembling in fear. I've yet to see a witch that could stand against a rhyming couplet and a labored metaphor."

"Just because you're frustrated, that doesn't give you the right to be insulting," said the monster.

Sir Thedeus snarled but checked his anger. He wasn't mad at Echo. Her curse was more limiting than most. He was, underneath it all, quite disgusted with himself. As a man, he'd faced every challenge with martial prowess, strength, and courage. As a bat, all he had left was the courage. He didn't know how to solve a problem that he couldn't just stab until it died.

"Echo, I apologize if I've offended ye."

"Don't worry about it. This is hard on all of us. But my metaphors aren't labored. Except for maybe one poem where I compared love to a kangaroo. I was going through my marsupial period. Dreadful batch of work then."

Sir Thedeus spread his wings and prepared to take flight.

"Where are you going?" asked Echo.

"To find a big, pointy rock. Coming along, lass?" He flew away.

"Wait for me." She floated after him invisibly.

"Good luck," said the monster under the bed.

The rest of the assembly continued their spirited discussion, and the monster was tempted to get up and find someplace quieter. But he was so very comfortable under Nessy's bed, having gotten settled in, and he didn't want her to have any trouble finding him when she came back, as he hoped she would. He closed his three gray eyes and sank deep in the darkness until their squabbling was little more than a distant chatter. He felt around for his books, caressing their covers. There were so many still unread. He clutched a thick one he'd just found that he was certain would be wonderfully entertaining, even though he hadn't seen the cover yet.

Meanwhile, outside the cot in the glow of torchlight, the debate raged. Only the toad prince and the rag doll were not involved, having slunk away from the main body to share a conversation.

"Are you feeling better?" he asked.

"Yes, thank you." She coyly averted her gaze, and it was very difficult to be coy with button eyes. "And how are you, sir? Does your stomach still trouble you?"

The toad frowned. "It's improper to discuss such things, m'lady."

"Nonsense. It's plain you are a born gentleman, and your discomfort is my discomfort."

"Then I am undoubtedly the most fortunate toad prince in this or any other accursed castle."

The doll brightened. Her stitched mouth stretched in a smile as wide as was proper around a fresh acquaintance. "You're a prince?"

The toad puffed out his chest proudly. "Firstborn son and heir to the throne of Neria by the Sea. And you, m'lady?"

She curtsied. "Princess of Ario of the Shire."

"Princess of Ario?" He hopped twice for joy then regained himself. "This is wonderful news. I was sent to rescue you, my princess." He held up his flippers. "Unfortunately, things didn't go as planned. Still, I've never given up hope. Love always finds a way. But why aren't you in the hall of paintings with the other royalty?"

"Margle said there wasn't enough room for another portrait. So he made me a rag doll, thinking it ironic in some fashion, I suppose." She fussed with her yarn hair and brushed the lint from her green dress. "I must look a mess. Oh dear, oh dear."

He hopped forward and took her hand. "On the contrary, your inner beauty shines through any shell that might strive to contain it."

She giggled.

"It is I who should be embarrassed." He croaked.

"No, good sir, you are certainly the handsomest figure of a toad any rag doll of a princess has ever had the privilege of being rescued by."

He stared deep into her button eyes. "Speaking of which, I've always heard that a kiss of true love can break a curse."

"As have I."

It occurred to neither that they'd just met, and that true love was perhaps expecting too much. For this prince and this princess were raised in a very traditional fashion, and knew the royal etiquette of love at first sight which taught quite plainly who they were supposed to love and how strongly.

"But is it proper for us to kiss so soon?" asked the doll.

"If it is improper, then so be it. I've searched too long not to claim the reward due me. With your permission, of course."

"Granted, my prince."

He puckered his wide mouth and leaned closer, but before their lips could meet, his stomach groaned, and he belched long and loudly and fragrantly.

"Oh, dear." He put a flipper over his mouth.

"It's fine. I don't have a nose."

He smiled. "Truly, you are a forgiving soul." He tightened and burped again, expelling a bit of fire this time.

"Are you certain you're feeling well, my prince?"

"It's nothing," he groaned bravely. "Just some indigestion. I'll be fine. I'll be—"

His chin puffed out. His body contorted. And he noisily vomited up a bit of bile and a small firefly. The sound was so loud and painfully disgusting as to bring all other discussion to an end.

The firefly shook the bile from her wings. Her tail flared a bright crimson. She glanced about the room.

"Hello, what do we have here?" Her eyes glinted, full of demonic mischief. "I claim this castle and all the damned souls within it."

The rat chuckled harshly. "You're too late. Someone else has already claimed it."

"She's going to feed us to a zombie legion," said the shadow.

"Mob," corrected the parrot.

The demon rose in the air. Her wings beat louder than a stampede of antelope. "We'll just see about that."

The toad prince convulsed as he vomited once again. Only this time, he didn't stop with one firefly. This time, he spewed forth a great swarm of them. Hundreds upon hundreds poured from his mouth. They filled the chamber with fire and cold, cruel laughter. Every other creature, screaming, dashed off in all directions, and the demon chased after them, leaving the chamber mostly deserted. Only the toad, the rag doll, and the monster under the bed remained.

"I hate demons," said the monster.

"You stayed," said the toad prince. He smiled, too weakened to do anything else.

"I shall always remain by your side, my brave prince."

"About that kiss, my princess"—he belched painfully—"perhaps it would be best if we put it off a while."

Nose or no nose, the doll heartily agreed.

Decapitated Dan howled with laughter. He did this quite regularly, for while he was very mad he was also a jolly fellow. Still, it was the former quality that kept away visitors, and Dan had to find his own amusement. This wasn't always easy for a skull, but he'd always lived mostly in his own head. He laughed for reasons all his own at little jokes only he heard, which even he couldn't always claim to understand. This joke, however, he understood perfectly well.

"It's time, isn't it? Oh ho, wonderful, wonderful."

Mister Bones had grown accustomed to Dan's rants, his strange little monologues. But these conversations weren't always as one-sided as it appeared. For madness and magic were strange bedfellows, and not every voice Decapitated Dan heard was a figment of his insanity.

The castle talked constantly. Only Dan was perceptive and deranged enough to decipher its booms and groans, its creaks and moans. Even then, the castle didn't always make sense, mostly because it was a very large thing with a very large soul and a very complicated mind. Dan caught only portions rumbling through the kitchen on their way to complete thoughts. It was like a thing in the shadows that couldn't be seen except for a small bit of color here and there that strayed into the light, trying to put together an ocean-sized puzzle with only a handful of pieces. But on occasion, the castle found focus for its colossal, rumbling will, and when it spoke—its many voices and hungers as one united desire—Dan understood.

He howled again. Alive, he'd often howled until his throat was raw, tears streaming from his eyes. He didn't have a throat or eyes anymore, so he had to watch himself, or he could howl for days on end. Even Dan might find that a tad peculiar.

He focused his empty sockets on the skeleton sitting at the table. "Ol' Mister Bones," he whispered. "Mister Bones, Mister Bones, Mister Bones. Can you hear it? Can you hear what ol' Dan hears? Of course you can. You're part of ol' Dan, you are. You can't deny that, can you?"

The skeleton did his best to ignore the chattering skull.

"Listen, Mister Bones. Listen close."

The kitchen rattled. Pots and pans banged against one another. The manacle around Mister Bones's ankle vibrated with sinister energy. He stood.

"Yes, yes, yes." Dan chortled. "Ol' Margle, he weren't so mad after all. He brought ol' Dan here with a purpose, you see. You and me, Mister Bones, we've a task to do. Not the task Margle intended, but he's not our master anymore. Not until he comes back, and if the castle has its way, he won't ever be coming back. The magic in these walls has better ideas than boring ol' vengeance. Tonight, you and me, Mister Bones, we get to strangle the whole world. Not just us, of course. We're more like a knuckle of a giant hand wrapped around the throat of the world, but it's still an honor to be invited." His voice grew rough and menacing. "To be there to hear the death rattle of creation itself."

The skeleton sat back down.

"Oh, you've got some spirit in you. It's that goody-good Nessy. She's polluted you, tainted you with her nicety and pleasantness. Doesn't matter though. She couldn't wipe it all away. It's still in there. I can feel it. We can feel it."

The castle moaned in agreement. Mister Bones's chain twisted and writhed like a serpent. He stood again.

"That's it. Oh, ol' Dan knew you wouldn't let him down. Come along now, we mustn't miss the fun."

Mister Bones moved slowly, inexorably toward the skull. Each step was easier than the last. His posture changed. He became a skulking, grasping creature, a slouching, sneaking monster. Reverently, he lifted Decapitated Dan off the spice rack and lowered the skull onto his neck.

He paused. Just for a moment.

"None of that, Mister Bones. Too late to turn back now."

The shackle whipped in agreement. Mister Bones shoved the skull into place.

"That's better. Oh so much better." Dan stretched. He stared at his fingers of white bone, opening and closing them. He knocked aside the spice rack. It broke apart, spilling multicolored grains across the floor. "Oh how long I've been waiting to do that."

The castle groaned impatiently. The shackle around Dan's ankle sprang open.

"Don't worry. Ol' Dan is on his way. He knows his part." He threw back his head and howled once more. And this time, he didn't stop.

# NINETEEN

Though The Door At The End Of The Hall had taken to wandering about the castle, it was waiting for Nessy and Tiama at its proper place when they arrived. Nessy had expected as much.

Tiama halted at the hall's end, far from the Door, as if pausing to savor a sacred moment. Nessy looked up at Gareth the gargoyle, who said nothing. He just gritted his stone teeth nervously. The Door was strangely quiet, perhaps sensing its time had finally come.

The wizardess strode down the hall. A cold breeze filtered down its length. Nessy felt the drop in temperature, but the draft itself barely touched her. Tiama's robes whipped softly. The wind grew harsher with each step, but she seemed its only target. It blasted her with gale force. Her hair and robes stretched behind her, ready to tear away from her thin body. The hall stretched one step for every two she took, and though the force of air threatened to snatch Tiama by her long sleeves and carry her away like a kite, she pressed on. Slowly. Inevitably.

Nessy wondered just why the Door would struggle so against Tiama. It wanted to be opened and she was here to do just that. The Door should've drawn her to it instead of pushing her away. As for Nessy and the nurgax, the gale seemed only a chill breeze. A trifle colder than the general drafts of the castle but nothing too bothersome, and almost welcoming for a forbidden portal of doom. She'd long ago accepted she'd never truly understand magic. Maybe no one ever did. Maybe even the greatest wizards just feigned comprehension, hiding their ignorance behind towering arrogance and fortresses of bluster. It would certainly go a long way toward explaining how often they were destroyed by the very forces they claimed to master.

Tiama and Nessy reached the Door. The winds buffeted Tiama as she put out a hand. Then the strangest thing happened. The Door At The End Of The Hall pulled away from her. The parchments nailed across it flailed, slicing her hands. The cuts to her left arm were so deep that the hand hung at her wrist by a few strands of flesh. There was no blood. Only some red sand and green mist wept from the wounds.

Tiama screamed in agony. Nessy was taken aback. She hadn't been sure the wizardess could even feel pain. Now Tiama howled as if her soul were being rent to pieces.

The Door howled along with her as if sharing her suffering. Her eyes burned with black fire that traveled along her eyelashes to her eyebrows and set her white hair ablaze in a pyre of smokeless, ebony flame.

No one understood magic, Nessy decided for certain.

Abruptly, Tiama's screams came to an end. Her face became the same hollow mask it always was. The flames died away. There wasn't any smoke, but Nessy smelled the stench of ash. The gale died as Tiama drew her mangled limbs into her long sleeves. She said nothing. Only stared at the Door in utter silence.

The nurgax whined curiously, but Nessy quieted it with a touch on the snout.

Tiama's left hand, whole and without a trace of damage, extended from her sleeve. She barely reached for the Door's handle when the hall roared. Something not quite invisible jumped from the Door and struck her. Tiama, both flesh and robes, crumbled into red dust.

The Door groaned with disappointment.

Nessy wasn't optimistic enough to think the enchantment on the Door had destroyed Tiama. The wizardess was far too powerful for that. While Nessy waited, she pondered why Tiama was having so much trouble with the Door, even if the magic guarding it was impressive. Perhaps even deceased, Margle possessed enough power to keep the Door sealed forever. It wouldn't save the castle from Tiama's wrath, but it would spare the world at least.

The dust exploded in a burst of flame that solidified into Tiama's gaunt form. She made no move toward the Door this time.

"Nessy, open the Door," Tiama commanded.

"But, my mistress, if you couldn't open it, how can I?"

Tiama glared. "Are you questioning me?"

Nessy bent low, turning her gaze to Tiama's feet. Or where Tiama's feet would've been had they not been covered by her sweeping robes. "No, my mistress, but—"

"Look at me."

Nessy raised her head until she looked the wizardess straight in her smoldering eyes. It was meant to intimidate, but Nessy didn't feel afraid. Tiama seemed somehow lessened.

"Do as I command, beast."

A suggestion of desperation slid beneath the surface of Tiama's cold voice. Nessy glanced at the Door; its timbers slanted in her direction.

"Do it!" It was the first time Tiama had shouted. Wrinkles creased her formerly porcelain features.

The nurgax growled. Nessy stroked its horn until it was calm.

"No." She was quite surprised to hear herself say the word. She wasn't the same kobold she had been only days ago, though she hadn't realized that until now.

"You dare defy me?"

"Yes, I believe I do." Nessy smiled. "If you want that Door opened, you'll have to open it yourself. If you can."

"My power is beyond your pathetic imagination."

"Very true." Nessy bowed and motioned toward the

Door. "So it shouldn't be very difficult to pry open a single stubborn door."

Tiama scowled. Her skin boiled. Liquid flame dripped from her eyes before her face snapped back into that preternatural blank.

"What makes you think I won't destroy you?"

"I'd be very surprised if you didn't. I've yet to meet a wizard who could control their temper. They're all rather like spoiled children." She grinned. It felt very nice to finally say the things she'd always thought.

"Don't you fear death, beast?"

Nessy shrugged. "Not really. A violent death is expected in my trade. I made my peace with it long ago."

Tiama stammered. "And what of your friends? The bat, the voice, the cat and the others? You do know I'll destroy them as well."

"I know, but I also know that whatever is behind that Door is a far greater evil than you. And behind that Door is where it will stay."

Tiama's eyebrows arched. "You would sacrifice every poor soul in this castle?"

"If I can save them, I will." Nessy sighed. "But if there's no other way, then so be it."

"You are far too practical for your own good, Nessy." The wizardess clasped her hands behind her back. "It's an admirable trait, I suppose. To a point."

"You can't open the Door, can you?"

Tiama shook her head. "Even I have my limits."

Speaking with Tiama as an equal wasn't so difficult. Nessy had never feared any of her masters, but she'd always feigned terror. She didn't see the point now.

"What makes you think *I* can?" she asked.

"I know you can."

Nessy studied the Door. The runes and glyphs upon it meant nothing to her, but she still had much the same impression. Why Margle had placed this burden upon her, she didn't understand.

"I'll never open it."

Cold mist leaked from the jamb as the Door grumbled.

"Then you'll leave me no choice but to destroy you and everything else in this castle," said Tiama.

"You were going to destroy most of it anyway. You said it yourself, there's nothing of value here for you. Why don't you just leave?"

"Are you appealing to my mercy?"

"Not your mercy. Your indifference. But if you must look at it in such terms, perhaps there would be nothing crueler than leaving them to suffer their curses. It could be said that death would be an act of compassion for most everyone here. And if that isn't a good enough reason for you, then how about the simple truth that the castle is destroying itself very nicely without any intervention on your part?"

Tiama chuckled dryly, as if the sound itself had to claw its way out of her throat. "Very good, Nessy. You're quite clever in your own way. I do confess, your argument makes a certain sense. But it doesn't matter. I shall smash this castle and everything in it to ruins. And I shall send those ruins so deep within the bowels of the earth that none will know it ever existed. It's the only option left to me."

She whirled and stretched out her hand a mere inch from Nessy's face. "All it takes is one touch, you know. Do you know what it's like to never feel the caress of warm flesh, to know only the icy tenderness of oblivion?" She drew back her hand and frowned.

Compassion swelled within Nessy. Tiama was as cursed as anyone else in this castle. That the curse was her own doing made it no less tragic.

Tiama's face hardened. "I don't need your pity, beast." She turned to the Door and spoke with her back to Nessy. "Let's play a game. Opportunity offers me so few amusements. Run. Run and hide in this home of yours. Hide from me as long as you can. Because when I do find you, and I will find you, I am going to pass the next one hundred years killing you over and over and over again. By the end, you shall curse me and everything you once held dear. And then we shall see which of us will be in need of pity."

Nessy stood there a moment and pondered. Every previous master had spoken endlessly of the torments they would inflict on her, but when it came right down to it, she always expected to be destroyed in a passing moment. Wizards considered their time far too valuable for anything more elaborate for a lowly kobold. Tiama's speech was very pretty, very wizardly, but it was yet another lie.

"I don't hear you running," said Tiama. "Has your terror frozen you to the spot? I was hoping for a little more sport."

Nessy didn't know what Tiama was scheming. She didn't think Tiama could be stopped, but Nessy owed it to her charges to take whatever chances were offered. And, whatever her reasons, Tiama had given Nessy more time to come up with schemes of her own. She turned and walked down the hall.

Tiama called after Nessy as she turned the corner. "Hide well. Don't make it too easy."

The nurgax growled.

Nessy traveled through the castle. Her mind wasn't on hiding. It was well past the time of waiting for Tiama to get bored and leave, which she certainly wasn't going to do. Nessy had to find a way to destroy the wizardess, or at the very least, remove her permanently from the castle. Her thoughts turned to the most dangerous areas of her home. The Catacombs were a maze of ravenous creatures. But Tiama couldn't be killed by terrible beasts. THE MONSTER THAT SHOULD NOT BE had proven that.

There was the Bottomless Pit, a yawning hole from which nothing ever reemerged. There was the Chamber of Blades, where guillotines and saws waited to chop and slice anything that entered. Or the Insatiate Furnace. Or the Tapestry of Emptiness. The Hall of the Blood Fountains. The Dungeon of Dismemberment. The Den of Blasted Pox. The problem wasn't in finding something suitably perilous, nor of luring her there. But so far there'd been no proof that anything could be more than a touch troublesome to the wizardess. And even that was a trifle optimistic.

Nessy decided then that she was contemplating the wrong question. Tiama couldn't be stopped, but she was still playing these strange games, involved in bizarre machinations. Wizards were eccentric, but they weren't generally stupid.

She thought of Margle. Compared to Tiama, he'd been quite sane and predictable. Nessy couldn't envision him giving her authority over The Door At The End Of The Hall. That thing that he feared so much placed in her care. He'd always been obnoxious, insulting, but she'd known he trusted her. She'd never suspected he'd trusted her that much.

So many questions assailed her that, for once, she refused to think about them anymore. She wasn't without her limits. She wandered quietly through the castle for a while without thinking much about where she was going until she opened a door and was nearly pierced by a crossbow bolt that buried itself in the wood a few inches above her head.

"Ye idiotic gnome," growled Sir Thedeus. "I told ye not to fire unless ye were sure 'twere her."

"I didn't fire it," said Gnick. "I'm in charge of aiming." The crossbow across his back was obviously intended for much larger hands. He let it slide off his shoulders and lowered it to the floor. "If you're going to blame someone, blame the weasel."

Dodger shrugged. "Sorry. I didn't realize how sensitive the trigger is."

"Ye have to be more careful." Sir Thedeus flew to Nessy's shoulder. "Are ye all right, lass? We dinna skewer ye?"

"I'm fine." Nessy tugged at the bolt, but it was firmly implanted in the door. She reached for the parchment hanging from the shaft.

"Dunna touch it, lass. 'Tis a rune spell that Yazpib supplied us. He says it should either turn the witch into a tree stump or give her a case of convulsing hiccups. He wasn't sure which. Lousy excuse for a wizard, if ye ask me, but he's all we have and either one should slow her down."

"And the bolts are purest silver," added Echo. "Mined from the Sacred Mountains."

"My idea," said Gnick. "Of course, there are only three in existence, and we just wasted one."

"We still have two more," said Dodger. "Now help me load again."

Gnick sighed. "It took us fifteen minutes last time, and I wasn't tired then."

Sir Thedeus flew to the crossbow and together with the gnome and the weasel, they tugged at the taut string. "And to give it that extra kick," he explained between grunts, "we dipped them in the blessed water of the Fount of the Clouded Heaven. Put yer back into it, lad."

Gnick just snarled.

"If this doesn't stop her then nothing will," said Sir Thedeus.

Nessy didn't quite agree, but she saw no reason to discourage their efforts. Instead, she joined in the tugging and seven minutes later, the crossbow was loaded again.

Sir Thedeus panted, his tongue darting in and out of his mouth. "How did ye escape, Nessy lass? We thought for sure ye were done for."

"She let me go."

"Let ye go? But why?"

Nessy had no response.

Dodger said, "There's a flock of demon fireflies terrorizing the west wing. Just thought you might want to know."

"Don't add to the lass's problems." Sir Thedeus perked up. "Ye needn't worry about it, Nessy. We'll handle it."

"Easy for you to say," griped Gnick. "You aren't the one who has to lug this thing through the corridors."

Nessy smiled. She wouldn't have faulted them for cowering in the shadows and hoping for these problems to fix themselves, but they were trying. Their efforts, while doomed to failure, were commendable. And touching. She couldn't think of a better group of friends, and she wasn't going to lose them to Tiama. Not if she could help it.

The demon could be contained. Nessy didn't know how to get the fireflies back into the Purple Room or if the enchantments that had once bound the demon within were still intact, but these all seemed minor concerns. That was the one benefit to having so many problems. Even the big ones were relatively small after a while.

A voice rolled from a darkened corner. "Nessy, Nessy, Nessy."

She recognized it immediately, and though it should've been the last thing she expected, she was no longer in a mood to be surprised.

Dan, no longer decapitated, strolled into the brighter torchlight. "I've found you, I have. Right where I knew you'd be." He leered, but a bare skull always leered. "I told you ol' Mister Bones and Dan would be the best of friends again, didn't I? And ol' Dan's word is as good as a viper's fang. And twice as sharp." He lurched forward, hands extended like grasping talons. "Come and give ol' Dan that hug I've been waiting so long for."

The nurgax pounced with a feral roar. It was the first time the creature had demonstrated outright hostility. Even when it had devoured Margle, it'd done so quite innocently. But it'd never liked Dan. The mad skeleton struck the creature aside with a single blow. The nurgax fell back with a yelp and a dark welt already visible on its snout.

"Naughty, naughty. I'll not be done in like Margle. I was always a strong boy, though mostly skin and bones. Now that I've lost the skin, you'd think I'd be the weaker for it, but appears I'm stronger still. Wonderfully strong." Dan chuckled. "Strong enough to choke the life out of anything I can wrap my hands around. But words . . . words so often fail us. Come here, Nessy. Let ol' Dan give you a demonstration."

"Fire," screamed Sir Thedeus.

Dodger pulled the trigger, and the bolt soared true. It passed through a gap in Dan's rib cage and buried itself in the stones behind him.

"Oh, damn. Ye blasted gnome, can ye not aim a'tall?"

"The time has come, Nessy," said Dan. "Margle's revenge is at hand. I'll strangle you, then that beast, then that bat. And nothing can stop me." He howled like a mad wolf. His skull twisted. He hiccuped loudly.

The rune spell stuck to his bones went up in a flash. He hiccuped again, louder this time. A third hiccup erupted with such force that his jaw slipped from its right hinge and wagged halfway off his skull. He shoved it back into place. "Oh now this is vexing."

Dan's bones rattled with every convulsing spasm. He clutched his abdomen, which he didn't technically have, and it helped to quiet his hiccups a little. "Don't think this'll stop ol' Dan. *Hic* Not for more than a minute. *Hic* Not for more than a—" He ground his teeth, fighting off the next wave. Ten seconds later, without uttering another peep, he stood straight. "There we go. Good as, good as, as . . ."

He unleashed a discordant blast, the kind of hiccup reserved for a drunken god after a millennium of debauchery. Dan fell to pieces.

"I don't like being vexed," he grumbled. "Sours my sunny disposition, it does."

The collection of bones rapidly pulled themselves together. Speed was more important than anatomy, and Dan lurched awkwardly on his hands as his skull swayed on the end of a femur. Another hiccup caused one of his limbs to fall apart, and he hopped around to maintain his balance.

"One second, Nessy. *Hic* Dan'll be right with you. *Hic*"

"You should run away, Nessy, while you can," suggested Echo. "We don't know how long the spell will last."

Nessy was growing tired of running from her problems, but she couldn't see any alternative. Even with his accursed hiccups, Dan was a great danger now that he had his body back. He was vulnerable, and the nurgax could easily devour his mad skull, but she didn't know the effect that might have on Mister Bones, who she still wanted to save if she could.

"Find someplace safe," she told the others. "And stay away from Tiama."

"We're just trying to help," said Echo.

"I know, but Tiama is reluctant to kill me. I don't think she'll hesitate with anyone else."

"I didn't want to do this anyway," griped Gnick. "Technically, I'm not supposed to leave the armory."

Sir Thedeus climbed on Nessy's shoulder. "We better leave, lass. The skeleton looks to be adjusting to the spell."

Dan glowered, having reassembled into an awkward configuration, resembling a centipede with various bones for legs. His pelvis perched atop his skull like a big white bow. Hiccups shook loose odds and ends.

Gnick and Dodger went off in one direction, while Nessy, Sir Thedeus on her shoulder, the nurgax by her side, and Echo hovering somewhere by her ear, headed in another.

"Ol' Dan will find you, sweet Nessy!" the skeleton shouted. "I'll find you!" A hiccup echoed along with the clatter of bones. "And I'll be in a most unpleasant humor when I do!"

They walked a while in silence.

"So what do we do now, Nessy?" asked Sir Thedeus.

"I'm not sure."

"But ye always have a plan, lass."

"Not this time." She stopped, and Sir Thedeus, shocked, tumbled from her shoulder.

"Ye canna give up. We need ye."

"He's right," said Echo. "We're not good for much ourselves."

Nessy frowned. "That's nonsense."

"'Tis true, Nessy." Sir Thedeus scaled her leg to return to his perch. "None of us are the heroes we once were."

"Ridiculous." She plucked him from her shoulder and held him in cupped hands. "Your curses define you only so much as you allow. I don't know why I should have to keep reminding you of that."

"Aye, but we still have to accept our limitations."

She put him back in place. "Acceptance is one thing. Allowing yourself to be defined by them is quite another."

"I suppose," said Echo. "But it's hard not to sometimes."

"We will break your curses. After we deal with these difficulties."

"But how can you be certain?" asked Echo. "It's so much to overcome."

"Because I choose to be certain." Nessy smiled. "Because I'll take hope over hopelessness any day."

"But it's not always easy, lass."

"It's all well and good to set reasonable goals, but when unreasonable goals are your only choice, you should always strive for them. Because it's not really a choice at all."

"I'd never thought of it like that," said Sir Thedeus. "So do ye truly think we have a chance?"

"There's always a chance."

They turned a corner. Tiama the Scarred stood before them. A faint smile hinted upon her lips. "There are no more chances."

Nessy backed away.

"Oh please don't tell me you're going to run now. What would be the point?"

While Nessy agreed, she still turned and bolted down the corridor.

# TWENTY

Tiama's laugh was as cold and lifeless as the wizardess herself. It chased Nessy through the halls. Nessy had a fine-tuned ear when it came to echoes, but she couldn't pinpoint exactly where it came from. One moment, it was behind her. The next, ahead of her. And sometimes, it seemed like every direction at once.

She ran because she couldn't think of anything else to do. She truly was out of ideas. It was an unusual occurrence. Nessy rarely found herself without a plan, even if it was only a vague outline of one. But she could see no course of action left except running and hoping that a solution of some sort would present itself. If kobolds had a god, she might even have prayed to him.

She paused at an intersection. That infernal laugh poured from the shadows to confuse her.

"The witch is everywhere," whispered Sir Thedeus.

"She can't be everywhere," said Echo.

Silence.

"Did we lose her?" asked Echo.

A new chuckle filled the air. Madly jovial, broken by hiccups.

"Dan." Sir Thedeus's large ears pivoted to find the source.

The skeleton was even more dangerous than Tiama, thought Nessy. The wizardess was hesitant to kill Nessy, but he wouldn't be.

"Neeesssyyyyy." He sang out her name again and again. "Neeeesssyyyyy. *Hic*"

"He's over there," said Echo, although she couldn't clarify her direction with any sort of gesture, so the remark was useless.

A door flew open and Dan came charging out. He had a strange run, legs spread wide, arms flailing in the air. And that peculiar hiccuping cackle.

Nessy dashed away. She didn't look back, but slowly, the click of his bones against stone faded. She stopped to catch her breath.

Tiama appeared. Whether she'd actually sneaked up on them or just appeared, Nessy couldn't say. She soared forward. Her entire body was aflame, rippling with black fire, and she howled like a specter.

Nessy ran again, and soon enough, the wizardess was lost somewhere in the chase until only the threatening silence remained. Over and over, the ritual repeated itself.

Tiama or Dan would chase Nessy a short while, only to fade into the shadows and reappear once again.

The nurgax whined.

"Why don't they get it over with?" asked Sir Thedeus.

Nessy knew why. Kobolds weren't strangers to the art of harrying, of chasing down prey until it was so exhausted and disoriented that it might blunder into a vulnerable position. They were trying to confuse her.

But though her body ached and she was a bit tired, she knew her castle. She was now in the pillar chamber, large and lined with thick marble columns. There were two doors out of it.

She opened one. Dan stood on the other side. He lunged at her, and though he should've caught her easily, she managed to slip from his strangling embrace. She threw open the second door, back the way she'd come. Tiama stood, somber-faced and eyes aflame, in the doorway. There was no escape now.

Tiama and Dan stood side by side. They were working together, and Nessy wondered what purpose could bring them together.

"Nessy, look," said Echo. "There's an exit behind us."

Nessy chided herself for making such an obvious mistake. She should've known her castle better. She dashed to it. Tiama and Dan strolled after her, as if they had all the time in the world.

The door was barred, and Nessy struggled to lift the wooden plank. It seemed as heavy as iron.

"Hurry, lass," urged Sir Thedeus.

She stopped.

"What are ye doing?"

She stepped back. "This door doesn't belong here."

He glanced back at their pursuers, drawing steadily closer. "Now isn't the time to be questioning any bit of good fortune that comes our way, lass."

It seemed the perfect time to Nessy. This was exactly what Tiama and Dan had worked so very hard to do, and they had almost succeeded.

"I know what you are," she said.

The Door growled as it cast away its illusion.

Nessy turned her back to it and faced the wizardess and the skeleton. "I'm not opening it." Her exhaustion fell aside, replaced by a quiet resolve. "I'm never opening it."

Dan chuckled. "I told you she wouldn't be tricked so easily."

The Door moaned.

"She's got a good head on her shoulders. Best thing to do in ol' Dan's opinion is to squeeze that little neck until it pops off."

Tiama held up a hand to keep him back. "Your defiance grows tiresome, Nessy."

"And I'm growing tired of this endless discussion." Nessy made a show of yawning. "You keep threatening to destroy me if I don't open that Door. I keep refusing. And yet, here I am, not destroyed."

The fire in Tiama's eyes surged, and smoke poured from

her sockets. "Very well. The time for reasonable discussion is over. You're quite right. I have no intention of killing you. Dead, you would be worthless to me. I was merely hoping to do this in a civilized manner. But I see now you've forced my hand. You've no one to blame but yourself. You'd be surprised the pain you might endure without dying. In truth, the most terrible pain is rarely fatal. It's a lesson you shall learn most intimately. Every stubbornness has its limits. We shall find yours. You shall beg for death's mercy, but I shall not grant it. Not until you open that Door. Only then will I give you that gift. Perhaps. If I'm feeling charitable." She grinned. "Although, to be perfectly honest, charity is not my strongest suit. Seize her, Dan."

The nurgax leapt upon the skeleton, clamping its mouth around one arm. Dan growled with annoyance. With his free hand, he grabbed the nurgax by the horn and threw it down to the floor. He punched it once across the jaw, knocking loose several long, white fangs that clattered against the stone. The creature tumbled over, on the verge of unconsciousness.

He chuckled. "I said ol' Dan was strong, didn't I? Now let's have no more of this silliness." He wrapped his painful grip onto Nessy's shoulder. "Be reasonable. I don't like torture. *Hic* I may be mad, but I'd rather just kill you. *Hic* The suffering never appealed much to me. Ol' Dan just likes the pretty pretty death rattle."

But he saw that Nessy wasn't about to change her mind and sighed.

"Have it your way then. *Hic*"

A steel gauntlet wrapped around the skeleton's own neck suddenly. The Blue Paladin hoisted Dan high in the air. Though his every move was a rattle of armor, somehow he'd sneaked up on them. The Paladin raised his other hand and with a single finger, flicked the skull from Dan's shoulders. The skull bounced to the far end of the pillar chamber.

"No fair! No fair!" he cried.

The Paladin backhanded Tiama, hurling the wizardess away. She lay on the floor, a broken heap. The Paladin brushed the kobold gently aside. Behind him, the army of empty armors stood ready. The strange new tendency of things to suddenly appear no longer surprised Nessy.

"I was wondering when you'd find me." Tiama rose, much to no one's surprise. "Do you really think you can stop me?"

The Paladin held high his massive battle-ax. Tiama laughed, and this time, somewhere under it all, there was a trace of honest amusement. Then the Blue Paladin lowered his ax, and the armors charged forth. There were no war cries, no bloodthirsty whoops, but they clanged and banged, rattled and clattered. The dragon armor's steps thundered loudest of all. With its wide strides, it reached Tiama first. It reared up and brought all its weight down upon her, crushing her beneath its two unforgiving gauntlets. The brick floor buckled, threatening to give way. The dragon raised its helmet as if unleashing a victory call.

The army circled around.

"She isn't dead, is she?" asked Nessy.

The Blue Paladin shook his helmet.

"Can she die?"

He shrugged.

The chamber trembled.

The Paladin motioned for Nessy to step back. He clutched his battle-ax. His army readied their spears and swords. The stone armor of the rock brute pounded its granite fists together.

"Should we leave them to their business?" asked Sir Thedeus.

Echo said, "If they don't stop her, I don't think we'll be in any less danger anywhere else. Not in the long run."

"Easy for ye to say, lass. Ye haven't a body to get hurt."

The rumbling grew louder. Cracks rolled up the pillars, shedding chips of marble. The dragon armor struggled to hold Tiama down.

"You can't tell me you're willing to miss this," said Echo.

Sir Thedeus grinned. "Aye. But it might be wise to step back a bit."

Nessy grabbed the stunned nurgax by the tail and attempted to pull it to a safer distance. Mister Bones came to her aid. He wasn't as strong without Dan atop his neck, but they managed to drag the creature behind a pillar.

She thanked him, and Decapitated Dan, clutched under Mister Bones's arm, scowled. "Already back to your goody goodness. Ol' Dan's disappointed in you, body of mine."

The tremors ceased, and all was quiet. The dragon armor lowered its helmet and carefully opened its gauntlets. Even the armors seemed to wait with bated breath for what would happen next. A ball of red flame shot straight into the dragon's helmet. Though it had no eyes, it clawed and beat at the fire. Its panicked sways sent its tail sweeping across the room. Several armors were batted aside, breaking into pieces.

Tiama waved her hands about, casting bolts of green and purple in every direction. Those armors struck fell apart on the floor. Several suits got close enough to stab her with their swords without much effect. She stood unaffected by the blades running through her flesh.

The rock brute smashed Tiama beneath its relentless fists. The first blow staggered her. The second brought her to her knees. The third and fourth dropped her prostrate. Again and again, the brute struck until its enemy ceased to move, until her skin burst at the seams. There was no blood. Tiama had been filled with only red sand and white flames.

The Blue Paladin stepped forward and raised his mighty ax to deliver the deathblow. The brute held her down that the Paladin might finish the job with a clean beheading. He swung with every ounce of his considerable might. Tiama, looking very much like a doll without stuffing, swiveled and caught the blade's edge in her hand. Her eyes flashed, and both the Paladin and the rock brute were hurled away by invisible force. The Paladin struck a pillar with such power it collapsed, burying him. The rock brute crashed so hard against the ceiling that the stone armor shattered into a rain of dust and gravel and a few odd stones.

Several spears were thrown. They skewered Tiama impotently as she inflated again. The pixie leathers whirled about, lacerating her skin with a thousand cuts of their tiny daggers. The wizardess clapped her hands, and they burned away to ash.

Fire and magma dripped from her wounds. But Tiama kept smiling.

And the armors hesitated. For they had learned fear.

The dragon armor, having regained its senses, raised its long neck. Its helmet spewed forth a tremendous silver-and-gold gout. Tiama crossed her arms, and the fire splintered into a dozen smaller flames. They ricocheted through the chamber, blasting armors. In seconds, nothing was left of the army but mounds of broken, blackened steel.

The dragon, the last standing warrior, rattled its wings. The silver-and-gold flame collected into a ball above Tiama's head. She stopped smiling, shook her head as if no longer amused, and turned her back on the final suit.

It took one step forward. Her fireball launched itself into the dragon's face. Its helmet flew off its neck, and the dragon stood still for a very long moment.

Tiama sighed. "Somehow, I was expecting more."

The dragon armor fell apart, one piece at a time. Its neck brace collapsed. Then its wing sheaths. Then its arms and body and tail. Finally, its legs. The noise was almost musical. Like orcish war gongs, beautiful in a way but never a sound one was eager to hear.

The rubble shifted, and the Blue Paladin rose. His helmet swept the remains of his troops.

Tiama spoke, once again a lifeless creature. "I know you had to try, but this will come to pass. And in the end, you'll thank me for it."

The Paladin snatched up a nearby spear and rushed at her.

"Very well." Tiama's hair shimmered with fire. "I grow weary of this distraction. Let's finish it."

He knocked her aside with a blow of his elbow and hurled the weapon across the chamber. Nessy fell to her knees, lanced through her chest.

Sir Thedeus gasped, struggling for words.

"Oh no," said Echo. "Oh please no."

"Well, I didn't see that coming." Decapitated Dan frowned. "Though I enjoy a good surprise as much as the next gent, this is a turn not to ol' Dan's liking."

Tiama screamed, and the castle itself screamed with her. "What did you do? What did you do?" A pyre of black fire devoured her, and she disappeared. "What did you do?" her voice echoed from one end of the castle to the other.

"Nessy, lass. Hang on. Ye have to hang on." Sir Thedeus pleaded with teary eyes. "We need ye."

She drew in one last pained breath, and then she was still. Blood ran down the blade, dripping into a red pool.

"She's gone," said Echo.

"She canna be." Sir Thedeus whispered gently in her ear. "Come on, lass. Ye were always a stubborn one. Yer not going to let a little thing like this keep ye down, are ye?"

Mister Bones knelt down and closed her eyes.

"No need for all that gloom." Decapitated Dan chuckled. "She's just gone off to have a chat with ol' Margle, she has. He'll have some words for her, I'm sure."

"Shut up," said Echo. "Show some respect, you lunatic."

"Ol' Dan's got nothing but respect for the dead. Why do you think he's sent so many to their grave?" He stifled a giggle and clicked his teeth and said nothing else.

Sir Thedeus sat quietly for a very long time beside Nessy's body. He kept seeing her alive, thinking to catch signs of life. But they were just twitches of fur in the drafts of his imagination.

"Why?" he asked the Blue Paladin.

The Paladin offered no explanation. He bent down and stayed on one knee, helmet bowed as if in silent prayer. The nurgax howled a low, sad dirge, and curiously enough, the Door joined in with a mournful creak of its own.

# TWENTY-ONE

Nessy knew she was dead. She hadn't really known until after the fact. It'd happened so suddenly, and the living mind wasn't made to truly acknowledge mortality. But now that it'd come to pass, and her soul was freed from its delicate mortal flesh, she had no problem understanding her demise.

Nor did she have much trouble deducing where her spirit currently dwelt. To take it as it appeared was to see only the brick walls of the castle. But there was something more to it. She felt the warmth of vitality beneath her feet, the pulse of a living essence beating up and down the halls.

"What are you doing here, beast?" Margle stood before her.

She bowed to her former master, mostly from habit. "The same thing you are, I suppose."

A voice spoke up, and Nessy knew it belonged to the

castle itself. "Nothing leaves my comforting embrace without my master's permission." The voice was soft and delicate, not the voice of an accursed fortress, but a loving, cozy
cottage. "Not even souls. That's your doing, Margle. Or
have you forgotten the boundless greed which so defined
you in life and continues to do so even now in death?"

The wizard didn't reply. He stared coldly at Nessy.

"You killed me."

The castle laughed. "You killed yourself. Don't blame
her. But I suppose your arrogance was as unlimited as your
greed."

Margle glared everywhere at once, nowhere in particular. He thrust his fingers in Nessy's direction and muttered
an incantation, meaning to roast her from the inside out.
But he called upon magic he no longer had, and nothing
happened.

"If I must collect my vengeance with my own bare
hands, distasteful as that may be, then so be it."

He lunged, and she sank her teeth into the tender flesh
of his hands, just short of drawing blood. Although she
wasn't at all certain spirits had blood to draw.

He recoiled. His eyes widened. "You bit me!"

The castle laughed. "Very good. Though I would've
taken one or two of his fingers myself."

"You can't bite me." Margle rubbed the wound. "I'm
your master."

"You were my master." She bared her sharp teeth in a
friendly smile.

The torches around Nessy brightened while the others extinguished. Dark things, there was no other way to describe them, slithered from the shadows and wrapped around Margle, dragging him into the blackness, where his screams soon faded. The light returned, and he was gone.

"What did you do to him?" asked Nessy.

"No more than he deserved." The voice was now lower, harsher, tinged with grim humor. "Allow him to wrestle my shadows for a while. It should serve to distract them for a time."

Faint shrieks and howls, belonging to Margle and something else, reached Nessy's ears, and she frowned.

"Where do you find compassion for such a wicked soul?" said the castle. "Your sympathies are misplaced. My darkness is of Margle's own creation. He reaps only what he has sown."

She shrugged. She'd never seen the point in cruelty, even towards the cruel.

The halls dimmed, and several torches flared brightly. "Walk with me, Nessy. But stay in my light. My soul is a jumbled ocean, and many of the less pleasant things swimming within have grown restless of late. Unlike Margle, you haven't the wizardly training to withstand such spiritual torments."

The torches led her down the corridors and as Nessy listened, the castle explained.

"To understand the situation, you must understand the most basic philosophy of spells. This is a secret not many know because wizards and their ilk don't like to speak of it much. They like to pretend they're masters of magic, when in reality they are little more than tailors and seamstresses who stitch and weave their spells from a much larger tapestry. They snip off a little here, knit together two pieces there, trim a few unwanted bits. Those rejected scraps are tossed aside to be absorbed naturally back into that tapestry.

"But this is where Margle, in his all-consuming voracity, made his mistake. For greedy fool that he was, he refused to release those scraps. He threw them behind a special door in his castle for no other reason than he couldn't stand the notion of letting them go. They weren't of any use to him, these little pieces of unfinished magic. So they sat ignored behind that special door for a long, long time. Until something unforeseen started to happen.

"These scraps of enchantment and bits of sorcery began to evolve, to grow and change, to thrive in a fashion. Every spell cast added to the volatile mixture, this new life. And this went on for some time before Margle finally noticed it.

"He could've unmade it then. But in his arrogance, he didn't see it for what it might become. Instead, he was curious. So it was allowed to continue its evolution under Margle's study. But eventually, even his conceit couldn't hide the truth. That this experiment behind the Door had become too powerful, too dangerous and unpredictable. By then it was too late to destroy it. Magic is raw possibility, but too much possibility is only chaos. Oceans would boil.

Continents would sink. Monsters would tumble out of hellish worlds. Cats would start dancing, and geese would fly north for the winter, a season that would be only three minutes long. Those are just a sampling. The release of such unprecedented magical energies so suddenly would bring madness to the world.

"Margle's only choice was to contain the experiment. He hid it away behind potent enchantments to prevent it from ever escaping. There it waited, always changing, always growing, becoming. In time, it grew conscious of itself. It became aware of everything within it. And it learned."

The castle grew quiet. The torches dimmed.

"I learned terrible things, Nessy."

A chill breeze blasted through the hall, and she shuddered. For a long time, there was silence.

"You must understand," it said softly. "I was nurtured on Margle's twisted wizardry. Dark magic begets dark magic. I was weaned on cruelty. I knew little else. What else could I become but a terrible, malformed horror?"

"I understand." Nessy rubbed her hand in small comforting circles on a wall, and the castle seemed to perk up.

"That is where you came in. You were the first to demonstrate the virtue of compassion. That compassion lives within me, though it is a small thing, and my cruelty and madness hold greater sway. But I still seek my final form, and my many facets each struggle for dominance. It's a difficult battle, but the hope within me is that the finished design shall be something worthwhile. Perhaps on that day, the Door can finally be opened."

The soul of the castle paused, allowing Nessy to absorb all it had said. The torches led her up a flight of stairs to the tallest tower. The spirit castle was identical to the real thing except for its lack of furnishings and windows, but there was another difference in this chamber. A small table stood in the center of the room and a closed book sat atop it.

The chamber darkened. Margle was spat into the room through the doorway. He ungracefully landed on his face where he lay for a while moaning.

"Get up," commanded the castle. "Stop being so dramatic."

He rose slowly, and Nessy realized what a pathetic figure he'd become. Without his magic, he was just a little, unassuming man. His bare soul seemed a pitiable thing. She took his arm to steady him.

"Away, beast." He jerked back and nearly stumbled off balance. "Your touch disgusts me."

"Poor, poor Margle," said the castle. "You'll never learn. I suppose the same could be said for you, Nessy. Strange, how the same quality can be so reprehensible in one and commendable in another."

The voice sighed.

"Tell her about Tiama, Margle."

Margle snarled. "What are you blathering about? There is no Tiama. She's just a nightmare story shared amongst wizards."

"She was. Until you made her real."

"Tiama's a spell," realized Nessy aloud. "She's a spell to avenge Margle's death."

"Yes, yes, that was its purpose," said Margle. "But it wasn't to my liking. So I unmade it."

"And where do all your unwanted magics go?" The castle laughed long and hard. "They come to me. And though the wards that lock me behind the Door are powerful, I've grown strong enough to seep from my prison. When Margle died, my darker half found the power to raise her. But with new purpose. Still she couldn't escape without one final element: your permission, Nessy. Which, in ignorance, you granted."

Nessy frowned. If she'd only denied Tiama at the front door, none of this would've happened.

"You couldn't have known. You did only what you thought best. There is a balance to my soul, albeit a tenuous balance. When some of my evil escaped, so did a sliver of my good. It was a tiny bit of magic. Just enough to wake the enchanted armor of the Blue Paladin and his army. My good half hoped to destroy Tiama with these instruments, but her physical form is merely convenience. The evil magic that raised her can't be unmade. It must be returned whence it came. When my benevolent side realized this, it struck her in the only weakness she had, the one thing that it could do to prevent the Door from being opened."

The torches flickered and dimmed.

"I'm sorry, Nessy."

She smiled. "It had to be done."

"You're truly a forgiving soul." The lights brightened. "I have one more spell left, a single enchantment placed within me by Margle. With it, I can return my master to life. With it, I can thwart my darker half."

"Then return me to life that I may do that," shouted Margle, sounding rather childish.

"I can have only one master." The voice grew rough and cold. "Which of you that shall be has yet to be determined."

The torches flickered. Growls rolled up the stairs, and shadows crept along the walls.

"Though my darker half is stronger, this spell is one of life and healing. Thus, it falls within the domain of my more humane side. So I find myself in something of a dilemma.

"Margle, as a great wizard, has the might and knowledge to easily cast Tiama back into her prison. But he is also a wicked soul, beyond redemption, possessing not a single admirable quality. None that my kinder half finds admirable at the very least.

"Nessy is a splendid creature and someone from whom I believe I could learn much more. But she lacks power, and though I trust in her competence, I must question whether this problem is beyond her abilities."

The walls trembled. The stones under their feet shifted. A horrid wail filled the air.

"My darker half grows impatient. Tiama, in her blind

unchecked rage, might destroy the castle and everything in it, including herself." The moan chilled the air, and malignant shapes twisted through the cracks in the walls. "Perhaps that would be best."

Nessy stepped forward, although the great soul was all around her so it was a gesture more for herself than the castle. "I can stop her."

Margle laughed. "Don't be absurd."

"I can stop her."

"This is ridiculous!" shouted Margle. "You don't really see this as a debate, do you? I'm your master. I made you. You wouldn't exist without me. What has this dog done? Swept a few floors? Alphabetized a few books? Even those simple tasks were never to my satisfaction, and I will not compete with this thing." He kicked Nessy, and blindsided, she fell. Twice more he booted her as hard as his thin legs allowed. The twisted, smoky ghouls chuckled. He pulled back his foot for a fourth blow when Nessy sprang.

She latched her jaws onto his ankle, and he screamed. She discovered spirits did indeed bleed. His acrid blood burned her tongue, stung her gums. But she sank her teeth deeper. Margle howled, unable to shake her loose until she let go of her own accord.

She remained on all fours, growling, broken with aggressive barks. Her lips peeled back to show her sharp fangs, stained red, which were much longer and more pointed than Margle had ever noticed before. Her eyes, always bright and shiny, were now two black pearls of contempt.

"Even the most patient soul has her limits, master," said the castle. Its ghoulish shadows laughed at this too.

Nessy advanced. Margle retreated, limping on his savaged leg. She was a small creature, but without his wizardry he had little hope of preventing a mauling. She backed him against the wall, where he huddled, his arms and legs drawn tight. And he trembled in a puddle of his own blood.

"Don't. Don't hurt me."

But she so dearly wanted to. A bite for every insult. A slash of her claws for every inflicted bruise. A drop of blood for every accursed victim of his cruelty. It was no less than he deserved. Perhaps there was a point in cruelty to the cruel after all. Perhaps, bloodied and humiliated, Margle might finally learn the attraction of mercy. Probably not. But in a world without justice, perhaps vengeance was all one could hope for.

Her ears flattened. Drool dripped from her lips. The shadows tugged devilishly at the wizard's hair and robes. They whispered in his ear, musing on the tender pain soon to be his. And Margle wept. He sobbed and trembled. Snot dribbled down his lip.

She put a hand on his shoulder, and he jumped. Tears rolled down his face. But Nessy didn't bite. She wiped the drool from her lips and smiled softly. She shooed the shadows, brushing them away like buzzing insects, and helped him up. She glimpsed the confusion in his eyes. He didn't understand why she wasn't ripping him to pieces, and he most likely never would. She marveled how someone could know so much and so little at the same time.

The castle's voice was dark and low. "He hasn't earned your mercy."

Nessy replied, "Mercy isn't earned. It's given."

"This is something I find difficult to comprehend. I have too much wickedness within me." The voice changed. It remained harsh, but less so now. "But I'm right about you, Nessy. You've much to teach me. And Margle, simpering, miserable thing that he is, has exhausted his lessons."

The wizard offered no protest. He was too busy wiping away his tears.

"Before I return you to life, Nessy, I pose you this riddle. There is a door which must never be opened and a thing on the wrong side of that door. How do you get it back to where it belongs?"

Nessy thought for just a moment before reaching her answer. Upon hearing it, both the castle's good and evil halves laughed as one. The book floated from the table and into Nessy's hands.

"Read it, and be on your way. But take care. I haven't the power to thwart a second death."

Nessy glanced at Margle, who had regained his composure, although his arrogance was obviously lessened. "And what of him?"

"What of him? He deserves every torment he suffers. And more." The castle sighed deeply. "But I shall grant him mercy, even if I fail to see why I should. He shall be safe from my shadows, sheltered in the warmth of my charity. Now go. And may fortune favor you, my mistress."

Nessy opened the book. Strange letters danced on the pages. They glittered with soft light. She disappeared. The book fell to the floor, leaving Margle to the castle's tender mercies. He hobbled on his bloodied leg and snatched up the tome. But its pages were blank.

"The spell is gone," said the castle, and its dark phantoms howled with delight.

Margle winced. He was a spirit now, and his wound could bleed forever without killing him. His would be not an eternity of hellish agony but endless stinging annoyance. For the first time in his life or his death, a notion occurred to him. That maybe, just maybe, he had brought this on himself. But it was the merest inkling, and he quickly dismissed it.

"Cease your whimpering," groaned the castle. "Sit."

A chair appeared by the small table, and he used it. It wasn't comfortable in the least, but it eased the weight on his ankle.

"Dress that, would you?" said the castle. "You're bleeding all over my floors."

A roll of bandages lay on the table, and Margle bound his wounds. When he was done, he leaned back in his uncomfortable chair and felt just a little bit better.

In the highest tower of the castle's soul, the torches grew a little bit brighter and the shadows a little bit quieter.

Somewhere in its layered, colossal soul, the castle smiled, although it didn't know exactly why.

Sir Thedeus stood watch over Nessy's body. She was such a little creature, nothing much to look at, but it was as if her death had killed something inside him as well. He'd always been a fighter, never one to lie down and surrender. But now . . .

Now he wondered if he'd ever find the strength again.

It wasn't the curse of bat skin that contained him. Nessy had shown him more than once that power wasn't only found in physical might, but everything had changed. He glanced over at the dead kobold and grimaced.

But none took her demise worse than the nurgax. The purple beast had ceased its mourning. Now it just lay beside her in a grim imitation of death. It hadn't moved for over half an hour, and there was only the slightest indication that the creature was breathing at all.

"I can't believe she's gone either," said Echo softly. "What are we going to do?"

"Nothing. We do nothing, lass."

Decapitated Dan chortled.

Sir Thedeus snarled. "Canna ye keep that blasted madman quiet?"

"If death couldn't silence ol' Dan," he replied, "I don't see what chance any of you have."

Mister Bones dropped Dan onto the floor and sat atop

the skull. But Dan wouldn't be rendered mute so easily. He twisted on his jaw and muttered through clenched teeth.

"What would goody-good Nessy say seeing all of you in such a darkling gloom? She'd be disappointed, she would. Willing to give her life for the likes of you, and now all you do is sit around and pout." He wailed, throwing Mister Bones to the side. "Oh, poor are we! Poor are we! Nessy has perished, but we're the unfortunate ones, we are!"

Mister Bones snatched up Dan and struggled to hold his wagging jaw shut.

"You'll not shut me up, body of mine! I've learned from Nessy never to go quietly! I've learned, even if none of you whimpering flesh have!"

The skeleton clamped Dan tight, but Dan kept mumbling.

"Wait," said Sir Thedeus. "Let him speak."

Decapitated Dan howled. "Oh ho ho! Now you want to hear ol' Dan out! Not so mad now, am I?"

Sir Thedeus flew to Mister Bones's shoulder. "Yer a lunatic, lad. But ye've a point."

"I always have a point, though it's not always a point many would like to understand."

"Why would ye encourage us to fight?" asked Sir Thedeus. "I thought ye wanted the Door opened?"

"Oh, indeed I did." Decapitated Dan whistled. "But the advantage of lunacy is that I can change my mind whenever I bloody well feel like it. And now that ol' Dan's had some time to think on it, I'm not so sure I want the world to end today. So many interesting turns this day. Piqued my curiosity, it has. Brought to me a new perspective."

"And that's it?" asked Echo.

"Well, ol' Dan's a little bored as well. Should be worth a chuckle or two to watch you throw your lives away in a hopeless cause. Always enjoyed a hopeless cause, myself. And a massacre all the more."

"He's right," said Echo. "What chance do we have?"

"None." Sir Thedeus raised his tiny body high. "We've none a'tall. But we fight. And if we die, we do so with honor and courage."

Dan cackled. "And they call me mad."

The Blue Paladin jumped to his feet with a clatter. A swirl of colors settled onto Nessy's body and for a moment she was so bright it was painful to look at.

"Oh damn," said Dan. "I was hoping she'd be gone just a wee bit longer."

The glow faded, and she sat up and frowned at the spear buried in her heart. "Would you mind terribly . . . ?" she asked the Paladin.

He pulled the spear from her chest. The wound closed, and she drew in a deep breath. "Much better, thank you."

The nurgax howled with delight. It danced about Nessy on its two stumpy legs, singing an off-key warble as it licked her. She endured its joy a few moments before calming it with a stroke on the snout.

"'Tis a miracle!" Sir Thedeus flew to her side and

scrambled across her shoulders to confirm what his senses told him.

"No miracle. Just magic."

Her ears raised, stirred by a fresh tingle in the air. Something new was happening. She knew the castle's will now, its desires. This had been so for a long time. But now, the castle knew her will as well. It was a delicate connection. The castle's darkest desires lumbered like a terrific, crackling beast, whereas her will was a subtle thing astride the monster's shoulders, attempting to direct these desires to more positive ends. Or, at the very least, less dangerous ones.

It would be a difficult task, but she could manage it, for she was the castle's mistress. Her methods were far different from Margle's. But she would learn. And so would the castle.

The pillar chamber rumbled with the beating of a thousand tiny wings. The doors flew open, and a swarm of demonic fireflies flooded the room. They swirled about, laughing but not attacking yet. One insect with a flaming blue tail settled on Nessy's nose. It spoke, barely audible above the thundering noise.

"Hello, Nessy. I'd heard you'd been killed." The swarm chuckled, repeating the last word over and over again. "I'm pleased to see you weren't. How else could I collect your soul?"

"I don't have time for this." She brushed the firefly away.

The demon's tail turned bright orange. "Nessy, you've changed. There's something different about you. I'm not sure I like it."

"Off with ye," said Sir Thedeus. "We've got a witch to deal with."

The fireflies landed. They crawled across the floor like a living carpet. "I'm insulted. I'm far more dangerous than a meager witch."

"Not this witch."

The swarm spun around in a tornado of fiery rage. "I am queen of the underworld! This castle and all within it are mine to destroy; their souls shall sate my unholy appetites!"

"No one is dying today," said Nessy.

The demon laughed. "And what makes you think you can stop me?"

Nessy smiled. "Because I know your true name."

The fireflies buzzed angrily. "You're lying."

"Possibly, but I've always been a terrible liar."

A contingent of insects broke away and scrutinized Nessy's face. She stared back into the dozens of tiny red eyes, and she didn't blink.

"My dear little Nessy, I wonder, have you learned the art of deception? Is this what's become of your beautiful soul?" The demon mulled this over, whispering to herselves. "And, supposing that this is true, where did you learn this information which no living mortal knows?"

"Margle wrote it in a book, and I looked it up. Just in case I might need it."

"Am I to believe that Margle would leave such cherished information merely lying about?"

"It wasn't just sitting out for the world to find, but I know this castle very well." She shrugged. "In any case, it's your choice what to believe."

"You do know that any mortal that dares even whisper my true name shall perish beside me upon uttering the wicked syllable."

Nessy nodded. "I've already died once today, so death isn't that frightening a fate."

"She's lying," said a bug.

"Dare I take that chance?" asked a second.

"But I can't go back to my purple prison."

The swarm roared in unison. "I won't! I'd rather writhe in the pit forever and ever than spend another minute locked in that room by myself."

"Perhaps another arrangement could be made."

"Do you wish to bargain with me?" The swarm's flames flashed a rainbow of colors. "Only arrogant fools barter with demons."

"This isn't a bargain," said Nessy, never once dropping her smile. "This is a compromise."

The demon's thousand faces snarled. "There is no fouler word. I'd be the laughingstock of the underworld. No, Nessy. No, I call your bluff. Send me back to hell, but don't ask me to commit that blasphemy."

"If you insist." The kobold cleared her throat.

"Wait!" roared the demon. Her beating wings fell to a whisper. "You would, wouldn't you?"

"She would," said a fly buzzing in Nessy's ear.

"Without hesitation," added another bug crawling atop her head.

"Then this is the question that I must face. If you are not lying"—she paused to study the kobold up and down for nearly a minute—"if you are not lying, then I must either die or compro—" The word caught in her throats. "Do that thing which demons despise doing. Allow me a moment to discuss it amongst myselves."

"Certainly, but only a moment," agreed Nessy. "I haven't got all night."

The swarm flew to a corner and chattered in hushed tones. Everyone waited quietly. They dared not speak. Sir Thedeus paced Nessy's shoulders, and Echo whistled as she sometimes did when she was especially nervous.

A single firefly broke away and landed on the kobold's nose. "I've changed my mind, Nessy." Her tail shimmered soft red. "I think I like this new you after all. I like it very much."

The demon laughed a faint, chilling chuckle that sent shudders through everyone in the room, including Dan and the Paladin. Everyone but Nessy, who stood unflinching, her soft smile never dropping from her lips.

# TWENTY-TWO

Gareth the gargoyle stood watch over The Door At The End Of The Hall. It'd appeared at its proper place not long ago. Now it waited. Gareth, who'd spent years studying the Door, sensed impatience from it. It clanked its handle with steady rhythm, and the runed parchments swayed back and forth. Every so often, it creaked in a way that was not at all dissimilar to an irritated sigh. It was clearly waiting for something, and Gareth didn't want to imagine what that might be. But, as the mind is wont to do, he found himself guessing. They were all, without exception, terrible guesses. That is to say, the guesses in themselves weren't terrible, but every one was a horrifying possibility. Each more horrifying than the last. Until Gareth, having worked himself into a state of quiet panic, wished he could close his eyes and pretend he saw nothing. But Margle had denied him stony eyelids. So when Nessy arrived, all by herself, without even the nurgax at her side, he couldn't help but notice.

"What's going on around here?" he asked. "I thought you were done for. Where's Tiama?"

Nessy said nothing. She strolled quietly down the hall to stand a few feet from the Door. It growled at her, spitting steam from its edges.

"Are you feeling well, Nessy?" asked Gareth. The torches were inexplicably dim, and he couldn't quite make the kobold out in detail. She seemed somehow different.

"I'm fine," she replied, but there was something odd about her voice.

Before he could pursue the point, a cold wind blasted down the hallways. Dark shapes dripped from the cracks in the walls and dribbled into a large puddle behind Nessy. He was about to warn her when she turned around on her own, and watched, without a hint of emotion, as the blackness rose and congealed into a vague, womanish shape. Tiama the Scarred had never been more than passably human.

"Hello, Nessy. I know what you're doing. It won't work."

"Won't it?" asked Nessy. "There is a door which must never be opened and a thing on the wrong side of that door. How do you get it back where it belongs?"

Tiama chuckled. "You open that door. But you see, dearest Nessy, the moment you open that Door all the magic within will come flooding out. How do you intend to stop it?"

"By my will."

Tiama threw back her head and laughed, although it was nothing like a laugh, neither amused nor malicious, but empty. Like an echo of a sound that never was.

"You've overestimated yourself, Nessy. The castle's soul will crush you beneath its venomous might. You can't expect to stand against that."

"I can." It didn't sound like a boast, yet it lacked any trace of confidence as well. "I only need to do it for a moment. Just long enough."

Tiama knelt. "And supposing that you are able. What's to prevent me from killing you the moment the Door is open? Your will is formidable, I'll admit, but it won't do you much good when you're dead. And all it will take is a single touch." She reached out with her hand. Then withdrew it. "Not yet. Not until you've done what you've come to do."

"You've forgotten one thing."

Tiama stood. "Have I? What might that be?"

"I'm mistress of the castle, and, for all your power, you are just a piece of its leviathan soul. You're under my dominion."

"Absurd."

"Is it?"

Tiama shook her head. "Have you gone mad? There's no escape left you. You've no choice but to open the Door or die."

"That's very true. But since we both know I want to open it, I think you're the one who's been maneuvered into a trap." The torches flared brighter, casting unforgiving light on the pallid, hairless complexion of a not-quite-finished kobold. "Amorphous."

The protean sludge dissolved into a yellow puddle.

Tiama whirled. At the other end of the hall, the real Nessy stood with Sir Thedeus perched on her shoulder, the nurgax, Mister Bones, and Decapitated Dan at her side, and the Blue Paladin behind her.

"You were right, Nessy." Echo whipped invisibly down the hall to her companions. "It worked."

The wizardess bared her teeth in a snarl that seemed quite genuine. "How?"

"You believed because I wanted you to believe." Nessy smiled. "Is my will so puny a thing now?"

Nessy raised her arms and spoke her levitation incantation. The bar across the Door slid aside and clattered to the floor. With a triumphant bellow, the dark portal swung wide and spewed forth a thousand hideous phantoms, all cackling and howling and screeching.

Nessy held her hands up. "Stop."

The command was spoken quietly, without force. Yet the tide ceased. The shadows, muttering and hissing, receded.

"Impressive, Nessy. I've underestimated you." Tiama's human form lost much of its shape, dripping and blending with the darkness swimming around it. "But it won't be enough." Her eyes blazed with flame. The deluge wailed and crept forward with the slow certainty of a river of molasses.

Nessy stood her ground. Her brow knit in a tight V, burying her eyes into blackened slits of determination. The darkness rolled to a stop at her feet. Claws and tentacles reached onto the bricks and struggled to pull themselves another inch so the evil might devour this last stubborn obstacle to its release. Hungry jaws snapped and clicked at Nessy's nose. The supernatural weight pushed against her, and she tried to push back. But the tide was inevitable, unstoppable. She'd never get it behind the Door again. She barely had the strength to hold it at bay, and that strength was fading all too quickly. But she didn't back down. Not one step.

An unexpected newfound strength patched up her crumbling willpower, and she realized that Tiama had been right. Nessy wasn't strong enough to stop the darkened castle's soul by herself. But she'd forgotten an essential truth of Margle's castle.

One was never really alone.

She mentally shoved the darkness while taking a step forward. The evil receded, just out of her reach.

"Ye did it, 'lass." Sir Thedeus clung fast to his perch on her shoulder. Though his body was tiny, his courage was boundless. And his stubbornness was a tower.

She smiled. "We did it."

She put her hand on the nurgax's horn. The purple creature cooed, offering her its strength as well. It hadn't the force of Sir Thedeus's, but it was enough to bring a pained roar from the writhing evil. Mister Bones put a hand on her shoulder, adding his own silent determination. Decapitated Dan, much to Nessy's surprise, cackled as he cast a few drops of his maddened tenacity to their side.

The castle roared loudly enough to nearly knock everyone off their feet.

Tiama trembled ever so slightly. "It won't be enough. Even with every accursed soul behind you, nothing can stand against the monstrous storm that has been brewing. Its fury shall consume you."

Nessy closed her eyes. She felt the castle all around her. There was darkness, evil, and cruelty. But there were also little spots of gentle warmth. These were the residents of the castle. Some were warmer than others. But in each, even the most wicked, was a speck of something good. As mistress of the castle, she summoned forth those drops of willpower, those dollops of courage and compassion, pinches of unyielding obstinacy. Individually, they were nothing before the madness of the castle's twisted spirit, but together, they were a great, invisible army standing as surely by her side as were the nurgax, Sir Thedeus, and the Paladin.

The power flooded into her, and she sparkled with a brilliant golden nimbus. Cool, blue fire filled her eyes. The shrieking, howling phantoms retreated behind Tiama, clinging to her hair and robes.

"Get back where you belong," commanded Nessy.

The smoldering red flames in Tiama's eyes erupted, consuming her face. The skin melted away to reveal a shapeless thing, a skull made of ash and smoke. She spoke and gouts of multicolored fire exploded from her maw.

"Is that all you have?"

She laughed, but this hideous chuckle possessed a quality Nessy had yet to see from the wizardess: fear. And the shadows, the many horrid facets of the castle's malign soul, all wore the same ghastly terror upon their perverted countenances.

Nessy frowned. There was a time for patience and there was a time for discipline. She'd had enough. She bared her teeth in a snarl and growled. It was the exact growl, stern yet calm, that her mother had used with her as a disobedient pup.

"Get back."

The tide of phantoms ebbed. Some were more stubborn than others, but all slunk back into the welcoming blackness behind the Door's threshold. All but Tiama, the last and most resolute portion of the castle's evil. She took a single step forward. Her veil of humanity fell away. She was nothing but red sand, black smoke and white fire. She stretched a gnarled, crimson claw against Nessy's shining light. The fingers smoldered, but she pushed forward with an agonized howl.

One touch. That was all it would take. From behind the threshold, the phantoms encouraged her with a chorus of shrieks. Her inhuman body broke apart, re-formed, and broke apart again and again. But she pushed on, and when she was a mere inch from that fatal caress, a grin spread across her ashen visage.

A single demonic firefly rocketed from around the corner and hurled herself into the wizardess's hand. The claw disintegrated, and Tiama stumbled back. She clutched the burning stump. It re-formed into warped talons.

Another firefly landed on Nessy's nose. "Remember your promise."

Nessy nodded, and the demon chuckled.

Her swarm poured down the corridor, hundreds of flaming insects launched into Tiama. Each blast tore away pieces of her skeletal body, but she re-formed almost as quickly. Still, every blow pushed her back a little, and soon she was on the edge of the threshold. The flames in her eyes had all but died away, but she held onto the jamb with tight, knotted fingers.

The last firefly atop Nessy's nose shrugged her wings. "That's all I have."

If Tiama was to return, then all the pieces of the castle's soul must go with her. Even the good. The Blue Paladin strode forward. He paused, waved good-bye, took Tiama's wasted form in his two gauntlets and, as she wailed in protest, dragged her across the threshold.

Nessy and the others ran to the Door and tried to throw it shut. She almost succeeded, but her glow had faded. The shadows were still pushing back. The nurgax and Mister Bones added their muscle, but it still wasn't enough. The Door slid open half an inch. Slivers of shadow struggled to wedge it further.

Sir Thedeus jumped from Nessy's shoulders and braced

his tiny body against further advance. "Come on, lads. Put yer backs into it!"

Nessy's aura was nearly gone, and without that, their might wasn't up to the task.

A shaggy beast lumbered around the corner. It was ten feet of coarse, green fur with a great toothy mouth, three gray eyes, and a strange hat atop its flat head. The creature snatched up the iron bar and shoved the Door closed with one hand. Its nostrils flared in a wet snort as it dropped the bar into place.

Instantly, all was quiet. Nessy sat on the floor, finding she was too exhausted to stand. The last of her glow faded from her hands, but a hint of azure light glinted in her eyes. It would never quite go away.

She glanced up at the tall, wide beast, and she recognized his three silver eyes, and his funny hat that wasn't a hat at all. It was her cot.

"Thank you."

The monster under her bed shrugged. "No problem."

The Door At The End Of The Hall heaved a very long, very disappointed sigh.

# TWENTY-THREE

The hard work of the next few days consumed all of Nessy's attention. There was much to be done. Added to all her normal responsibilities, which had not vanished simply because Margle had died, was the trail of chaos left in Tiama's wake. The now-inanimate armors needed to be repaired and returned to the armory, which needed to be dusted and cleaned. Gnick's devotion to his silver gnome duty had lessened, and she was only too glad to help him in that monumental task.

Gnick checked an empty helmet for any signs of lingering life. "Hello? Anyone in there?" He twice rapped his knuckles on its shiny surface before stacking it on the cart. "I don't know if we'll ever get them all back together."

"We will. Eventually." She studied a spear, its tip red with encrusted blood, her very own blood. She decided to keep that one for herself. As a memento. Another she handed to a throng of dust pixies. The little sprites scrambled off to the armory, leaving tiny tracks of dirt. She ignored that. One task at a time.

The nurgax raised its head curiously. That meant Echo was here.

"The wedding's about to start."

Nessy had nearly forgotten, which was proof of just how busy she'd been. She set down a shield on a pile of them and asked Gnick if he were coming. He mumbled something about being too busy and hating weddings anyway, and she left him to his work.

The castle didn't have a proper chapel, but arrangements were made in the observatory. It was a little out of the way, but a lovely place for the ceremony. One of the few rooms with sunshine, and Ivy had managed to sprout a rainbow of colorful roses along the walls. It was positively beautiful. There weren't any chairs, so everyone sat on the floor. Only a small selection of the castle's residents were here, as the observatory wasn't very big, but the toad prince and doll princess had wanted an intimate affair.

Nessy slipped past a ghost and a snake to sit at an open spot between Yazpib the Magnificent and Fortune.

"I thought you might be late," whispered Yazpib.

"Are ye an idiot?" Sir Thedeus flew down from somewhere to land on the kobold's shoulder. "Nessy's never late."

She glanced to the bride and groom bathed in the golden light of the afternoon. The prince wore a little crown upon his head, and the princess a veil Nessy had knitted for her.

"I love weddings," said Echo.

"Watching weddings wills me to wanton weeping," agreed Olivia the owl, who'd forsaken her day's rest to attend the event.

"This'll never work," said Yazpib. "My brother's curses won't break so easily."

The presiding fern shook his leaves, and the ceremony began.

"I wrote the ceremony," said Echo.

"Love is like a flower," started the fern. "When watered by the fountain of tenderness and sunned by the light of giving and nurtured by the dirt of an open heart . . ."

Sir Thedeus repressed a chuckle by clearing his throat. "Beautiful, lass. Just beautiful."

"Let the leaves of your love shelter you from the cold rain of discontent," continued the fern.

Sir Thedeus buried a snort, but when the priest warned of the lumberjack of jealousy, the bat only managed to hold back his fit of laughter by digging his fangs into his lip. The ceremony was short, which greatly pleased Nessy, who still had much to do. The fern pronounced the prince and princess married under the laws of heaven and earth, and they leaned in for their kiss.

"It's not going to work," said Yazpib again.

And it didn't. For one brief moment, there was a pause of disappointment from the audience, but the moment passed. Their congratulatory cheers filled the observatory. Sir Thedeus whooped and flew somersaults in the air. The nurgax, full of the spirit of the occasion, danced about with surprising grace while gleefully whistling. Even Nessy threw back her head and unleashed a joyful howl.

The rag doll threw her small bouquet into the crowd. Olivia soared through the air to catch it in her talons. She circled the room.

Morton the mouse gazed up at her. "She'd make a beautiful bride."

Nessy smiled. Perhaps another wedding was on the way.

"I told you it wouldn't work," said Yazpib.

Sir Thedeus landed atop Nessy's shoulder. "Congratulations, laddie. Ye were finally right about something."

Nessy stood.

Fortune stretched. "Where are you going?"

"I've things to do."

"But you'll miss the reception," said Dodger from between Nessy's feet.

"I really don't have the time." She took a step but something snagged her. The nurgax held her by the sleeve.

"I shouldn't."

Sir Thedeus shook his head. "Ye should. If anyone's earned a bit o' fun, lassie, it's ye."

The crowd fell quiet again. The toad prince hopped forward. "We'd be honored by your attendance."

"Yes, Nessy," agreed the doll princess. "Please, come."

The nurgax whined playfully and slapped its wet tongue across Nessy's face.

Her mind ran through her list of chores. There was nothing terribly pressing, nothing that couldn't wait until morning. Though it was against her nature to put things off, she supposed that if the castle hadn't fallen apart after the last few days, it would stand for one more wasted night.

"Well, perhaps half an hour."

The gathering cheered.

The reception was a gala affair. Everyone who could show up did, and there was much rejoicing and celebration. There was dancing and food, and Nessy had had absolutely nothing to do with any of it. For once, she was allowed to simply enjoy herself without worrying about keeping things in order. The experience was strange, but not in an unpleasant way. She even shared a dance with Sir Thedeus, although he did complain that she led. There wasn't much he could do about it though, considering his feet didn't even reach the floor.

It went late into the night, but Nessy decided to retire early from the celebration. She excused herself from the party, and she, the nurgax, and Sir Thedeus headed for her bedroom. They stopped only briefly at the kitchen to bid its residents good night.

Mister Bones had willingly shackled himself back where he belonged, and Decapitated Dan had a new place by the sink. The mad skull rested comfortably on a cushion Nessy had supplied him. He'd almost destroyed the world, true, but in the end he'd proven helpful. He'd earned a comfortable pillow at the very least. On the table, in a small glass jar, a demon firefly buzzed. She was just one of many such fireflies scattered throughout the castle. The demon wasn't free, but at least she wasn't alone anymore.

"Pleasant dreams," she said.

"Yes, yes," agreed Dan. "Only the sweetest dreams for the sweetest girl."

The demon and the skull shared a wicked chuckle.

"I dunna know if 'tis such a good idea to leave those two together," observed Sir Thedeus.

Good sense told Nessy much the same, but she'd given her word, which was very important to her. If her castle was to become something worthwhile, she had to set a good example.

Her castle.

The thought made her smile every time. The blue light twinkled in her eyes. Of course, it wasn't only her castle anymore. It belonged to everyone who called it home. In that way at least, their curses were a little lessened.

The castle had already changed in many small ways. Its torches burned brighter, its air was fresher, and its rumblings and creakings less ominous. Even The Door At The End Of The Hall remained in its place.

"Nessy, lass, I've been thinking," said Sir Thedeus. "I canna help but wonder about Margle. Are ye sure he's well and truly dead?"

"I don't really know."

"And the castle's soul. How can we be certain some of it dinna slip out when we were closing the Door? I'm almost positive I saw something creeping away into the darkness after. And even if I only imagined it, I dunna think it far-fetched that there are still other evil magics creeping about these halls."

"It's possible," she agreed.

"And our curses. We've yet to break a single one."

"We will."

Nessy pushed open the guest room door. It'd taken some time, but she'd finally made the room livable. Specks of jabberwock paste remained here and there, and an odor lingered, but that could wait until tomorrow. Tonight, she was finally going to sleep in her new room. The gray-eyed monster had already moved in. His shaggy, green bulk hid beneath the darkness under the bed. It was an impossible fit, but no less so than his previous home.

Nessy leaned the spear that had killed her in a corner and plumped up a thick pillow beside the fireplace for the nurgax. It sat without being told. She petted it for a while until its purring stopped and it fell asleep.

The monster under the bed fidgeted and shifted, grumbled and grunted.

"Comfortable yet?" she asked.

His three eyes glared from the shadows. "It took me years to get settled in properly under that cot."

"At least this bed is bigger."

"Too big. The cot was cozy. A nice, snug fit."

"You're welcome to go back there."

He snorted. "I'll get used to it."

A clatter arose from the hallway. A gray fog floated through the door, dropping stones and pebbles onto the floor.

"The gorgon haze," said Sir Thedeus. "Curse me for a fool, I'd forgotten about that."

She hadn't. She plucked a pouch from her belt, poured the powder into her hand, and blew. The white frost enveloped and devoured the haze within moments. It even turned the stones back into air.

She muttered softly and levitated herself onto the bed. She could've just hopped up, but she liked to practice whenever she could. Magic seemed a little easier every day.

"So many problems." Sir Thedeus asked, "How can ye not be worried, lass?"

She placed him on the pillow beside her. "Get some sleep. We've a busy day tomorrow."

He laid down his head, and soon he, too, was fast asleep. He'd been more tired than he'd wanted to admit. As for herself, she wasn't quite as tired as she'd first thought.

"Nessy?" asked the monster under her bed.

"Yes?"

"Would you like to do some reading tonight?"

"Not tonight."

He sighed.

She said, "But I do know a story. I'll tell it to you tomorrow, if you like."

"What's it about?"

"A castle. One filled with magic and wonders."

"And curses?" asked the monster.

"Indeed."

"Oh, I don't know. Doesn't sound very interesting. Are there any barbarians in it?"

"No, but there's a monster," she said. "He lives under a bed."

"Is he important?"

"Very. You could even say he's the hero."

The monster laughed. "Oh, I can't wait."

Nessy lay back on her new bed and listened to the crackle of the fire. Sir Thedeus was wrong. She did worry, about all the little things that had to be done tomorrow, and all the other things she didn't even know about yet but were out there waiting for her.

But worrying was her job.

She fell asleep with a slight smile on her face.

"Good night, Nessy." The monster closed his eyes and vanished into the deep, comforting darkness.

The bedroom torches dimmed and, with a gentle rumble, the castle drifted off to sleep with its mistress.

# TOR

Voted

**#1 Science Fiction Publisher
25 Years in a Row**

by the *Locus* Readers' Poll

———•———

Please join us at the website below
for more information about this
author and other science fiction,
fantasy, and horror selections, and to
sign up for our monthly newsletter!

**www.tor-forge.com**